I0831291

The Ghosts of Hawthorn, Missouri

Heroes of Hawthorn, Volume 1

James Peet

Published by Persimmon, 2018.

THE GHOSTS OF HAWTHORN, MISSOURI

First edition. May 1, 2018.

ISBN: 978-1-64440-060-9

Written by James Peet.

Zero

The days were numbered for the part of town known as Jackass Flats. It was a place that always smelled of rainy mildew, and was hazy with the ghosts of those who succumbed to the heartbreak of their own failed hope. It was a place that seemed to eagerly anticipate the apocalypse. It would come soon enough.

Hawthorn Baptist Church was being built in the place where mobile homes with no electricity once housed families escaping the penetrating, deadly Missouri winters and summers. Those trailers – once refuges for hungry bodies bogged down by the water-soaked clothes caked in mud from walking home from the bus stop in the rain – were now being sold for scrap at Reggie Walter's salvage yard.

Back before the earthquake decimated it once again, back before the earth erupted in fury and erased it from the planet to start anew, this part of town was called Jackass Flats. It was lousy with Hawthorn and Dogwood trees, dropping green and white blossoms mercilessly all year alongside the trash and, in concert with general neglect, smothered the grass to a dry, brown death.

People on the north side of town were happy to see Jackass Flats go. They liked their houses clean and new, untainted by the smell of the south Hawthorn houses' rust and wood rot. It must have been an act of God, they figured, and welcomed it. The events that occurred were too well timed to not be from either God or the Devil himself, and either way, it was all a part of a plan.

Before all of that, Hawthorn Baptist Church tried to quell the fire of Jackass Flats through reconstruction. The Cue 'n Brew got a facelift – a more welcoming neon sign and brand new tables imported from nobody knows where, along with a more attractive staff of women, some of them poached from north Hawthorn. Jackass Flats got a new grocery store and a new clinic, of which the attached pharmacy had a security system only seen at big box retailers.

But the center of it all, which the neighborhood orbited, the Groce Trailer Park, with its rusted lemon yellow metal mobile homes and life-hardened chain smokers who lived there, was about to be wiped. Most people, including the residents, were quietly happy about it.

Change and hardships were something to which the residents of Jackass Flats were accustomed. They did not extend to the world hard feelings for the cards they had repeatedly been dealt for generations. No, they just rolled with it and strapped the additional weight to their backs, content to carry the more prosperous world's burdens, perhaps because those burdens weren't always evident to them.

Jackass Flats, for all of the miscreants it held in its bosom, was a quiet place. Save for the occasional rock music blasting from backyard sheds or car backfires, people mostly held together silently. Children just sat on the edge of the playground instead of playing. They did nothing much but stare at the grey sky, and threw rocks at the corroded swings and slides, coexisting with the teenagers and degenerate women picking up rides from strangers on the other side of the playground.

Occasionally, from the vantage point of that playground, the children would see a figure – sometimes a woman, sometimes a man, sometimes a child just like they were - walking down the gravel road adjacent to them. A translucent boundary separated them. On one side of it, kids were kicking rocks and humming with a casual enjoyment of life, as adults with nothing better to do watched passively to make sure their kids didn't run into traffic.

On the other side of this boundary were the kids from Jackass Flats – unnoticed or unattended by their parents – watching the happy, well-nourished souls on the other side of the park. They looked on with the kind of envy that makes a person ache a little in his stomach.

Sometimes this figure from across the way would be leading a child by the hand or a dog by the leash, and sometimes they would be wearing gym clothes and running shoes, and sometimes they would be wearing a brightly colored dress from the department store at the mall in north Hawthorn. Whatever the case, the children would look at this figure walking on the outskirts of their bubble with faint hope.

One day, they could have that kind of life, too – a life where their skin was clean and their bellies were full, and their eyes didn't reflect the dirty faces of their brothers and sisters. Instead, they would reflect the bright outline of the sun and the moon. They would reflect a life free and clear of hunger and drunken drama.

JACKASS FLATS WAS STARTED as, in a jagged sort of way, a dare to God, and so it was no surprise that it ended with so much rancor.

Its original residents came from the nearby town of Lampe. The Lampe Church of God split into two factions. The rift began when part of the congregation, after a spirited conversation during a potluck dinner, voiced their collective belief that once God saved you, no matter what you did, you were always saved.

This notion was violently resisted by the majority of Lampe Church of God. It started out as a cold war; a dissipating bond where certain women – "sisters" – no longer spoke to each other during church fellowship. Their cool civility soon gave way to near-seismic feuding that even the nearby New Madrid Fault Line couldn't manage.

The folks who would become immigrants to Hawthorn were accused of witchcraft, as many people were in those days – a logical conclusion to war against ideological minorities. Unwelcome in the town of Hawthorn from day one, they set up shop with their own church on the south side of town, in an abandoned carriage house.

The pastor of this church was a good-looking, charismatic white man in his twenties. He preached a modern sermon and fashioned himself after contemporary renderings of Jesus – long hair, a beard, and soft-spoken nature. It was quite a simple play, really, and it attracted many women from both north and south Hawthorn, who convinced their husbands to start attending this strange new church. Before they even knew it, they had created south Hawthorn and had taken hold of it.

Things fell apart, however, when this young pastor, named Stephen Shrine, lost his mind in a whirlwind of ego and lust and "married" a former slave whose name no one can seem to remember these days - after which, she bore his child. There was no denying the child was of mixed race. His skin was just caramel enough to look different from both of his parents, and most certainly from the white folks in town and the few Black folks who hadn't moved north to Kansas City, or east to St. Louis. And actually, there was little room to deny that the child, named Ethan, was Stephen's: they both had striking blue eyes and the same dust-colored birthmark over one of them.

The young American government gave Stephen Shrine fifty acres and a musket, as they did all white men that year. He made sure to push the process through as soon as the local government discovered his lover was pregnant, so that his family could have wealth to pass down.

Stephen's wife was found dead shortly after that with a shotgun wound between her eyes.

Stephen found her body first. Her facial expression didn't display horror or pain; instead, it was inscrutable, almost peaceful. The wound, directly between her eyebrows, dripped down her nose all the way down to her chin, forming a border between the left and right side of her quickly graying face.

Stephen stared into his dead wife's gelatin eyes for a few minutes. There was no time for emotion. Not fury or sadness, just wonder.

It finally happened, he thought to himself. *Now what?*

No one questioned her mysterious murder. Stephen knew that the law in town not only would decline to help, but were likely involved in her death in the first place. She was laid to rest in the first grave of what would become a massive cemetery on a steep hill in south Hawthorn, holding the corpses of many prominent townspeople over the centuries. Her grave is one with her husband's and only bears his name.

After Stephen's wife passed away, the congregation of Hawthorn Baptist Church dwindled because Stephen's spark had left him, and his sermons became increasingly slurred and unhinged.

Stephen Shrine's spirit was stolen. The world had beaten him before he had a chance to turn 30.

The Klan, in the middle of the night, hanged him on the last day of April. Stephen barely resisted. Ethan was spared, and taken to an orphanage. He lived to old, bitter age, and became an infamous miscreant, living in the belly of south Hawthorn – which coincidentally or not, was nicknamed Jackass Flats right after Ethan was hit by a train in the middle of the night.

The moniker Jackass Flats had been bandied about jokingly before Ethan's death, but after, the name stuck for over a hundred years. It finally died along with the town itself, before both were resurrected.

The pendulum swung a few dozen more times over the years, and the landscape of Jackass Flats, despite its ugly name, became quite beautiful from a distance. Those Hawthorn and Dogwood trees gave it a lovely appearance from Heaven, but perhaps not from the ground, where you could see it up close. The residents were too caught up in their daily lives, sharing their energy and their food stamps just to survive.

That is until Father Redmond came to Jackass Flats to save it, and for better or worse stirred up long-dormant life in people, like the cicadas that hid in the Hawthorn trees in summertime.

One

Music was the thing that gave Terrence his life. It gave him something to hide behind. It gave him an alternate identity in which he could immerse his body and mind when the rest of the world got too loud.

After he lost his mind, he could not clearly remember the first five years of his life. His only real childhood memory was playing the piano. It was the first thing he did after coming home from school.

His mother, noticing Terrence's bloodshot eyes and swollen cheeks, let him play as long as he wanted, despite the fact that she worked the night shift at the pie factory all the way in Springfield and needed the sleep.

She let him play. He played for hours until the joints closest to his brown fingertips pulsated with the arthritic ache of overwork.

He occasionally remembered in the middle of his playing to look over his shoulder to see his mother fidgeting with a lit cigarette, staring at him like he came not from her but from outer space.

A sensitive Black boy, she thought.

Ain't no way of life harder in this world than for a sensitive Black boy.

She never said a word and mostly never paid him mind while he was playing. But when he was done, she gave him a creaky smile - always looking down and never at him - and erupted into a round of applause - flicking ashes all over the kitchen table, some of them still lit.

Nine-year-old Terrence had built up internal strength on his own. He was ashamed of his parents' weaknesses. He hated his father's histrionics, and how booze was likely the only thing keeping him from some sort of dramatic suicide.

He hated how Marianne, his mother, forced him to pick cotton alongside his white classmate, Toby McAdams, whose father owned the farm.

He hated how patronizing the McAdams family was to them; he hated how his mother lapped it up for a few flimsy silver coins at the end of the day.

He hated the heat.

This diverse fanning of hatred within his spirit had strengthened his resolve. Outwardly, it aged his face, every muscle in it scrunching until it had an involuntary hardness.

Inwardly, it gave Terrence a tough, steely gut. It made the world less intimidating to be always angry at it.

You can take shit off this world if you want, he said to himself, grunting as he picked cotton. *But one day, this world will be taking shit off of me.*

He refused to give his soul to a world that still thought of him as not wholly a person.

One afternoon, toward the end of his shift, a policeman Terrence had never seen before drove up. Earl McAdams, the owner of the farm, perked his ears until he saw officer Grady get out of the car - all three hundred pounds of him.

Grady waddled over to where McAdams was, wiping his brow with his left hand, and concealing the right one in his belt.

"It's a hot one today!" Grady said in a good-ole-boy accent.

"Yessir. I reckon it is," McAdams said with a smile.

Grady and Terrence's eyes met. Grady recognized the glare of a criminal when he saw one, whether or not he had committed a crime.

Grady tipped his hat to Terrence as he spoke to McAdams. "Good thing you have your mules to pick up the slack for ya."

Lightning struck Terrence. The words came down through his skull and gave his temper a jolt of electricity.

He looked at his mother. She tensed the lower part of her face into a slight grimace, but her eyes went glassy. She looked down, sullen, as she continued with her work.

Terrence was not accustomed to this sort of outward attitude from white folks. They were almost always polite to him, though Terrence could still sense the disgust that they so crudely attempted to suppress behind a bland half-grin - and that alone was enough to sour him.

He knew it was far worse a little bit south, in Arkansas and beyond. When Terrence was just old enough to speak, the Haight family took their one and only family vacation to Silver Springs, Arkansas, to see the nation's most giant statue of Jesus Christ.

Martin, the family patriarch who had not yet given his youth over to the numbness of whiskey, pulled over to put some gas in their rickety car.

Terrence had overheard many of the white children point at cars like his at the grocery store and casually refer to them as "nigger cars," and ever since he heard it the first time, he rode slouched over in the passenger seat, looking down and tuning out the world around him.

A portly white man, sucking on a cigarillo, shuffled over to their car, tipped his hat, and looked into the window. He smiled – until he saw who was inside.

"Uh," this elderly white man said to this nervous Black family, "we closed, sir," he said to Martin.

"I understand," Martin said, knowing very well they weren't closed. "But we in a bind, here," he said, pointing at his gas gauge. "Could you help us out? I'll pay you extra."

This old white man leaned into the window, resting his hands on the ledge. He looked at Martin, then Marianne, then ultimately laid his dark eyes on Terrence, who met his gaze with fury.

"Get outta here, man," the white attendant said. "We closed."

Martin noticed another younger white man in the doorway, with his arms crossed. He started walking across the dirt parking lot toward them, and he looked angry.

The two white men exchanged angry words – too far away for the family to hear - before the younger man jogged to the car.

Martin had one hand on the ignition keys, and one grip on the gun he kept hidden under the seat.

"Don't," Marianne said under her breath. "Let's go."

"Don't leave!" The other white man called out while jogging. "We ain't closed."

He filled up Martin's tank free of charge, as he knew better than his father that they couldn't afford to let any customers leave angry.

The Haights being the only family of color in Jackass Flats left a young Terrence little option but to keep to himself. He had no friends; had no use for them, even though Toby McAdams had desperately tried to befriend him that summer.

Terrence could always sniff out awareness of 'Other'-ness in the white people of Jackass Flats that turned his stomach. It was an awful burden to carry having empathy as a person who's different, and it wore on his mind with a slow tick until he gave in and finally went crazy.

It was the night of Grady's casual insult years prior that Terrence set fire to the McAdams cotton fields, which kept him clothed and fed in the months between school sessions.

His rage billowed smoke inside his head all day long; it never subsided.

When Terrence first had the inkling to burn down the field, he was lying in bed meditating on his own sweatless, raging internal heat. That inkling became a multi-layered mission the longer he thought about it. Violence melted into poetic justice the more he allowed his hot emotions to mingle with his cold pragmatism.

He decided that he'd rather burn it down than have to spend another day watching his mother bow down and carry the burden of failing her son – showing him true hopelessness in the name of survival.

Still, he considered what his mother would say.

I ain't raisin' no hoodlum, she'd say. *You angry? Take it out on the work. It'll make you work faster. Let's get it done. I'm saving for your college. Ain't no son of mine getting into that crap.*

It was a decision he did not take lightly.

After exploring several scenarios, he deemed his original plan the best one. Terrence burned a large chunk of the cotton field with his father's cigarette lighter and a few mouthfuls of diesel he siphoned out of a nearby tractor.

He crouched down in the dark, lighting each plant one by one, turning the blue glow of the moon that the cotton reflected into a violent green-yellow until he was satisfied. He watched for a bit to make sure the fire caught, and then he ran away, resisting the urge to enjoy the spectacle of the lake of fire he created.

It was a not a well-planned crime, but there had been a series of arsons in town with no suspects. The police, including Grady, just assumed this was another one, though he always suspected young Terrence was behind them all.

The night terrors began right before puberty. Terrence was terrorized in his sleep by owls with demonic glowing eyes, simpering serpents, and wolves with metallic teeth. The dreams were so real that they were no longer dreams, and was what some say broke his mind. But to Terrence, they were what made him sane. These dreams opened his eyes.

He ran through the south Hawthorn woods in the dead of night. Mud grabbed hold of his feet, holding them to the earth and slowing him down. Serpents hung off of branches, staring at him and sleepily hissing, but never striking. When the mud got too thick for him to run, his tired, sore legs shook, but he never fell. He stood there in the gluey mud, working his frantic breathing into a meditative, musical sigh. He waited.

The owl, with its glowing green eyes and blood on its beak, perched itself on a branch directly in front of Terrence, in the middle of a hissing audience of branch-dancing serpents.

This owl - this demon - didn't make a sound, but the light from its eyes grew brighter until the tree branches cast shadows on the wilted brown crops that surrounded them for many acres.

Then came the wolf.

The wolf always showed up a few minutes later. He stood guard behind Terrence with quiet strength. Then, the lightning storm began.

When the rain started in these dreams of Terrence's, it was never the cool dampening showers that pierced the heat in the brutality of a Missouri summer afternoon.

This rain was warm and red – it was blood.

Streak lightning taunted Terrence, striking around his shivering body, but it never hit him. Thunder crashed furiously, and the lightning-induced fire that spread quickly among the dry field of dead crops cast a heat over Terrence that made him wish for death.

Am I dead? Terrence would wonder right before he woke up in the realm that he seemed to primarily exist - in his bed, staring at the portrait of a nude blonde woman taped to the ceiling that he ripped out of his father's magazines.

"What's 'a matter with you?" His mother would open the door and say through the crack in it, breaking up the light from the hallway.

"Nothin'," Terrence would say.

"You have a bad dream?"

"Yes, ma'am."

"Just pray 'bout it," his exhausted mother would say before going back into the bowels of the house. "You'll be all right."

These dreams followed him all day. It was like he never wholly woke up, just entered a different level of sleep.

As the dreams became more frequent over the years, Terrence's reality became a rippled pond, bending and wrinkling and showing itself to be just a transparent veneer, and proving the things around him to be paper-thin projections by which he would never be fooled.

If Terrence decided he did not want to be Black, if he decided that he did not want to be a man or even a person, he could transcend his personhood and numb the sensation of a vivid, violent world at his whims. It was a power he had learned to control, and make potent on command.

Nothing mattered, he resolved, and so nothing fazed him.

As he went through the tunnel of dingy light that was his adolescence, the testosterone in his blood gave his spiritual powers an aggressive quality. His eyes had an involuntary intensity. His gaze could burn through metal.

"You're so funny," his first girlfriend, a white princess named Donna, said during a secret rendezvous. Her chin rested on his chest as she looked up at him. Her naked breasts stuck to both Terrence's waxy skin, and the metal of the car hood upon which they laid.

"Why am I funny?" Terrence said on his back with his head cradled in his hands, staring at the sky.

"Your brow is always furrowed," she said. "Even your glances are stares."

"Nah," Terrence said with a smirk. "That can't be right."

Donna giggled. "Yeah," she said. "Even while you sleep."

Terrence made eye contact with Donna. "I'm happy, though. Don't worry about it."

Donna said, "Sometimes I wonder what you're thinking about so hard." She gazed into his emerald eyes, which always pierced through whatever met his scrutiny.

It occurred to Terrence that if he explained what he was thinking about, Donna still wouldn't understand.

So instead, he laid with her night after night, always before Donna's dinnertime, diving into her skin and scraping the bottom of her chest in search of a spirit, so that it could meet his. He did it desperately and with despair, unable to suavely face the panic that came with the realization that this girl he had such affection for could not match him in passion, and therefore, could not stay with him for long.

In fact, it ended even before Terrence could have predicted when his worst fear came true. His worst fear was not being caught by Donna's father. No, even more frightening to Terrence was being caught by his mother.

His mother, in turn, held a strenuous fear of catching him with a white girl like she had caught her husband and a local barfly in the utility closet a week before Terrence's twelfth birthday.

Marianne walked in on the traumatizing image of her son's muscular backside as he devoured a white woman's body, seeming to soak in it. Terrence loved physically to such a severe extent that it often felt spiritual when in fact it was not.

Still, his mother was fooled. She saw the intensity of Terrence's pleasure – the serpent-awakening pumping of his hips and his stoic, trance-like expression, his muted grunting, and it was too much for Marianne to process.

When Marianne saw the abomination (who had captured her only son between her white legs), her eyes calloused and her equilibrium failed her. She fell backward, the crown of her head splitting the hollow paneling on the wall.

Terrence's eyes moved backward from his laser-focus on Donna's body, and he leaped from his bed, attempting to cover himself.

Donna screamed when she saw Marianne on the floor.

Marianne crawled away from the doorframe, panting moderately.

She did not ever acknowledge what she had seen, but still, she did not ever completely get over it.

Terrence was her only child. Marianne could not have another child after Terrence's difficult birth, and she was secretly happy about these circumstances.

It was her husband who taught her how to hold a baby – cradling the head and not the neck, appearing warm in the face. "Babies can pick up on that kind of stuff, baby," Martin said. "You gotta learn to smile."

"He gotta funny looking head," Marianne said. "It's long and bumpy."

"You gotta shape it," Martin said.

"What's that mean?" Marianne replied, awkwardly cradling her baby.

"Just rub it, honey," Martin said. "Keep rubbing his head."

For all of Martin's failings as a husband and a father, he loved Marianne. Although, he didn't understand her strange thought processes. His wife seemed to make less sense to him with each passing year. Every birthday brought a colder chill to her demeanor than the one before it, and her brain seemed to evolve too fast to bother to remind her mouth to speak. When she did speak, Marianne slurred her words, biting her bottom lip at the end of each sentence.

He considered taking Marianne to a doctor. However, he didn't want his wife to end up like his mother, who lived in a state institution after a crude lobotomy - drooling on herself until she finally died of loneliness.

Martin loved Marianne and was patient with her. In fact, the only time Martin lost his cool with Marianne was when she was off in one of her dazes and dropped hot ashes into Terrence's crib, hitting him in the eye.

What disturbed Martin so much was not that he had slapped his wife, but that his first instinct was to assume that Marianne was burning her baby on purpose.

Marianne had all but exited her body after Terrence was born. He took everything from her, and it didn't seem like he aimed to give it back any time soon, with his giant green eyes and insatiable appetite. In the first years of Terrence's life, Marianne developed sore, chapped nipples, a lazy demeanor, and a hunched-over gait.

She rarely ate, and only slightly more often spoke. She silently stared out of windows and smoked cigarettes, but not much else. If not for the constant cycle of smoke through her mouth and nostrils, an observer might think she was catatonic.

SIXTEEN-YEAR-OLD TERRENCE woke in the middle of the night. He felt a pair of eyes glaring at him. It was a familiar kind of glare as if his reflection was watching him sleep. He looked down to see his father, half drunk, sitting on the floor of Terrence's bedroom. The room was muggy, with the smell of beer and sweat stagnating in the air.

"Dad?" Terrence called out faintly.

"Yes," Martin said, sniffling. "It's me."

"What are you doing, dad?"

Martin shifted positions, then laid back on the carpet and rubbed his eyes. "I failed," he said in a sniveling baritone that made him appear pitiful. "I can't do it no more."

Terrence stayed silent. He knew what was coming.

He saw it in the way his father averted his eyes away from his mother during meals – always smiling at his wife while looking at the floor.

He could sense the love Martin had for his wife give way to impatience. He heard it in his father's sighs; his grunting in lieu of hellos.

After a while, family dinners seemed more like dining with strangers. However, a young man who sprang from their loins but who no longer needed either of them held these strangers together.

They became indifferent toward each other but courteous and kind which suited them, as they were both secretly afraid that they were incapable of living without each other.

"She'll get better," Terrence said to his incoherent father, not believing his own words for an instant. "You just gotta pray about it."

Martin laughed bitterly through his tears. "You sound like your mama," he said. "Praying ain't never done nothing for us. You need to get over that."

Terrence looked up at his ceiling, or where it would be if it weren't swallowed in darkness.

"If you're gonna leave us," Terrence said, "I reckon you should just go on. Make it easy on yourself."

"I need to say goodbye to your mom—"

"No," Terrence surprised himself with his stern tone. "You'll kill her. Then I'll be left here to pick up the pieces. Just be on your way."

"I'll send some money back," Martin said. "When I get a job, I mean. I promise."

Terrence rolled over on his side. "Don't bother," he said, facing away from his father. "Live your life. We'll be all right."

He allowed his father to fall asleep on the floor next to his bed.

When Martin sobered up, Terrence made Martin and Marianne eggs with black coffee. Martin never left, except eventually through death.

At age 18, Terrence figured he had looked after his family enough, and joined the army. His mother took the news surprisingly well, considering Terrence joined during wartime.

"You okay, mama?" He asked her, stooping his head and widening his eyes. He broke the news to her, and she stayed silent for several seconds after.

Marianne smiled a tortured kind of smile. "Yeah," she said through a thick wall of anxiety. "You do what you need to do."

He told his father the news that night as he laid on Terrence's bedroom floor, but Martin was too drunk to remember. Terrence never got a chance to tell him while he was sober because they never spoke when Martin was sober.

"Army, huh?" Martin said tepidly.

"Yeah," Terrence said. "What you think?"

"I think if you tryin' to make it in a white man's world, that's a good place to start," Martin said. "I never could hack it. But if you can, more power to you."

"Might as well try while I'm young and able," Terrence said. "I want to go to college."

"You know they ain't giving Black folks that shit, right?" Martin said. "Only white folks get that kind of hand-out. They'll just let you do the grunt work and get shot at."

"Then I'll pay for it," Terrence said defiantly.

"Hey," Martin said almost defensively, "If you got it figured out, more power to ya'. Do better than me, and I'll die happy."

WHEN TERRENCE WAS FINISHED with the Army, aged 21, he went to school at Southwest Missouri State University, where he was a dutiful, above-average student. One of the only Black men on campus, Terrence studied, wrote, and barely made a sound while walking across the stage at graduation.

He went to graduate school, aiming to become a music instructor. He became engaged to Donna, who was thrilled at the prospect of marriage even if it meant complete disconnection from her family. She wanted a dull, soft life, raising children and pleasing her man. Terrence wanted happiness and nothing more, and he loved Donna. It held together for as long as it should have.

Donna eventually became irritated by her complacency, which manifested into what men call jealous ways. Every move Terrence made, every look he gave her, every look he didn't give to her, was a topic of argument.

Terrence found himself occasionally, flinchingly, looking at Donna as an Other - an archetype of oppressive, emotional turmoil that he so despised as a child and that had made him so angry.

He had fallen in love with Donna for no other reason than her willingness to look him in the eye, unlike every other person he ever met. But now, she was becoming one of them: someone who considered him slightly less than human. He started to feel like a fetish, a mule, just as Grady called him and his mother all those years ago.

Once he concluded that no woman in Jackass Flats could ever really love him as an equal, leaving her was easy. And Donna took it well.

“Just tell me,” Donna said, looking down, “is there someone else?”

“No,” Terrence said. “I still love you, D. But we ain’t fitting.”

“We ain’t fit for a while,” Donna said through tears. Then she smiled. “But when we did, that was real nice. You made me feel like you loved me. I never felt that before.”

Terrence grabbed Donna’s hand. He kissed it. Donna blushed.

“You think we’ll ever have that again?” Donna asked, bashfully.

“You will, if you want it,” Terrence said. “I don’t know that I do.”

“Was it so bad?” Donna asked. “Was it so bad that you don’t want to do it again?”

“It was good,” Terrence said. “Real good. But once was enough for me. I want to feel something else for a while.”

“You mean, something bad?” Donna asked, confused but intrigued.

“I don’t know, D,” Terrence said. “I just want to feel everything. Love is just one thing.”

Donna tilted her head.

“It’s a wonderful thing,” Terrence said. “But I need to savor this loss I’m feeling.”

“But why?” Donna asked pleadingly.

Terrence shrugged with tears in his own eyes. “Maybe to prepare, or something,” he said, looking at the stars.

He turned and looked at Donna after she didn’t respond. “You know what I mean?” He asked. “It’s coming soon, I think.”

Donna grabbed Terrence’s arm and rested her head in his armpit. "I don’t get it," she said. "But you do what you need to do to be happy." She stroked his chest, occasionally reaching up to dry his tears.

"More loss," Terrence finally said. "I think my life will be nothing but a series of losses, and I need to make my peace with it now."

“You don’t know that for sure,” Donna said. “But I understand what you mean.”

"You're the best D," Terrence said. "Someday you'll get the man you really deserve."

"Maybe," Donna said dreamily. "Maybe not. Either way, I'll be fine."

"Okay," Terrence said, squeezing Donna closer. "I'll be fine too."

"Promise?" Donna asked.

"I'll try my best to. How about that?" Terrence said. "Just for you."

"You'd better," Donna said.

Terrence stroked Donna's hair. "You're such a worry wart," he said.

After a few more late-night rendezvous, Donna moved on. She ran away, married someone rich, and had children. Terrence got two letters from Donna – one to inform him of her upcoming wedding, and one when she had her first child. Terrence never responded, and so she decided it best to respect his boundaries.

Finding a job after the military was difficult for Terrence, just as his father predicted. No public school would hire a Black man as a full-time teacher, even though it was starting to become uncouth to say such things openly. Terrence did odd jobs around town. He always made sure to go above and beyond, building trust and good relationships around town – both for business and for kinship.

He also convinced Billy Joe to let him play his electric piano at the Cue 'n Brew on slow nights.

"You don't have to pay me nothin'," Terrence said. "I'll just put out a jar."

"Then why you doin' it, son?" Billy Joe asked, hung over and impatient.

"Because I love it," Terrence said. "What other reason do I need?"

Billy Joe threw up his hands. "All right Terrence," he said. "Mondays are slow, and sometimes Wednesdays, too, but we get a lot of after church crowds on Wednesdays."

"My lyrics are clean," Terrence assured Billy Joe. "I mostly just play, anyway. I'll even turn my back. They won't even know I'm here."

Billy Joe waved him silent. "Okay, okay, I get it," he said. He extended his hand. "We have a deal."

Terrence shook Billy Joe's hand firmly and quickly. "Thank you, sir."

"Call me Billy Joe," he replied.

The first night Terrence played his electric piano, facing the wall near the men's room, a portly bald man stopped to watch. Terrence felt this man's burning eyes. He occasionally turned and smiled at him, until the song was finished.

The bald man rested his hands on the waist of his khakis.

"You're extraordinary," this man said, sounding almost smitten.

Terrence nodded. "Thank you, sir."

The man handed Terrence a business card. "You want to make some steady money playing music, call me," he said.

Terrence looked at the card.

FATHER HAROLD REDMOND

Pastor, Hawthorn Baptist Church

Terrence called the next day, but Redmond seemed surprised by the call, only pretending to remember Terrence at first.

"Oh, yes!" Harold exclaimed. "The piano man."

"Yes, Father," Terrence said with a polite chuckle.

They spoke for a while about God, and about the importance of music.

"I think music is the closest you can get to God without dying or praying," Harold Redmond said.

"I heard that," Terrence replied.

"So, listen," Harold said, changing the tone. "I'm kind of new in town, and I'm rebuilding a church."

"Okay," Terrence said, awaiting the point.

"I have a background in music, myself," Harold said.

"Oh yeah?" Terrence mimed interest. "What'd you play?"

"Business side," Harold said. "Christian music, mostly. I'm out of that game now."

"You felt the calling, huh?" Terrence asked.

"Yessir," Harold said. "Anyway, I got a couple of propositions for ya."

"Great," Terrence said. "I'd love to hear them."

"One, I'd like you to play at church on Sundays," Redmond said. "I'll pay you."

"Sounds good," Terrence said.

"Do you know hymnals?" Harold asked.

"If not, I can learn in a whip-stitch," Terrence said.

"The second thing is, I've been trying to get piano lessons for my son," Redmond continued.

"I see," Terrence said. "How old is he?"

"About six," Redmond said. "He's...kind of difficult. Are you good with kids?"

"Not really, to be honest," Terrence said. "Not small ones anyway."

"I see," Redmond said. "What about high school age?"

"Maybe," Terrence said. "You know of a gig like that?"

"I'm going to be frank with you Terrence," Redmond said. "Because I like you."

"Okay."

"A public school in this town would never hire you as a teacher," Redmond said. "Not a full-time one, anyway."

"Not surprising," Terrence said. "I figured."

"But I do know of a music teacher who needs an assistant," Redmond said. "If you want, I can get you hooked up."

"Mister," Terrence asked, "may I ask why you're doing this for me?"

"Because I heard you play," Redmond said. "And music is the one thing that's going to save us all from going crazy one of these days after we done ruined everything else."

TERRENCE GOT WHAT HE was looking for in being alone. He was an assistant to the music instructor during the day and ate his mother's cooking every evening. He was comfortable - and for the moment, that was enough for him.

Being in transit from one phase of life to another was the point of being among the living, Terrence reckoned, and the buried thrill of it was the only thing that kept Terrence going.

He turned 25. He turned around twice, his father died, and then he was 26.

He blinked. 27. His mother died in the middle of the night at the kitchen table, her cigarette burned all the way down, leaving blisters on her fingers.

He closed his eyes tightly, hoping to block out the world for a while.

Terrence finally opened his eyes, and he had nothing but a painfully empty but bloated gut, a dead mother and father, and some four-years-recycled lesson plans.

Unlike the white boys of Hawthorn, Terrence had no gilded cage to seek refuge, whose brassy metal he could bang against in furious rebellion as he'd seen them do so often.

What made those white boys so wily, anyway? He wondered. *Did they just not know any better?*

The dreams started again. The owl came back, and the wolf did too.

But in this series of dreams, he was at Fog Creek, bordering what was now McAdams' new row crops, and the subject of many lurid rumors.

In waking life, Fog Creek unofficially split north and south Hawthorn. One side of the bank was littered with food wrappers, hypodermic needles, and used condoms. But in Terrence's dreams - which he was finally beginning to reckon with - both sides of the bank looked equally bare, holding nothing but dead, wet weeds.

He sat at the edge of the creek, dipping his toes in the water. Looking at his wet toes in the blue hue of the moon, he noticed thick red syrup creeping down his foot. It was blood.

Then he heard a light splash from the middle of the creek, followed by the hiss of the serpent. The snake crept his scaly head out of the water and rose – up, up, up, all the way up - to Terrence's eye level.

A beautiful if truncated hoot echoed through the darkness as if it were being carried through the haze – the same haze that draped the moon in a sheer blanket.

From above, the owl fluttered its wings right above the serpent, which stayed still and stiff at Terrence's eye level.

This cued the wolf, which stood behind Terrence, and growled when Terrence turned to him, showing silver, metallic fangs.

All three creatures watched as Terrence sat on the edge of the south bank. The owl and serpent's eyes both tracked Terrence's gaze while the wolf stood guard, making sure he didn't try to escape.

Terrence stood up. The wolf did too.

Terrence looked straight upward. The moon grew bigger and brighter by the second, devouring the sky, cosmic inch by cosmic inch. The atmosphere became glowing white, and everything looked fluorescent.

Terrence put one foot in front of the other, edging them into the mud of the creek.

"Is this what you want?" Terrence said to the owl. "Do you want me to drown?"

Their eyes locked on each other as Terrence lowered into the water. His knees, his thighs, his belly button, his nipples, his Adam's apple, his lips, his nose, his eyebrows, his scalp – swallowed whole by dirty water.

Just before Terrence woke up, water filled his lungs as he looked at himself in the reflection of the moon. This growing, glowing orb hovered over the water and was colored amber by a murky layer of rippled water.

Terrence's brown face blended with the amber tint seamlessly, which made him look omnipresent. He was the guardian of Hawthorn or the world – he wasn't sure, and it didn't matter to him. He didn't want it.

Thin red ribbons of blood floated above his head as he sunk to the bottom of the creek, weighed heavy by his thoughts, and by the thoughts of the people he was charged with watching over.

He woke up a different man, and it was no surprise to him. He immediately realized it. He rose out of bed wholly drenched – to the extent that he wondered if it was sweat or the water from Fog Creek.

As time quickly wore on, Terrence was more and more unencumbered by tradition, and the trouble of his childhood became spotty in his mind.

He let his hair grow out. His brow stayed furrowed, only relaxing when he caught the attention of the students. Terrence was pleased when his words could connect to an audience despite this spiritual shift he was enduring. It let him know he was going to be okay during the whole damn thing.

At first, this change in Terrence brought on frenetic energy in him. But as he grew comfortable with himself, his brown skin, and his glitchy soul, he slumped his hips and relaxed into his heels, and walked with both authority over his fellow citizens, and submission to the dark magic of the universe that showed him how to finally feel like a human.

He opened every class by playing the piano, for which he had to ask permission from the grouchy old teacher he assisted. He sat at the keys with his back turned to his students as they marched in - slovenly and drowsy after a greasy cafeteria lunch.

Terrence's head bobbed as he played, mimicking a possessed person, emphasizing the drama of the music. The students grudgingly, with rolling eyes, admired their teacher's brilliance - one girl in particular.

Her name was Patty. She was a sophomore at Esther B. Williams high school. She was beautiful in the way that maize is beautiful, or hard lightning storms. She had a front chipped tooth and swollen, pink lips that were perpetually chapped. She had the practiced, wayward strut of a fallen princess, but the clothes she wore came from the donation box converted from an old dumpster in front of the McAdams Market.

Still, Patty got what she wanted from the older men around her – her pastors and teachers. She learned to leverage what she perceived as her power – in her view, the only weapon a girl honestly had over authority.

She enjoyed bending the morals of old men and defiling their rigid reverence to their wives. It let her know that no man could ever get over on her just because they sat comfortably on top of the food chain.

There was something to be said, she thought, for the power of the feminine mystique. Men are simple, and they crave complexity. Except when men get it, it becomes the thing from which they seek to escape as her father did more often than not during drunken nights at the Cue 'n Brew.

Patty didn't hang out at the park soliciting the attention of older men like a typical teenage hustler. She coaxed the attention out of them. Once she got them alone, she pulled it all out of them as quickly as she could have pulled off their ties – but didn't. She let the more common girls do that. She was saving herself; maybe not for marriage, but for as long as she could.

All she had to do was listen to them. Not touch – never touch. But listen to them. In return, they not only gave her good grades but a tacit pass into adulthood. Those grades would launch her into a college career neither she or her family could pay for, and the approval let her know just how easy navigating the adult world would prove to be – as long as she made it there in one piece.

Patty perfected her technique on nearly every male teacher at Esther B. Williams. Many loved her - and in an odd way, she loved them back.

She had a magical way about her, propping up her youth while hiding her experience just below the surface. Even though she could have gotten good grades on her own - and easily - she recognized the value of seduction for a woman who wanted to succeed alongside the men who were so clearly intellectually inferior to her. Men were gifted with aggression. Women were gifted with cunning.

The skill of seduction was more valuable than popular friends. It was more powerful than money. Because, as she learned on the playground when she needed to ply other kids' lunches from their boxes to bring home for dinner, a seductive personality is how you gain those things that a girl needs to survive.

But Patty resisted the temptation to make Terrence a victim of her seductive spirit, for a couple of reasons.

Terrence seemed fragile to Patty.

Most men understood that their relationships with Patty must be brief, as one could only rely on the cover of darkness for so long. But Terrence's own essence had a delicate music embedded inside, and Patty feared what that might mean when it came to end it with Terrence. It's the gentle soul, or fragile ego, that most violently riots when bruised one time too many.

Patty's other reason was selfish.

She wished to avoid being called a nigger-lover, or worse consequences that stemmed from being a white girl involved with a person of color, let alone someone so much older, let alone a teacher.

Even though she had been promised love from every man who was tasked with caring for her, and some people even knew about it, and most everyone else suspected it, no one cared that much.

Men are pigs, and they do what they can get away with, most people thought. It's up to the girls to control not only their own minds and libidos, but also the minds and libidos of the men who threaten their chastity.

And a Black man?

Even the poorest and dumbest of white girls should know better than to throw themselves away like that, they said to each other in constant whispers.

The implication, Patty recognized, was that Terrence was not gifted with even the most basic human restraint – he was not a complete person.

He looked different, and that dictated that he must be different. He must be, according to the rest of the world, an animal of some sort.

In the eyes of the world, he was less than her in some ways and less than her other lovers. Patty thought it was unfair, because she had a great affection for Terrence, if from a distance.

But what can you do? Patty concluded. *That's the way the world works.*

"Mr. Haight," Patty said, firmly but smoothly, standing behind him. Terrence stopped playing and turned around to see Patty's bashful face.

Patty stammered a bit. "What song is that?" She finally asked after seconds of fielding Terrence's fiery gaze.

Terrence blinked twice. "You can call me Terrence," he said, almost whispering. He turned back around and started playing again. Patty pulled up a chair.

She watched Terrence sway and feel what he was playing. He appeared to feel sounds like he felt his own toes.

He was letting his murky energy loose onto the keys, each finger casually forcing noise from the guts of the piano.

The strength of his fingers and their deliberate tapping aroused Patty's interest.

What was behind such grace and such force?

Terrence's eyes expressed a deep comfort - a feeling of control that he did not show much evidence of in any other waking moment.

Terrence no longer looked wild to Patty, or even exotic. He looked like a person she wanted to know.

After he was done playing, he closed the piano and turned around to face Patty. He leaned back with his knees apart, his untied shoelaces appearing to keep him tethered to the ground.

Patty sat directly across from him, with her hands collapsed in her lap; imitating the mature ladies she observed having coffee at the Hawthorn café.

"What do you want?" Terrence asked after a few seconds of silence.

Patty continued to stammer. "What – what song is that?"

Terrence crossed his legs and squinted his eyes. "Why do you ask?"

"Because it's beautiful," Patty replied.

Terrence's mouth slowly widened into a grin.

"Thank you," Terrence said. "I wrote it."

Patty nodded. "It's beautiful," she repeated.

Terrence's smile opened to reveal a series of off-white, slightly crooked teeth. Patty smiled too.

Their love story is a tale of an awkward dance between jittery spirits.

Neither of them knew what the other truly wanted, but they were desperate to learn. They never did learn, but they came to accept and appreciate each other as a stepping-stone to knowing about the world, and about themselves.

They walked each other through space and time at a respectful distance, finding a window to climb through together to observe the absurdity of life. Though they knew that their hearts would ultimately go to other - perhaps less deserving - keepers, the memory of this affair would be impressed on other lovers, unfairly or not.

Patty led Terrence down a county road past the persimmon tree, her arm linked with his, tugging with a little too much force.

She bent down to pick up a small, shriveled persimmon. She held it up to Terrence's right eye, and she swerved it into the grip of her front teeth, ripping the orange mush right from its core. She hocked it out onto the ground with full force, as a man would.

Terrence flinched. "What are you doing?"

"Give me your pocket knife," Patty said, putting a piece of the orange flesh behind Terrence's bottom lip.

"Mmm," Terrence said, swallowing it. "It's really sweet." He handed the knife to Patty. She flipped it open and carved the oak-colored seed in half. She opened it like a book. Her tiny thumb felt the ridges - her chipped, canary-colored nail polish eclipsing the imprint.

"A spoon," Patty said. "That means lots of snow."

Terrence shook his head to indicate he had no idea what Patty was talking about.

Patty scoffed. "Didn't your granddaddy teach you nothin'? Inside the persimmon is a knife shape, a spoon shape, or a fork shape. A spoon means cold winter," she explained. "Lots of snow."

"I think your granddaddy was full of it, girl," Terrence said. "More full of shit than a Christmas turkey." Terrence laughed, making Patty blush with aggravation.

"He ain't never been wrong!" Patty exclaimed. "Except he beat up my grandma when she didn't mind him."

"What would your granddaddy think about me?" Terrence said, shuffling his feet as he walked.

"He grew up in a different time, Terrence," Patty said.

"So? What's so different about these days? That's just some mess white people say," he said. He realized he was perhaps being too candid with this sixteen-year-old girl.

"So what would your granddaddy think about me?" Patty said, putting her hands on her hips.

"My granddaddy's dead," Terrence said.

"What if he wasn't dead?" Patty asked, undeterred. "What would he think of me if he was still here?"

Terrence looked off toward the fading sun. "I reckon you're right," Terrence said.

"Mmm-hm," Patty said, pulling Terrence closer to her. "Sorry, but it's cold," she said. "Don't get any ideas."

"Wouldn't dream of it, Your Highness," Terrence said.

A vehicle drove down an adjacent road. The couple saw it through the trees and heard the tires wreck through gravel. They froze for a second, looking at each other like doomed deer.

Terrence, without saying a word, put up his quilted hood - hiding his face in cloth and shadow - and put on his gloves. As the truck drove past them, Terrence turned his head away toward the tree line.

"He's gone," Patty said as they walked. Terrence kept his hood up anyway.

Two

Long before she was ready to shave her legs, Shelly Guile decided that if she were to ever do anything with her life, she would have to do it under the wing of a man who inherited his power.

She knew that she would still have to fight for her power, of course - in the same way that the cats who hung around the rain gutters fought with the groundhogs for squatter's rights every summer.

But whatever she needed, she'd fight for it, and she'd get it.

She came of age in a trailer before the term "trailer trash" had taken hold in popular culture and permeated playgrounds as one of many brutal insults children hurled at each other. In her fantastical reality, Shelly Guile was perfectly, adequately middle class, despite all evidence to the contrary.

Her grandfather Lloyd raised Shelly after her birth mother gave up custody and her grandmother died unexpectedly. It was with Lloyd that Shelly perfected the spell she would later cast on so many older men. Her brand of magic was a mix of spiritual seduction and affected naivety. It usually worked - like when she applied for a job at the drive-in before she was legally old enough to work; or when she got caught by the janitor smoking under the Hawthorn tree on the outskirts of the campus of Esther B. Williams high school and knew that after-school detention meant a whipping from Lloyd.

Shelly sat back as ladylike as she knew how, watching with pleasure as the weak, amoral men with whom she entangled herself tromped over their entire lives – destroying everything they claimed to love like big stupid monsters, while she quietly bled them out.

Some men were easier targets than others. Some remained relatively unscathed by her serpentine spirit, while some were utterly destroyed from the inside out.

Shelly made old men feel things that were unfamiliar to them – long forgotten spritely energy - and in turn the men fell for her quickly. That left a nagging problem - guilt, from which she could never completely shake free from her conscience. It didn't stop her, but it kept her from sleeping soundly sometimes.

She spent her entire childhood forming this mold for herself – a look that girls would imitate. She put plastic general store berets in her hair that pinned back her brunette bangs, and painted her lips a shade of pink she made herself by mixing rose and maroon shades ordered from girly catalogs.

Shelly Guile always aimed for plasticine perfection, with even her flaws calculatedly on display. The other girls contorted themselves to try to fit into this mold. Patty worked the hardest, and so she was crowned Shelly's best friend since the seventh grade.

It was the day after she saw her friend Patty and what she had been up to – and with whom, that Shelly executed her cruel plan. It was a mix of girlish jealousy and emotional vacuity that had led her to follow Patty after school in her father's truck. She figured Patty was up to something. Patty had broken too many after-school plans to not be. Usually when Shelly asked Patty to do something, the answer was a sheepish yes.

It wasn't that difficult to catch them. Patty was a loner. Shelly had plucked her from the underpinnings of the trailer park and polished her up back in junior high. As such, Patty had no idea how much potential power and beauty she held. Their friendship would never work otherwise.

Usually Patty took the boys Shelly was done with walking along County Highway 505. But there she was, in broad daylight like a damn fool, with a man over a foot taller than she. Deducing it was Terrence that Patty was with was a little harder. Eventually, after a sleepless night of thorough examination and tossing and turning, Shelly settled on a lucky guess.

Shelly passed Patty and Terrence in her father's black pickup truck on that day, kicking up dust and throwing rocks onto the pleats of both of their pants. Patty was so stricken by the thought of getting caught with Terrence that it hadn't occurred to her who might be in that truck, even though she had seen it a thousand times. It only mattered that a Hawthornite was in it. None of them could be trusted.

When she saw Patty and Terrence walking together, Shelly's throat closed up. Her foot became heavy, and the cloud of dust that trailed Lloyd's truck got engorged and puffy but dissipated quickly like ashes.

Shelly laid awake all that night, wondering what Patty and Terrence saw in each other. Her feelings were inscrutable to her. All she knew was that she felt all mixed up and her stomach pained her. She had a bad taste in her mouth that came from her tongue tightening up on itself.

So she stared at the ceiling and worried. Though she tried not to plot against her friend, the plan stitched itself together in her mind, and Shelly didn't resist.

The next day in between classes, Shelly followed the beautiful piano music that scored her impending betrayal as she walked into music class early with an authoritative strut. She slammed the door behind her and guarded her breastbone with her textbooks.

Terrence quit playing the piano and looked over at her, slightly perturbed with her intrusion.

The two locked eyes. Shelly momentarily forgot why she was there. Tears streamed down her face. She caught the tears in her palms and discarded them in slight embarrassment.

"I saw you," was all Shelly could say with a quivering chin, her back pressed against the door. "I saw you together."

Terrence's face dropped. He said nothing.

"And it ain't right," Shelly said.

Terrence directly stared at Shelly, hoping she was a hallucination and that she would go away. After minutes of silence, she disappeared into the rectangular peninsula of the hallway. Shelly was stunned at what she had just done, as was Terrence.

Shelly was furious, but she didn't know why or at whom, exactly. So, in an attempt to right some wrong that she couldn't quite figure out, she found a way to keep her fury choked down. She greeted Patty in the cafeteria with a beaming smile. The pulsating humid vengeance calmed a bit within Shelly, as the two girls talked about silly things.

"I have a secret," Shelly finally said in between smatterings of girlish giggling and gossip.

Patty put in two sticks of gum. Her eyes lit up. "Tell me," she said.

"I'm in love," Shelly said. "With a teacher."

A chill befell Patty. "Oh?" She asked through a thick tension in her throat. "Like a real teacher?"

"I can't tell you," Shelly said. "If anyone knew, the whole town would string us both up."

There was only one teacher in Hawthorn who was off-limits; or rather, a teacher's assistant. The chill in Patty's spine became frenzied static.

"Does he love you back?" Patty asked. Her insides revolted against the walls of her abdomen.

Shelly watched as Patty melted down into rose-colored jelly. "I think so," Shelly said with a strange affection for her target. "Promise you won't tell."

"I promise," Patty whispered through tight lips, her heartbreak quickly turning to wrath before Shelly's eyes.

Three

Lloyd Guile lived in a yard filled with trees. His doublewide trailer shimmered through swaying earth tones of bark and leaves. The tin can trailer served as a beacon for Shelly on many late nights with full moons, and early morning rides home during the summer, blurry with fading drunkenness. She looked upon it as a girl scout would look at the northern lights.

Lloyd's wife, Gerty, died one windy March night after a nasty bout with pneumonia. As with most people who managed to flee Hawthorn, it was a funeral that managed to pull Shelly back. It was Gerty's funeral that marked the first time Shelly had set foot in Hawthorn since she started college. After a few days, she swore she'd never come back.

A lot had changed for Shelly in four years, but the community of Jackass Flats remained unchanged in the sludge of comfortable malaise.

Shelly had shacked up with a railway worker named Dwight Wright in Carbondale, Illinois, and they had a little boy named Daniel. Shelly commuted to college and picked Daniel up from daycare every day after class.

Dwight Wright was a hard worker, a passable partner, and an utter failure as a father. He looked at his son Daniel, who shared Dwight's blazing blue eyes (minus the inflamed blood vessels) and platinum hair, with distrust. Dwight spoke to his son politely and fettered. Dwight always wondered what this boy thought of him, and he suspected Daniel looked upon him with pity or disgust.

One morning, Daniel was seated in his high chair eating cereal with his hands as he observed his father stumbling around the kitchen in a drunken stupor. Dwight fumbled his hands around the cupboards, looking for a block of Ramen to boil. He threw a handful of chopped onions into the water, from which the steam started to build.

In a cartoonish sequence, Dwight somehow managed to knock the water off of the stove and onto his dirty white shoes. The scalding water splashed on top of the thin fabric of Dwight's swap-meet slippers; it rushed up his ankle and scalded his skin. As Dwight danced in agony and cursed more than he ever did in his life, he looked over at Daniel to see him smiling, then laughing – a toddler's relentless giggle.

Daniel's laughing broke Dwight's pitiful heart, which was already bogged down with bourbon. Dwight expressed this hurt as cursing and yelling toward his baby son - who in turn laughed even harder. No matter what Dwight said or how red his face got or how much he howled in pain, Daniel laughed at him. Shelly entered the room, put her hands on her hips, and scoped the scene. She started laughing, too.

Daniel was a sensitive boy, however. Had Dwight been a little brighter, he would have recognized that Daniel inherited this from him. Daniel contorted his face when cars backfired around the trailer park or when his parents yelled at each other in drawn out screaming matches. His eyes and their brows, as well as his cheeks changed shape tirelessly and displayed every emotion for all to see. His intensity endeared him to adults as a baby, but it would be something to mask later in life.

It was no surprise to see Dwight's note before he left for good. It was scrawled on a receipt in second grader's handwriting and stuck upside down to the refrigerator – probably in the hope that Shelly wouldn't see it right away, giving him a substantial head start had she even bothered to go after him.

Daniel was the first to see the note. He actually was in second grade and hadn't yet mastered reading in cursive, let alone in upside down chicken scratch. Even without reading it, he knew what the note said. His father would never write anything down unless there was no other way to communicate. Daniel wasn't even sure that his father could read. On the few occasions he saw his father reading the paper, he observed him flipping through it quickly, seemingly only looking at the pictures and occasionally muttering, "This country is going to Hell."

After she got used to the idea of Dwight being gone, Shelly gathered her breath and nursed her pride back to health. She plotted.

She ended up spending the cash Dwight left in her nightstand on an old Cadillac, an action figure set Daniel wanted for his birthday, and a basket full of Avon makeup from the frumpy teenager from down the road that Dwight always flirted with to no avail.

One day while Daniel was at school, Shelly packed the Cadillac full of Daniel's things and two of her favorite sundresses. She picked up Daniel from school and drove two hundred and fifty-seven miles to Lloyd's house.

Shelly arrived loudly, the rattle of the engine working with the wind to rock the dead leaves and gumballs off of the trees.

"Oh, bother," Shelly said under her breath as gumballs dropped on the roof of her car, waking Daniel in the back seat.

"Mama," Daniel said groggily, "Where are we?"

"Uh," Shelly said nervously, biting her nails as she put the Cadillac in park. "We're home." She looked back at Daniel and smiled. Daniel looked over Shelly's shoulder at the tin can trailer reflecting the sun.

Lloyd stumbled out in a stained wife-beater shirt and equally stained white briefs. He held a shotgun and stumbled around with it as if he was half-asleep. Shelly shrieked, and Daniel froze. Lloyd shielded his eyes from the sun to get a look at them.

"For God's sake," Shelly whispered.

"Mama?" A confused Daniel whimpered.

"S'okay, doll," Shelly said. "That's grandpa. He's...confused."

Grandpa?

"Shelly?" Lloyd shouted. "That you?"

Shelly cranked down the window. "It's me, dad," Shelly yelled.

The three sat and ate dinner at the same kitchen table that a teenaged Shelly once spent a year sewing together her own prom dress.

Shelly clicked her manicured nails against the fiberglass tabletop and hovered over her dinner plate, cradling her head with her free hand. She stared off into space, only breaking back into the present when she caught Daniel giving her an extended glare. She smiled at him.

Lloyd ate loudly. "So the dumb bastard finally bailed, huh?" He said with food at the back of his mouth. "I'll hand it to him; he lasted longer than I thought he would."

"Thanks, daddy," Shelly said, drained and defeated.

Lloyd reached across the table and tweaked Shelly's nose.

"He's a damn fool, leaving my beautiful baby like that," he said. "You think he found another woman?"

Shelly scoffed. "Just one?"

Lloyd seemed surprised at Shelly's unvarnished honesty. "We're all jackasses, sweetheart," Lloyd said in a saccharine tone.

"Don't I know it," Shelly mumbled. She threw her paper napkin on top of her plate. "I'm taking a bath," she said on her way out of the room.

"Don't flush the toilet before you run the water," Lloyd said. "It'll freeze your knockers off."

"Lovely," she called out from the bathroom.

Daniel gave his grandpa a hopeful grin.

"Go get your grandpa a beer, squirt," Lloyd said gruffly. "I'll give you a taste of it if you hurry."

"I'm not supposed to drink beer," Daniel said. "Mama says it'll stunt my growth."

"Nah, that's just an old wife's tale," Lloyd said. He pinched Daniel just above his nipple. "It'll put hair on your chest."

There was a fire in Shelly that would not go out. In the life of her dreams, everything was crushed velvet and expensive wine. Living with her father at the age of twenty-eight was just a penance to pay for her lack of humility, but one day soon, she'd rise above these folks in town, and she'd never have to watch her father spit tobacco into a beer can on Saturday night again.

For the first time since she'd arrived back in Jackass Flats, she put on makeup with the assistance of her compact mirror and the nickel-plated toaster. She smacked her lips and lifted her breasts like she was 16 again. It had been three months since Dwight or any other man had touched her, but she found the pheromones somewhere within her and put them to good use.

Shelly strutted to her car, and once inside checked her reflection yet again in the rearview mirror. She placed cat-eye-shaped sunglasses over her eyes, shielding them from the world, and she drove off.

As her foot lay more heavily upon the gas pedal, Shelly daydreamed. She passed dirty, shirtless children playing in the yards of their dirty, floorless houses.

Usually, she'd look upon them with pity and light disgust – as well as discomfort for how familiar the sight was. The feeling of being one with this town, absorbed under the surface of Jackass Flats - it was like forcing an emerald diamond into a garbage disposal.

But today, she paid them no mind. This world would soon be hers. These filthy creatures would soon be left behind.

Her rusty Cadillac parked in front of Hawthorn Baptist Church. Shelly was still in the hypnosis of her daydreams. Her body waited for her mind to catch up. She saw before her a quaint brick building with a neon-backlit wooden cross protruding from its backside.

It's not so scary, she thought. *Kind of cute, really.*

After a moment, Shelly's hand lifted the car door handle. Her feet, in thrift shop stilettos, wobbled a bit as she walked. She felt compelled to take them off, but she fended off this uncouth fantasy. Once her mind zapped back into place, she regained her composure and ignored her pain.

The musty smell of the church foyer grounded her. Her head stopped spinning. She heard the whispers of an old woman praying near the front of the sanctuary.

Shelly walked down the aisle of the church she got baptized in, her purse guarding her breasts. She sat down and looked ahead, her sunglasses still standing guard over her eyes. Shelly recognized this praying woman as Mrs. Redmond, pastor Harold Redmond's wife. She looked straightforward as not to disturb Mrs. Redmond.

Mrs. Redmond finally looked over at Shelly. "Welcome," she said. "Do you need to be alone?"

"No, ma'am," Shelly said. "I was just waiting for you to finish your prayer."

Mrs. Redmond smiled a row of straight, gray teeth. "Prayer?" she repeated back. "I wasn't praying, dear." Mrs. Redmond looked polite and perplexed. *If she wasn't praying,* Shelly thought, *she must have been talking to herself.*

"Do you know where I might find information about a job here?" Shelly asked, ignoring the peculiarity of Mrs. Redmond.

"A job? Here?" Mrs. Redmond asked.

"Yes," Shelly said. She dug through the wilderness inside of her purse to find the classified ad. She unfolded the ad just as carefully as she cut it out. "This ad says you're looking for a secretary."

"Oh," Mrs. Redmond said, taking the creased paper and holding it at arm's length, not even looking at it, then handing it back. "You ought to talk to my husband, Father Redmond." Shelly took the clipping, and Mrs. Redmond smiled. She blinked a few times in rapid succession.

"I see," Shelly said, a little uneasy. "Is Father Redmond available?"

"He went on a house call," Mrs. Redmond said. "If you like, I can lead you to his office. He'll be back shortly."

Harold Redmond's office was decorated like a Roman Coliseum. There were gold curtains draped over an oversized portrait of The Last Supper. His desk was plated with faux-marble, and his bookshelves were gilded in gold. Even his paperweights were chunks of fool's gold.

Shelly sat with her legs crossed. Her sharp knees tested the limits of her tan pantyhose. Her foot swayed circularly in anticipation. She checked her lips in her compact mirror for signs of smudging and looked over her shoulder to make sure Father Redmond wasn't nearby.

Finally, Redmond entered the office. He was a tall, paunchy man, with bifocal glasses and a spot of hair on an otherwise bald head. Despite his slovenly appearance, his energy was that of a man with too much authority. It made Shelly uncomfortable.

He seemed slightly startled to see Shelly. "Oh," Redmond said. "Hello."

Shelly stood to greet Father Redmond. She extended her hand. "Mr. Redmond, my name is Shelly Guile," she said with a speech pattern exhilarated by nerves. "I'm here for the secretary job."

To Shelly's slight surprise, Harold Redmond took her hand and kissed the top of it. He caressed it with his thumb, maintaining a tight grip on it. "Please, have a seat," he said with hungry eyes. "No need to be so formal." He walked behind his desk and had a seat himself.

Redmond sat back in his chair and cradled the back of his bald head with this hands. His bent elbows looked like pasty wings. He grinned with his eyes fixed on Shelly's. "Can you type?" He asked.

"Yes. I took a typing class in high school," Shelly said. "That wasn't an awful long time ago. I also graduated from - "

"How fast can you type?" Redmond interrupted.

"How fast?" Shelly repeated.

"Mmm-hmm," Redmond murmured, nodding his head. "How many words per minute?"

Shelly thought quickly. "About ninety," she said, lying.

"Ninety, huh?" Redmond said. He winked and smirked. "That's pretty fast."

Shelly smiled so tightly her lips cracked.

"You're a lovely young lady," Father Redmond said. "I'm surprised you even want to work."

"Why is that?" Shelly asked, her perky facade starting to wear thin.

"Are you married?" Redmond asked her. Shelly squirmed a bit at this question.

"Sort of," Shelly said, looking down at her throbbing feet. "He went to work one morning a few months ago, and never came back. I guess he's working overtime."

Redmond shook his head, feigning sympathy. "That's a real shame. I'm sorry to hear that."

"Thank you," Shelly said. She was uncomfortable and little agitated at the line of questions.

"A beautiful woman like you shouldn't spend one night alone," Redmond said.

"I'm not alone exactly," Shelly said. "I have a son."

"Mmm," Redmond said, nodding. "What's his name?"

"Daniel," Shelly said quietly.

"Daniel," Redmond whispered to himself. He met Shelly's eyes and smiled. "That's a nice strong name. Biblical."

"Like Daniel and the lion's den," Shelly said with a dry chuckle.

"Exactly," Redmond said with emphasis. "Are you well-versed in the Bible?" Redmond asked. "Do you have a church background?"

Shelly blinked twice and grinned. Her upper lip began to sweat. "You're the one who baptized me, Father," she said.

Father Redmond laughed with his belly. "Forgive me, darlin'. I've performed a lot of those over the years."

"It wasn't at this church, of course," Shelly said. "It was on the other side of town."

Harold Redmond nodded. "We've been very fortunate," he said. "God has blessed us with all of this." He raised his hands in praise.

"Looks like it," Shelly replied, darting her eyes around the room.

"And as such," Redmond said, "we receive a lot of phone calls on some days. Are you good on the phone?"

"Yes. I –"

"Because some girls just say they're good on the phone to get the job, but trust me: you either are, or you aren't," Redmond said. "It's not something you learn by doing."

"People say they are soothed by my voice," Shelly said. She couldn't think of anything else to say but that.

Harold Redmond remained leaned back in his chair. "Yes, I'm sure they do," he said with a Cheshire grin.

Redmond's eyes moved up and down Shelly's body. He zeroed in on her legs. "Your dress..."

"Is it too short?" Shelly asked, beginning to ramble. "I'm sorry. I should have known, coming to a church. But you see, it's laundry day, and I just moved back to town..."

Redmond shook his head no and held his hand up to halt her from speaking. Shelly noticed that Redmond kept sniffing and scratching his nose. Shelly also saw that during the fifteen minutes in which they spoke, he barely blinked.

"Can you stand up for me?" Redmond asked from behind his desk.

"Stand up?" Shelly asked, equal parts confused, knowing, and frustrated.

Father Redmond nodded yes impatiently. He twirled his pudgy finger into an invisible smoke ring. His eyes were stern, and his eyebrows were raised as if Shelly had asked a stupid question and no words were necessary – just a moment of silence, so this pure little lamb in a yellow sundress could feel the weight of his implication.

Father Redmond looked at Shelly like he was about to eat her alive as he got up from his desk and circled her. She placed her hands on her lower abdomen, and they started to quiver. Her arms guarded her rib cage. Redmond slid his hands onto hers from behind, stabilizing them while pressing his erection into her posterior.

Shelly jerked reflexively as her mind froze.

"Don't be afraid," Redmond cooed into Shelly's ear. He smelled of musky cologne and thin, putrid sweat. "No matter what happens, while you're under my wing, you're still a woman of God," he said.

Holding firmly on her arms, he then pressed on the back of her head, forcing Shelly's face onto the surface of his desk, wrinkling documents and scraping her eyelid on a copper paperweight shaped like The Holy Cross. She squeaked and whimpered.

"What are you doing?" Shelly asked, her words muffled.

"Be quiet," Redmond said more forcefully than before.

She didn't know whether the warm liquid dripping down her face and damning up on her cheekbones was a buildup of tears or blood.

As Father Redmond penetrated Shelly, he grunted in grotesque conquest. Shelly's insides - from the nerves in her painted toes to her intestines to her skull - felt cold and stiff and tingly, yet hot as molten lava beneath her clammy skin. Her buttocks tingled as if it had lost circulation.

As Father Redmond continued to thrust, the entire bottom half of Shelly's body was numb, and the tingling in her buttocks intensified into such heat that they melted her legs into a liquefied wax. She tried her best to stand up - and when that failed, she decided that she just had to get through it.

In her mind, she went somewhere else – somewhere she had never been; somewhere she couldn't describe or comprehend. She went into oblivion for a little while.

Suddenly, Father Redmond moaned and collapsed. He exhaled rapidly, feeling a mix of perverse victory and physical relief. He stroked the back of Shelly's sweaty hair as if to thank her. Redmond raised himself off of her and glanced at his palm, acknowledging the stickiness of Shelly's hairspray. He wiped his hand on his briefs. He buttoned his pants, catching his breath.

Shelly laid facedown on the desk, letting her bosom and stomach muscles hold her up, as her legs had buckled and were useless. Her feet dangled off the vinyl floor a half-inch - one stiletto on, and one somewhere across the room.

Father Redmond chuckled as he caught his breath. He wiped his forehead with a nearby baby wipe. He put the box of baby wipes and a bleach-stained towel that smelled of fabric softener next to Shelly's head as she looked straight ahead. She leaned on the desk, her eyes refusing to blink.

He placed a hardcover Bible on top of this stack of rags.

"There's some Band-Aids in my desk if you need 'em," Father Redmond said. "Looks like you got a little scrape there." He pointed to his temple.

Shelly said nothing as the same tears that formed fifteen minutes prior refused to come out. Father Redmond leaned over and observed that he could see the whites of her eyes.

"Take all the time you need," Redmond said as he started toward the door. "I'll be in the sanctuary."

Shelly, using her upper body strength to raise herself up slowly, turned her chin toward Redmond and nodded ever so lightly, eyes wide open.

"Welcome back to Hawthorn," Redmond said, opening the door and taking a step out. "And welcome aboard. Hopefully I'll see you Monday. Have a blessed weekend."

Shelly stood up after she heard the door shut, giving way to the ache in her back and the raw burning between her legs. Emptied and hollowed out with shaking kneecaps, Shelly used her upper body strength to knock the Bible off of the desk in a quick flash of fury.

A yellow envelope flung itself out of the Bible, now lying spine-up on the floor.

She found her other shoe and torn underwear under Redmond's desk and slid them on using numb arms and fingers. As she was mentally preparing to leave, Shelly looked back and took the envelope out from underneath the opened Bible.

The envelope said in black block letters: "TO SECRETARY INTERVIEWEE." Shelly stared at it for what seemed to her like several minutes. She contemplated not opening it, but her curiosity took over, and she ripped it open. She turned it upside down, shaking it. Falling to the floor like wafting leaves were two one thousand dollar bills. She looked at the money on the floor. The tears crept outside the pink flesh of the corner of her eyes. She felt her chin dimple into a thousand little pricks before catching hold of herself and neutralizing her expression.

She held the money in front of her stone face – and finally, the tears fell. She sat in the chair across from Father Redmond's desk, practically falling into it, and stared at that copper, blood-spotted crucifix paperweight for a good fifteen minutes.

Shelly sat there for so long that to her, time itself became arbitrary markers of unremarkable happenings.

Take all the time you need, he said. Shelly blinked a few times and thought of Daniel.

All the time you need, he said. Shelly wondered where Dwight had run off.

All the time, he said. Shelly wondered how often, exactly.

Time, he said. What was the point?

That was the point of it: to sit in the chair next to where she had just been violated and to stare at the room until she had shrunk the mental image of her rape down to nothing.

Shelly willed herself to disregard the nasty, evil world and questions of morality and the reprehensible things people do to each other; the pain of being a woman while struggling to be seen as a whole person.

Shelly floated so far above her own tragedy that life itself didn't matter anymore. Shelly had to make it okay not for herself, but for Daniel. This is what kept her from falling to pieces that day. It's why she took the money home. It's why she decided to come back on Monday - right then, right there. What were her other options, exactly? To live with her disgusting grandfather until he croaked?

What an heiress I'd make, Shelly joked silently to herself, as she finally broke into laughing sobs.

So she shoved the pain she felt below, into the same abyss that she discarded all of the things that got in the way of her living without fear. She walked through the church foyer with a terrible secret – one she intended to keep for the rest of her life.

She caught Mrs. Redmond dusting an already-clean table in the foyer. "Will you be joining the team, dear?" Mrs. Redmond asked cheerily. "The Good Lord knows we need the help."

Shelly nodded and opened her mouth to speak. She croaked at first, but she cleared her throat and masked her pain with a smile. "I believe so, yes," Shelly said with a teardrop in her throat.

As soon as she closed the heavy oak door behind her and her wet cheeks met the humid midday air, she ripped off her shoes and walked barefoot to the car. The gravel that covered the parking lot pricked indentions into the bottoms of her feet; her soles stung and scalded on thousands of sharp tiny rocks shaped like shards of broken glass, which heated like coals under the unforgiving sun.

Shelly drove home silent and barefoot, dwelling on the mercifully shallow physical discomfort of her raw, dusty soles.

The other pain she felt was sunken deep inside, hiding behind her eyes - which were gilded in tears that she just wouldn't allow to fall.

She could see her face in the rearview mirror out of the corner of her eye, and it took her remaining strength to not at least glimpse at herself. She knew her beauty was ruined for the day. Instead, she listened to the radio, even though the music coming out of the speakers hit her ears like white noise.

SHELLY FOUND DANIEL asleep on the living room floor. Lloyd was passed out on the couch, his chin toward the ceiling, head hanging back and his mouth agape. His throat was emanating the sound of a chainsaw.

Shelly knelt down to Daniel. Her knees ached with the acid of overworked muscles. She stroked Daniel's platinum hair and wiped wetness from his cheek. She laid on the floor, her knees to her stomach, and pulled him close. Daniel exhaled out of his deep slumber.

"Mama," Daniel slurred.

"Yes, baby?" Shelly said, her voice shaking.

"How long do we have to stay here?" Daniel asked with a frog in his throat, his eyes still closed.

"Everything's gonna be all right, Danny," Shelly said. "We'll be back on our own soon. Just you and me."

Shelly smelled on Daniel's breath the familiar salty-wheat stench of the cheap beer her father had kept strewn about the house in half-empty cans since Shelly was old enough to have a sense of self.

Once she washed off the events of the afternoon in the rusty shower, she heard a chainsaw out in the yard, buzzing in harmony with Lloyd's motorized snoring.

Through the screen door, standing in nothing but a peach towel, she saw a Black man in a straw hat doing his best to cut down one of the Hawthorn trees Lloyd always complained about. She fastened her towel, put on her robe and slippers, and walked toward this man, who was fighting with a jangly chainsaw. Judging from how old it looked, it was undoubtedly taken from Lloyd's back shed.

She saw the back of him – dark complexion; sweat dripping down his neck, his white shirt sticky, revealing the musculature of manual labor. She realized she knew this man from long ago, and felt immediate shame. It was too late to turn back.

Terrence turned and tipped his hat, uneasy at the undressed state of this weary woman standing before him.

"Hello, ma'am," Terrence said. "You live here with that old man?"

Shelly nodded. "For now."

"He hired me to cut down this tree. You from around here?" Terrence asked, killing the chainsaw engine. "You look like somebody I know."

"I used to live here," Shelly said. "But then I moved away."

Terrence nodded with a smirk. "Missouri has a wicked way of always sucking you back in to where you began, don't it?" He said. "Almost no use in leaving to begin with."

Shelly half-smiled. "Yeah, I suppose it does," she muttered with slight sadness.

Terrence removed his glove. "I'm Terrence," he said, extending his hand. "Welcome back."

"I'm Shelly," she said, extending one hand and keeping her towel up with the other.

"I know who you are," Terrence said, eyes widening. "I remember you, now that I got a good look at you."

Shelly turned red. "Sorry about my...wardrobe," she said. "It's been a long day."

"I hear that," Terrence said.

"Can I get you a glass of tea or lemonade?" Shelly said. "I could make some."

“That’s kind of you, but I’m about to give up on this old piece of junk,” Terrence said, swinging the chainsaw to his side. “Have to come back tomorrow with my own.”

Shelly looked up above at the tangled web of tree branches. “You know, I used to have a clubhouse up in this here tree,” she said.

“I’m surprised your daddy wants to cut it down, then,” Terrence said. “It’s perfectly healthy.”

“He probably doesn’t remember,” Shelly said, looking down. “Tornado got to it. Usually, I went up there to hide from him.” Shelly chuckled. Terrence nodded, making sure not to smile.

“He ain’t my daddy, anyway,” Shelly said. “But close enough, I guess.”

“Well, I best be going,” Terrence said after a moment of silence. “I'll be back Monday.”

“I’ll be here,” Shelly said. “Unless I’m at work.”

Terrence tipped his hat once more. “Then maybe I’ll see you Monday,” he said.

Shelly watched him as he got in his truck. Terrence caught her looking at him, and gave one more tip of his hat as he drove away. She recognized Terrence's face, name, voice, and mannerisms. What she didn't recognize was his nature.

Shelly remembered a jaded young man who assisted the music teacher, guarding his heart and his privacy with fervor.

This Terrence was different. She wondered what it was that changed him, and wished that whatever it was, it would happen to her, too. She walked back to her house, slightly dizzy from sensory overload, and wobbling from wearing heels earlier that day.

Shelly walked in to find an awakened Lloyd. He came alive when the screen door slammed. He stared at her with anger. “Don’t be flirting with the town nigger,” he snarled.

Shelly grimaced. “Excuse me?” She said, with uncovered strength in her voice.

Lloyd looked up from his beer, vacating all emotion from his face. He got up and walked to her. Shelly could smell his yeasty breath. “You heard me,” Lloyd said. “And I ain’t playing.” He threw his beer can against the wall. “The quickest way to get into trouble around here, in case you forgot, is to fuck around with the nigger from Jackass Flats," Lloyd said quietly, pointing his finger, grazing Shelly's nose. He sized up Shelly, smelling her fear, then walked to the bathroom.

Shelly hadn't forgotten the ordeal with Terrence. It could have ended much worse. Terrence could have been arrested, and if Patty's father was the sort, Terrence could have been killed. Nobody would have done anything about it except whisper amongst themselves.

Terrence had already shown great audacity in participating in any sort of misbehavior. The wrinkles of Jim Crow hadn't yet been fully ironed out in that part of the country. Terrence, from his colleagues' view, should have felt privileged by ever being hired to teach at all.

He had taught the white children of Hawthorn – those protestant families who could not afford to send their children to the private St. Denis academy, where one might avoid such a fiasco – for half a decade. It was his quiet nature and his complete dedication to the subject he taught – music – that kept him afloat for that long. He was careful not to know any student on a personal level. On the first day of each class, he gave the same short speech.

"Here in class you may call me Terrence," he said. "But outside of this class, you do not, will not, will not *ever* know me."

All of this was to avoid putting himself in a position where his intentions could be misconstrued. Merely walking down the street with brown skin could be taken as an act of violence on the psyche of white folks. The residents of Jackass Flats, no matter their social standing, needed someone on which they could spit. Nobody wanted to concede complete power to people who were merely born lucky. In their minds, they had a real shot at the American dream. In their minds, they were rich white folks in waiting.

Someone who looked like Terrence could never exist on the same social plane as they did; they would never allow it. All they had was their badge of white skin and not much else.

Terrence stayed in Hawthorn because he was born there. His presence was tolerated, and his daily work towards acceptance at some point dissolved into a feeling of pure, effortless living - nothing more, and nothing less. All he wanted was to go to his job, go home pleasantly drained from a day of playing and teaching music, and live quietly. To do this, he had to haunt the periphery of town, never making his presence known more than absolutely necessary. He only went to the grocery store when he saw the parking lot was nearly empty, and he sat in the back pew of the sanctuary on Sunday mornings.

Terrence's life fell apart shortly after Shelly Guile planted those seeds in Patty's mind. For reasons unknown even to her, Shelly aimed to trigger uniquely feminine jealousy in her friend. Shelly's manipulation of Patty was - as Shelly looked back, she realized - pure evil.

Patty was a simple girl whose soul was easily shattered. Once those seeds were planted, it only took a couple of hours for Patty's rage to bloom. And as such, Patty's actions set the course for her own bleak future. As Patty got older, she also haunted the periphery of town in self-exile.

Though they never so much as kissed, Patty and Terrence had allowed themselves to unravel in the safety of each other's gaze, ever so delicately. They had much in common, despite their troubling differences.

Terrence recognized the risk of befriending Patty. This is the man who declared that his students - who weren't that much younger than he was - would never know him. He had found something close to peace in solitude. Had he not seen a spiritual flare in Patty's eyes that told him it was okay to relax, he would have continued to be content in his uniquely pleasant version of loneliness.

But he also recognized that Patty didn't see an Other in Terrence. Her eyes didn't squint from the involuntary smirk of encountering a human oddity – a Black man from Jackass Flats.

But the reality was that Patty did see Terrence as an Other. She saw him as someone smarter. She saw him as gifted; anybody who can play the piano like that, she thought, must have a direct line to the Good Lord. In looking at Terrence's expressive face, she was never bored.

Still, it came as a surprise to her that she crumbled so easily when faced with Terrence's unseemly human traits. They were only friends, but Patty didn't usually make friends that fast. She thought it was special. She fantasized about their future, which involved scenes similar to those in her mother's romance novels.

When Shelly intimated that she and Terrence had carried on an affair and were in love, Patty's first instinct was to call Shelly a liar – which she was. The thought of Shelly stealing her only real friend swallowed her up instantly. Her rage boiled quickly but was left to simmer silently. So before that school day ended, she slid an anonymous note under the principal's office door.

"I would like to remain anonimuss, but I am an underage girl and I am having an affair with the music teacher, Terrence Haight. Please don't put him in jail. I still love him but the secret has become too much to handle on my own." Patty wrote it in block letters. It took her several minutes to write. She took breaks from writing so her tears wouldn't make the ink run - a romance novel cliché that even she couldn't stomach. She didn't want to be motivated by heartbreak; she insisted that anger take center stage for the first time in her life.

When the principal showed Terrence the note, he immediately recognized Patty's handwriting from homework assignments, despite her attempts to disguise it. Terrence said nothing, but tears started to cascade down his own cheeks - running the ink down beneath the blue lines of the notebook paper.

The principal looked at the wall behind Terrence with slight discomfort and let him cry for a minute. Even if it wasn't true, he knew he couldn't risk letting Terrence stay. If the town got wind of it, they'd string them both up.

Terrence went home without a fight.

It was the boredom of unemployment that threatened to break him again. The dreams returned, and his vision became murky once again. He woke up every day in a fog. He didn't move a muscle before ten a.m.

He looked out of his kitchen window one day and saw, in his own reflection, his mother staring back at him. Terrence shook his head vigorously but once he saw it, there was no un-seeing it.

He forced himself to be okay. He carried his mother's sorrow, as well as his own, around with him while he did odd jobs around Jackass Flats, and as many in north Hawthorn as he could find. To survive, he realized, he must live extra quietly, and with a smile. There was no room in his gut for fire, and there never could be again. After he made his peace with this, the only things he bothered to carry with him were the humility around his feet and a light tug of loneliness around his neck.

When Shelly came to him in a panic one morning years later - shoving her blonde, blue-eyed son toward him, Terrence could have leaped out of his skin. His chainsaw was running, and he was working on getting rid of the Hawthorn tree from the week before. Daniel's eyes and forehead glistened, as did the oily spots on the blade of Terrence's saw. The sun was already in full force.

"Terrence," Shelly yelled over the chainsaw motor. Terrence turned it off. Shelly was damn near out of breath.

"What's the matter?" Terrence said, dropping his saw, taking his right hand out of this leather glove and lightly placing it on Shelly's shoulder.

"I'm late for work," Shelly said, panting. "It's the first day of my stupid job, and my bastard father didn't come home last night, and my son—"

Terrence raised a calming hand to Shelly. He looked down to Daniel. "Hello, young man," Terrence said, kneeling down. He wasn't partial to kids since leaving his teaching job, but he tried his best. "You want to do some big boy work? I'll buy you a Coke."

"Okay," Daniel said, rolling his eyes. "But I like root beer, not Coke."

Shelly immediately started to dig into her purse to find spare change. Terrence put his palm on top of her shaky hands, dwarfing hers with his. "Get on to work, now," Terrence said. "We'll be just fine."

Shelly hugged Terrence's sweaty neck. "Thank you!" She said.

Shelly knelt down and gently tweaked Daniel's nose. "You be good for Terrence, Daniel."

If Marianne was watching this from the Hereafter, she was probably shaking her head. "Oh, that boy," she'd say to herself. "Will you never learn?"

Daniel watched in slight terror as his mother drove away by herself - the first time he could remember witnessing her doing so. Things were changing.

He looked up at this man with dark skin and intense eyes and, at the end of a stream of wandering thoughts, wondered what it would be like if Terrence were his father. *What a strange life that would be,* he thought with an uncomfortable snarl.

"You always this quiet?" Terrence asked Daniel, handing him loose tree branches. Daniel shrugged.

Daniel was usually quiet, but not to this extent. He felt it impolite to say - if he could even find the words to say it - but Terrence was the first Black person he'd ever laid eyes upon, not counting television.

Still, little Daniel couldn't see much difference between them try as he might. Terrence had the same accent when he cussed as did every man around town, and there was no reason to believe his feelings or thoughts ran any different. Terrence probably went to church and out to eat just like everyone else did. He was a boy once, just like Daniel was - and surely it wasn't that long ago.

SHELLY FUMBLED AROUND nervously at her desk for the first couple of hours of her first shift. Mrs. Redmond's presence was a strange source of comfort to her - her oblivious smile would continue, Shelly figured, even if she was being boiled alive like a frog.

Eventually, Shelly ran out of things to fiddle with and Mrs. Redmond relaxed into a comfortable, blinkless gaze at the wall across the room. The clock struck nine. Mrs. Redmond turned her head and widened her smile. "Don't worry," she assured Shelly. "Daddy's always late in the mornings."

Mr. Redmond came in around a quarter 'til ten. He sashayed into the office wearing dark mirrored sunglasses, a tight trench coat, and a scarf. He turned on his heels and bent down to kiss his wife on her forehead. She squinted like a puppy.

"Any messages, mama?" Redmond asked. Before Mrs. Redmond could answer, he noticed Shelly sitting hunched at her desk.

"You came back," Redmond said to Shelly, pleasantly surprised.

"Well...yes," Shelly said. She chuckled uncomfortably.

"Good deal," Redmond said softly, his rising cheekbones pushing his shades up. He sniffled and rubbed the cartilage of his nose. "Did Mrs. Redmond teach you the phone?"

"Oh, I know -"

"She knows the phone already," Mrs. Redmond said.

Father Redmond clasped his hands. "Excellent," he said. "Did I get any messages?"

Shelly handed Father Redmond a bunch of neon-colored sticky notes. He nodded, filed through them quickly, and retreated to his office. He slammed the door.

"He didn't have any corrections to your messages," Mrs. Redmond said, astonished.

"Does he usually have corrections to phone memos?" Shelly asked.

Mrs. Redmond nodded. "He has corrections to everything," she whispered. "He likes you. He's a tough man to please."

Shelly tried to figure out the dynamic. The Redmonds, as peculiar as they were - working from a dreary, dark basement - seemed to be successful despite their eccentricities. Mrs. Redmond was a lonesome woman who appeared to be ushered in from half a century ago. She wore a bun of hair on top of her head, no makeup, and flannel floral dresses that, Shelly guessed, she made by hand. Mrs. Redmond couldn't have been much older than Shelly herself – no wrinkles, despite a constant grin - but looked like she could be her mother.

Father Redmond, on the other hand, had an odd charisma mixed with something sly and sinister. He had already shown Shelly that he was capable of cruelty, carried out without emotion.

Shelly of course hated him, but she decided to play the long game. When Redmond spilled his wicked seed during Shelly's job interview, he fertilized dormant rage in Shelly that she aimed to use to lift up her life, and more importantly, the life of her only son. Revenge would wait.

DANIEL STOOD BACK WHILE Terrence ran a chainsaw against the stubborn Hawthorn tree. He shielded his eyes from the sun, creating shadows over the sparks and flares and broken pieces of sunlight - spraying like fireworks, making the day great.

After hearing a strange noise, Daniel felt himself being suddenly swept up. Terrence had run behind Daniel, grabbed him near his ribcage, and placed him on his shoulders.

Daniel's sneakers swung against Terrence's chest, as Terrence held Daniel's wrists with his giant hands to keep him from falling over. As Terrence ran across the yard, the boy sat perched on his shoulders, terrified and swaying.

"What're you doing, mister?" Daniel asked loudly. "I don't like heights."

Terrence knelt down and lifted Daniel over his head, putting his feet back on the ground. Daniel stood in front of Terrence. Terrence then pointed. "Just watch," he said. "You ever seen a tree fall over?"

"Just on TV," Daniel said. Terrence laughed. They took out the cotton from their ears and sat back on the grass.

"Get comfortable," Terrence said. "Looks like we gon' be here a while."

They watched as the tree inched down.

"This is usually more fun," Terrence said after half an hour, his chin resting on his upper chest.

"Can't we push it over?" Daniel asked.

"We could, maybe," Terrence said. "But don't tell your mama."

This excited Daniel. "Okay. Let's go," he said.

Terrence looked at Daniel for a while, weighing out the dangers ahead.

"All right," Terrence finally said. "Let's go."

Daniel didn't do much except provide moral support while Terrence pushed and grunted against the tree in vain. Terrence stood back with his hand on his hips. "Well, scratch that idea."

"I'll get us some sodas from inside," Daniel said.

"You sure your granddad is okay with that?" Terrence asked.

"Who cares if he is?" Daniel said with a twisted chuckle. "I hate him."

"Ain't healthy to hate," Terrence said. "But a soda sounds good, so go on ahead."

They drank their store-brand colas and watched the tree finally fall dramatically, creaking and cracking the whole way down. The tree fell swiftly, and the branches broke its fall, dulling its thud against the ground.

"Why'd you cut down that tree, anyway?" Daniel asked. "It wasn't dyin' or nothin'."

"Because your grandpa paid me to," Terrence said. "He said it messes up his antenna reception."

"No it doesn't," Daniel said. "TV works fine."

"Well then, if I had to guess," Terrence surmised, "this tree holds some bad memories."

"What do you mean?"

"Folks in town always want to tear down memories," Terrence said. "They want that bush tore out, that shed broke down and burned, this tree gone," he said. "Usually it's because they remind them of something they don't want to remember. They can't afford to move away, so...'let's just burn it all down and start over.'"

"I don't get it," Daniel said.

"You probably will someday," Terrence said.

A beige car pulled up to the house. Terrence and Daniel watched from a distance as Billy Joe who owned the Cue 'n Brew dragged an unconscious Lloyd out of the back seat. He piled him up on the front steps. He looked around to see if anyone was watching, and caught Daniel and Terrence looking from afar, nonchalantly drinking from soda cans.

Billy Joe tipped his cowboy hat to acknowledge them, got into his car and peeled out, slinging gravel.

"Go on and get in the truck," Terrence said to Daniel. "I got some walnuts in there." Daniel obeyed.

Terrence put Lloyd over his shoulder and carried him inside. Lloyd cursed him under his breath, and Terrence just mumbled back: "Yeah, shut up you old drunk. I'm saving you from getting your ass sunburned off."

Terrence left Lloyd in the bathtub in case he got sick, and put a note on the front door for Shelly.

Shelly drove home with a new wad of cash in her purse. She rolled down the windows so her face would air dry before she got home.

She went in to find Lloyd drinking a beer on the couch with a frozen steak on his face.

"Rough night?" Shelly said, tossing her keys on the counter. Lloyd grunted in response. "Where's Danny?" She asked.

"I'll tell you where he is," Lloyd said with a growl. "He's with that nigger."

"What are you talking about?" Shelly put her hands on her hips.

"You heard me," Lloyd said, indignant. "He went home with the guy I hired to cut down that damn tree. I told you about messing with him. Maybe one day you'll start listening."

"How do you know he's with Terrence?"

Lloyd pulled out Terrence's note, crumpled and wet with sweat. He tossed it at her. "Left a love note. Didn't know the nigger could read."

"Could you stop using that word?" Shelly said. "It makes you sound even dumber than you are."

"My apologies, princess," Lloyd said with bitter sarcasm.

Shelly drove around Jackass Flats looking for Terrence's truck. She decided spur of the moment to recreate her old bus route.

She had ridden the bus, which drove the same route from Kindergarten until she got her driver's license at age 17. She remembered her old route by heart and even did a rolling stop with her Cadillac at all the same houses. She stopped at Patty's old house longer than anywhere. The old baby blue shutters had faded to light grey, bleached by the sun and disregarded by owners for a couple of decades.

When Terrence left school and didn't return, Shelly sensed a growing distance between she and Patty. Finally, Patty decided to eat lunch alone one day, and that was that. Shelly Guile didn't beg for friends, and she found a new group of girls to boss around. Patty was okay by herself, mourning the loss of her friend - not Shelly, but Terrence, whom she had truly loved.

Shelly waited for a while, her hands gripping the steering wheel, to see if Patty - or anyone - still lived in this decrepit old house. After a few minutes of staring and waiting, Shelly started to run low of gas, so she went on her way.

She found Terrence's truck outside of the house in which he had always lived. She knocked on the door. There was no answer. She put her ear to the door and listened as choppy piano playing began and finished, and started again.

The clumsy pecking stopped again. "That's pretty good for a first try," Terrence said, creating a space in his mind for patience with children. "You just played the first measure of the song."

"It doesn't sound like yours does," Daniel said, pouting a bit.

"Well if you start now," Terrence said, "by the time you're an old man like me, you'll be able to play it blindfolded."

"Can you play it blindfolded?" Daniel asked.

Terrence laughed. "I'm sure I could," he said. “I don't think I've ever tried to play that way before."

Shelly's knocking startled both men. "That's your mama," Terrence said.

Daniel got up and opened the door. Shelly looked down at her doe-eyed boy and hugged his neck.

"Mmm, I've missed you darlin'," Shelly said, breathing in the sweaty stench of her son. "Were you good for Terrence?"

"We cut down a tree and then played piano," Daniel said.

"My, my! What a busy day! Go wait in the car," Shelly said. "I'll be out in a minute."

Daniel ran outside. He turned around and waved at Terrence. Terrence waved back.

"I hope you don't mind that I brought him home with me," Terrence said.

"No, of course not," Shelly said. "Thank you for watching him for me." Shelly pulled out a few twenties and handed them to Terrence.

"No, that's okay, miss," Terrence said.

"Please, I insist," Shelly said. "And please call me Shelly." Terrence took the money sheepishly.

"In fact," Shelly continued, digging into her purse, "I'd like to offer you a sort of job watching him. If you wanted the money."

"I'm a little out of practice dealing with kids, mi—I mean Shelly," Terrence said with a nervous chuckle.

"Oh, you'll be fine!" Shelly said, waving that thought away as she gave up looking for whatever she was looking for in her purse. "Kids aren't as difficult as they seem. Just look at Daniel today. He never opens up like that to strangers."

"Well, I'd have to take him with me to work around town," Terrence said. "You think you'd be okay with that? It's dirty work."

"He needs to learn man's business," Shelly said, looking down, digging in her purse again. "He's got the whole summer off, so I don't see why not."

"You think your pappy would be okay with that?" Terrence said.

"What's Lloyd got to do with it?" Shelly said defensively. She looked Terrence in the eye while continuing to caress the inside of her bag. "Daniel's mine, not his." Terrence nodded silently.

Shelly finally found what she was looking for in her purse: a small white card. She handed it to him. "Here's my work number," Shelly said. "I gave you one hundred. I can give you fifty more when the week's over. I have weekends off, so I won't need any help then."

"That's mighty generous of you, Shelly," Terrence said. "But don't put yourself out."

Shelly sighed. "I think we're finally going to get on our feet," she said with a smile. "We'll see what happens."

Terrence didn't know what to make of this statement, but he nodded in acknowledgment all the same. "That's good! That's good!" He said with a chuckle.

Shelly made eye contact with Terrence for a minute, to get a read on him. "Okay," Shelly finally said. "So we'll see you in the morning?"

Terrence nodded again. "Yes'm," he said. "See you in the morning."

Shelly leaped at Terrence and hugged him tightly. "Oh, thank you so much," she said, truly relieved. "You don't know what this means to us."

Terrence patted Shelly's back, careful not to lean into the embrace too much, or to give in to his instinct to smell her hair.

"Okay, get on home now," Terrence said. "We've all had a long day."

The next morning, Shelly came into work a bit early to find Mrs. Redmond tacking up a flyer advertising a house for rent.

"Good morning, dear!" Mrs. Redmond said to the open door without even looking.

"Good morning," Shelly said. "What's this?"

"What's what?" Mrs. Redmond asked, puzzled. Shelly pointed at the handbill Mrs. Redmond had just tacked up.

"Oh, just some things daddy - I mean, Father Redmond - wanted me to put up," Mrs. Redmond said.

"You have a house for rent?" Shelly asked, looking at the flyer on the bulletin board. Mrs. Redmond parroted her motion, looking at it for perhaps the first time.

"Oh, that's our parsonage," Mrs. Redmond said, quickly scanning the grainy black-and-white photograph. "We moved to north Hawthorn. I guess the board approved the rental."

"Do you think I could maybe rent it?" Shelly asked with wide eyes. "You could take it directly off my paycheck."

"Well, that sounds fair," Mrs. Redmond said.

Father Redmond seemed fairly excited about this arrangement. He drove Shelly to the house on her lunch break. It was a doublewide mobile home, set on painted concrete blocks. It was nicer than anything Shelly had ever lived in - nicer than any man, Dwight or Lloyd - had given her.

Before Shelly could get out of the car to look inside the home, Father Redmond grabbed her thigh.

"The rent is negotiable, you know," Father Redmond said. "I know you're on hard times."

Shelly tried her best to ease the tension in her muscles and to smile. "Thank you, Father," she said.

Shelly was barely in the house when Father Redmond began pawing at her and removing her jacket. She kept up his pace and pretty soon, they were both standing naked in an awkward embrace.

Before Redmond could think about logistics, Shelly knocked him on the floor using a technique from her college self-defense class. This startled Redmond, as Shelly had the advantage – straddling him, her hands were firmly around his neck as she had her way with him.

"Shut up," Shelly interrupted Redmond every time he opened his mouth to speak. "I'm almost done," she said.

His eyes became wider than she thought possible when, in one smooth action, she whipped his leather belt from his pants, which were sitting in a pile nearby, and wrapped it around Redmond's neck.

The closer she could feel him getting to the finish, the tighter the belt became until Redmond's face looked like a giant, pulsating red grape. She finished quietly, to his relief. The vein in her forehead became visible, and she exhaled harshly and collapsed over the top of his potbelly.

Redmond, exhilarated and satisfied, tried to grab Shelly's face to kiss her on her mouth, but she only relented a peck to him, before getting up. She dressed quickly.

"Next time," Shelly said, out of breath, "I may or may not let up on that belt."

Bewildered, Redmond left quietly.

"Thanks for the house," Shelly said as Redmond stumbled outside.

Four

Daniel and Shelly moved in right away. They didn't tell Lloyd beforehand, because he hadn't come home for two days. They were able to escape unnoticed, shoving their clothes and shoes and photographs into trash bags and the suitcases that Shelly received as wedding gifts and hightailing it out of there as fast as they could.

Shelly giggled to herself as she unpacked boxes, thinking of Lloyd coming home in a stupor and finding the TV trays gone. He'd probably get furious and trash whatever was left in the house, before getting drunk again.

"Mama," Daniel whined, "How much more do we have to unpack?"

"Just enough to clear the living room," Shelly said. "We're having company over tonight." This struck fear in Daniel.

"Is Terrence coming?" Daniel asked.

"No, Danny," Shelly said. "A boy named Eric is coming, though, and I want you to be nice to him. It's about time you started making some friends your own age."

"Kids my age are stupid," Daniel said.

"Yeah," Shelly said, putting wine glasses in the cabinet. "But maybe Eric won't be."

"I doubt it."

Mrs. Redmond came in with store-bought lasagna while Shelly was in the shower. Daniel looked at her, his face frozen in anxiety.

Mrs. Redmond chuckled. "Sorry for not knocking, dear," she said. "I have my hands full."

Mrs. Redmond put down her lasagna and raced toward Daniel. She embraced him in a tight bear hug, pressing the boy's face into her breasts. "You must be Daniel," she said. "Your mother talks about you all the time."

Daniel tried to speak, but his words got muffled in the squishy bosom of this strange woman.

Behind her stood a small boy with a mean look on his face. He had a shaved head and a red Kool-Aid mustache. He was carrying two 2-liter colas. "Mom," he said, "These are heavy."

"Put them over there, Eric, next to the food," Mrs. Redmond said with slight impatience. "Come say hi to Daniel."

Eric's eyes were wild, yet stern. He seemed like the type of boy who picked his scabs and chased girls with toads.

"Hi to Daniel," Eric said from across the room.

Mrs. Redmond leaned in and whispered to Daniel, "He's just a bit shy."

They ate the lasagna and drank the Coca-Cola with ice busted out of plastic trays. Eric played with his food, while his parents ignored him. Father Redmond only spoke when he was scolding Eric.

"Stop playing with your food, boy," Redmond said. Eric just rolled his eyes and gave the top of his lasagna a splat with a fork.

"Boys, if you're done eating, why don't you go play while we clean up," Shelly said.

Daniel glared at Eric with flared nostrils. "Do you like video games?" He asked.

The boys sat in the living room and fought space aliens for a while, but Eric got restless. "This is boring," Eric said, setting down his controller. "Let's go outside."

Eric Redmond was trouble from the minute he was born. He came out of the womb with pneumonia. When Eric was a baby, he refused to be held. When his mother tried, he would scream, cry, and hold his breath until he passed out.

When the Redmonds moved from Nashville to Hawthorn Missouri to start over, Eric was unmoved by the whole thing. People and places and things meant very little to him. Staring at the surface of things bored him.

He was an outcast in school. He was recognized as brilliant by the guidance counselor and by teachers, but he refused to learn the conventional way - with books and activities. Instead, he observed his classmates as if they were zoo animals. It was this attitude that bonded Eric and Daniel - a disdain for children their own age, and outright contempt for most authority figures.

Whereas Daniel moseyed along, quietly obeying no matter how he felt, Eric was defiant from the day he could speak. His first word was "no," and he had picked it up from watching his father's sermon. He was unimpressed by most of his father's teachings, but he liked his musical speaking style, particularly the way he yelled "No!" After asking rhetorical questions to the congregation – even when the questions didn't make sense, just sounded good.

"Do we want to live amongst the poor in spirit? Do we want to speak to the fragile egos of the average human? The ungrateful degenerates that have left us in ruin? No!" Redmond said on television, elongating the "o" and giving it a beat or two, emphasizing his southern drawl. "But we do it because we love the world, just like God loves the world."

Eric recognized the power of words in getting ahead. He had an appetite for expression - not to be heard, but as a means to an end. He saw the small empire his father was building, and though he felt indifferent towards him and never let him know he was paying any attention at all, he learned a great deal through observation.

Daniel gleaned what he could from his mother, but he quickly learned that her strategic thinking and seductive qualities were a matter of female survival - "girl stuff." He would have to find his own way to meet his needs, and he learned most of what he knew about manhood from the one summer he spent with Terrence.

His father Dwight was an ill-mannered alcoholic who, like so many fathers brought up in the ruins of the Midwest, was mostly absent. He had been missing for over half of Daniel's life. The half during which Dwight was present, he had failed to gain the respect of his son.

When Dwight came to the door of their new home one afternoon, it took Daniel several seconds to remember who Dwight even was, despite the fact that they looked very similar.

"Hey buddy," Dwight said, speech slightly slurred. "Your mama home?"

"Who's asking?" Daniel said.

The embarrassment of his own son not knowing who he was swished together with the alcohol in his belly, and his temper ignited. "I'm your goddamn dad, Daniel," he said. "Get your ass inside and get your mom."

Daniel glared at him and stood still. Terrence, who was over for dinner, heard the commotion and moved behind him.

"What's going on?" Terrence said with scrunched eyebrows.

Dwight laughed. "You gotta be kidding me," he said. His loud cackle awakened Shelly's maternal protective instinct and she rushed outside, pushing Terrence and Daniel inside the house. She practically closed the door in Daniel's face.

"I'll be right out," Shelly said, before closing the door. "Everything is fine."

"Who is that man?" Terrence asked Daniel, slightly unnerved.

Daniel shrugged. "Nobody." After a second of silence, he said, "He says he's my dad, but I don't know."

Terrence had half a mind to go outside and pick Dwight Wright up by his throat, dangling his toes against the floor of the patio. But he knew that if he did, he'd have to leave town - immediately if the neighbors saw.

It was an anxiety that had weighed on him his entire life.

Don't screw up. Shenanigans are only for white men.

Terrence could feel it: he just screwed up. Being seen alone in a white woman's home, especially when that white woman had a jealous ex-husband, was asking for trouble. He considered the awful possibilities. None were as hurtful as leaving Shelly and Daniel alone in this new world of theirs. But he imagined, for his safety and theirs, that this would be their last meeting.

Daniel grabbed two of Terrence's fingers and led him to the kitchen. "Let's go play cards," Daniel said as if to comfort this man who lorded over him, this man who only wanted to protect him and his mother. Terrence looked back at the closed door, listening to the estranged couple argue over the entire world that lay between them.

"Tell me you're not...*with* him," Dwight said with a severe cringe. "I think my damn head might explode."

"Not that it's any of your business, Dwight," Shelly said with a sneer, "But he's just a friend. He's good with Danny."

Dwight started to cry. "Oh, Jesus, Shelly!" He wailed. "What are you doing? You're gonna kill me dead."

"Pull yourself together, Dwight," Shelly said, rolling her eyes. "You took off, remember?"

Dwight collected himself. "You're right," he said twice. "But I'm here to fix what I done wrong."

"Mmm-hmm," Shelly said. "That's nice." She crossed her arms. Dwight tried to caress her arm, but she swatted it away. His eyes widened.

"You really are screwing him, aren't you?" Dwight said, putting his hands behind his head and sobbing. "Oh, Jesus, you are!"

"I said get a hold of yourself!" Shelly barked. "Jesus. The neighbors."

Dwight got wild-eyed, and his anger came back, layered on top of his frantic tears. His voice got louder, and his body got more animated.

"Oh, you don't want the neighbors to know you're fucking a nigger!" He screeched.

Shelly leaned against the porch column, her arms crossed. He came close to her, cradling her face in his hand. He spoke in a breathy, shivering whisper.

"You're going to regret this," he said with his finger in her face. He then pointed towards the house. "He's going to regret this, too."

"You really oughta' watch your drinking before you come over here," Shelly said. "You look crazy."

Dwight rushed Shelly, and she screamed. Suddenly, the front door swung open and Daniel came barging out. He pushed Dwight's shins, tipping him over into the bushes. Shelly put her hand over her mouth.

"Daniel, go inside!" Shelly yelled.

Dwight hobbled up, staggering with bloodshot eyes. He started to walk toward Daniel, who ran behind Terrence and hid.

Dwight shook his head. "I'll be goddamned if I'm going to let some porch monkey steal my family away," he said. He put his fists up.

"Dwight, stop it!" Shelly said, tears forming.

Terrence stood there, steely eyes, arms to his side, lips slightly pursed. He became a barrier, unwilling to break eye contact.

"Get on home, now," Terrence said. "You ain't welcome here."

Dwight laughed through tears. "You sure you wanna do this, nigger?" Terrence didn't move his stance or his face in any way.

"I ain't wanting to hurt you," Terrence said.

"This ain't over," Dwight said with a quivering voice. He walked backward, got on his bicycle and rode away.

In the hours after Dwight left, Shelly was outwardly calm, but her voice still shook. Terrence went into town and got Shelly cigarettes - a habit she quit years ago.

"Please don't judge me," she told Terrence over glasses of sweet tea, smoke swirling from underneath the table. "It's just been a stressful ordeal, moving and all."

"I think I should stay here tonight," Terrence said. "On the couch, of course."

"You think that's a good idea?" Shelly said, lighting another cigarette, depleted of emotion.

"I'd feel better," Terrence said. "I'll be worried."

Shelly stood up and touched Terrence's face. "You're a beautiful person. You know that?" She said.

Terrence blushed and turned his head away.

"I'm going to bed," Shelly said. "There's whiskey in the cabinet and clean towels in the dryer. Make yourself at home."

Shelly walked out of the kitchen, drunk on sleep deprivation and shocked nerves.

Terrence laid on the couch and stared up at the ceiling. He felt rushes of anxiety wash over his face before subsiding to his better nature. He closed his eyes, and before he could really start dreaming, he heard the sobs of a young boy beneath him, lying on the floor.

"Daniel," Terrence said, "what's the matter?"

"We ain't never gonna be normal, are we?" Daniel asked Terrence.

Terrence sighed, unable to lie to him. "No, probably not," he said quietly.

"Do you think other kids have to deal with this kinda shit?" Daniel asked.

"Watch your mouth, young man," Terrence said. "And yeah. I think a lot of kids do."

"Well, I think most people aren't meant to be parents," Daniel said. "All they do is wreck everything."

"You're right about that, Danny," Terrence said. "But listen. Someday, you're gonna really like not being normal. You're better than normal," Terrence said. "You got gifts."

Daniel rolled over, turning his back to Terrence. "Yeah, well, I ain't never asked for no gifts."

Terrence had been preparing for fatherhood since he was a boy. He had to have similar talks with his own father - a child inside of a man's frail, gin-soaked body. Daniel was the inverse: a fully-grown soul trapped inside a small boy's frame. Terrence waited until Daniel was asleep, and draped an afghan over his body. He placed a pillow under his head.

Shelly got a promotion of sorts. Father Redmond granted her idea of a daycare for the church's children. She was to start it out of the parsonage in which she lived. Once it grew too big, the daycare would move to the basement of the old Hawthorn Baptist Church in south Jackass Flats.

Father Redmond would make appearances to the children in costume. On Christmas, he'd dress like Jesus, and Mrs. Redmond would play Santa Claus, wearing a terrifying rubber mask that made several children cry.

On Easter, he'd once again play Jesus, and poor Mrs. Redmond would be stuck inside of a hot bunny suit, which was similarly terrifying.

Holidays were Father Redmond's favorite days because he would have the opportunity to explain to the children that most holidays were, in actuality, pagan conspiracies. Though they should graciously accept any gifts given to them by their parents out of respect, he said, they should also be aware that there is no such thing as Santa Claus, the Easter Bunny, or the Tooth Fairy.

The irony of these lectures was not lost on Eric, who attended the daycare while Mr. and Mrs. Redmond pilfered in the church offices all day.

"If the Tooth Fairy ain't real," Eric said to Daniel while they were playing with army men, "then how do we know Jesus is real?"

Daniel's eyes got wide. "You can't say stuff like that," he said.

"Why not?" Eric asked. "Who says?"

"Your daddy and Jesus," Daniel said.

"My daddy is as dumb as a tractor tire," Eric said. "He don't know shit."

Eric was alone in his assessment of his father. The congregation of Hawthorn Baptist Church grew - so much in fact, that they re-opened the old, dilapidated Jackass Flats location and had second, third, and fourth services on Sunday afternoons, sometimes going until midnight. It seemed everyone in town was attending.

Harold Redmond wasn't much on the eyes. Eric heard a lady liken him to Mr. Potatohead, which made him laugh. But he had that special something that movie stars and evil dictators have, and people fell in love with him.

Redmond got a local high school student to start filming his sermons, and he put them on public access. He bought a large movie theater screen off of the closed multiplex for the Jackass Flats location to play his sermons, so he didn't have to show up in person. Still, people were just as happy to see a mere projection of this man who spoke with the timbre of someone who had the golden ticket to Heaven. He merely put down a red carpet in the foyer of the church leading down the aisle toward the screen, and he hired a band, with Terrence on electric piano. People ate it up.

Redmond sweated and sniffled through his sermons, hiding behind violet colored aviator sunglasses, and preaching messages considered progressive in some ways, and odd and oppressive in others.

He had a peculiar fixation on demonizing homosexuality and adultery, though he had partaken in both with members of the congregation.

He was vehemently anti-racism. "The Bible never said anything about prejudice against people of different races," he said during several sermons. "Did you know that Jesus was probably Black?" This was a tougher sell, but it still somehow sold.

The only person in the whole congregation who wasn't impressed by Redmond was his son, Eric. He and Daniel sat next to each other every Sunday. Though Daniel found it peculiar to have a friend his own age, he was a captive audience for Eric because Daniel was so meek, he'd never turn away someone who wanted to be his friend; it seemed too cruel, and life was lonely enough as it was.

If not for Eric, Daniel might have been swept away by the town's infatuation with this authoritative preacher. But watching Eric's face through the sermons was enough to convince him that Father Redmond wasn't much of a father to his son. How could he be any good to anybody else?

He observed his mother's behavior around Father Redmond. She always seemed tense. She may have been smiling, but her jaw was clenched. He could practically see her skin crawl every time he touched her.

Shelly was determined to crawl out of Jackass Flats once and for all, and on her own merits. She kept a jar by her bed in which she deposited money to one-day move abroad - perhaps Paris. She started it when she quit smoking, putting the money she would spend on her pack-a-day habit away in the form of coins, mostly.

"Can I come, too?" Daniel asked one day as Shelly put some coins in the jar.

"You'll be grown by then," Shelly said, leafing through a catalog. "You'll have your own life."

"What if I don't have my own life?" Daniel asked.

"Then sure," Shelly said. "You can come."

Shelly tolerated Redmond's lecherous behavior, resisting only in spirit. Eventually, their encounters stopped. Redmond promoted Shelly to daycare manager, and he hired a young effeminate boy who just graduated high school to be her replacement as a secretary. She often wondered if this boy was subjected to the same abuse that Shelly was. Shelly also fantasized about the boy's future beyond Hawthorn, hoping that whatever he was looking for - whatever his ambition - he found. Allowing Redmond's greasy hands to touch their bodies had surely built up some sort of karmic debt in their favor.

It was at Shelly's persistent request that Redmond hired Terrence as a full-time groundskeeper as well as part-time Sunday morning musician. Terrence began music lessons again, and though he could afford to move out of the shack in which he lived, he didn't really see the point. It was paid for, and as far as Terrence was concerned, he'd happily die of old age in Jackass Flats.

Everything in Jackass Flats was looking up, and the residents credited Father Redmond. Most residents had contact with the church in some way, even if they were members of another church. Some worked for the church, cooking and cleaning up after potluck dinners at which the whole town was invited. Some only showed up to be fed. Some were the beneficiaries of the church's charitable endeavors, such as a weekly food bank for those in need - which was most of Jackass Flats, at least in those first few years.

The new pharmacy was made possible by a substantial gift from the church. Redmond, a self-styled champion of the poor, began a needle exchange program for local junkies, no questions asked. Inside each plastic bag of clean needles was a tiny, fortune cookie-sized card with an inspirational message, stamped with Father Harold Redmond's signature. The old church on the south side of town was eventually converted into a clinic of sorts, providing a cot for all kinds of disenfranchised souls, from the drunk and disorderly for one night, as well as drifters for as long as they needed. They were sent on their way with pamphlets for Hawthorn's own brand of Alcoholics Anonymous - tweaked to make Redmond, not God, the center of the program. Many did show up for meetings, if only for donuts. Still, they showed up, and they praised Redmond as well as Jesus for making their lives better.

AS THE CONGREGATION grew, so did the production budget for Hawthorn Baptist Church's public access program. They now had three cameras - two pointed at Mr. and Mrs. Redmond, and one aimed at the swollen, rowdy crowd.

The pulpit was decorated similarly to Redmond's office - gaudy and royal blue with gold effects. Even Redmond's sunglasses got darker and larger. His voice got louder. He mimed deeper confidence.

Mrs. Redmond mostly sat there nodding and tersely smiling at Redmond's words - terrified of being on camera, yet grinning and seeming oblivious. Redmond had dressed her up in off-the-rack gowns from the mall in Branson. Her odd proportions made every dress look like a sequined potato sack.

Daniel knew his mother was an unhappy woman. She strived all those years to be independent, but she was crushingly lonely. Though she was somewhat disgusted by Father Redmond, Shelly pined for his attention and spoke about him glowingly. She taped his show to watch during her wine and Valium filled evenings, getting wasted more on Redmond's charisma. Redmond had a strange hold on Shelly, but it wasn't just her. It was the whole town.

Father Redmond was now a local celebrity, and Shelly had always fantasized about being famous; and, if not famous, then at least important. Though she had earned her spot in Redmond's cabal, she was falling out of favor with the pastor. New women seemed to take her place - one new secretary after another, never lasting for more than a month.

Daniel watched his mother deteriorate. When Lloyd finally kicked the bucket, Daniel was afraid of what would become of her. Shelly did in fact hate Lloyd, and by all appearances was glad he was dead. However, when a man leaves - even in death - it leaves a child feeling empty and perhaps even a little guilty.

It no longer felt right to Shelly to call her adopted father a bastard, a drunk, a waste of space; for he no longer took up space. After his pine box was laid into the ground, his trailer was hauled away by the owner and sold for scrap at

Reggie's. His trailer was the last one of its kind remaining in the whole town of Hawthorn, except for mobile homes like Shelly's that had concrete foundations and was nicer than some of the "real" houses in town.

In the midst of her grief, she saw a quacky pill dispenser of a psychiatrist that Redmond had suggested. He worked at the south Hawthorn clinic two days a week. Every time Shelly complained of anxiety or sadness, or simply felt the need to share pieces of her life with this psychiatrist, he upped her Valium dosage. By the end of that year, she was pretty much a drooling zombie. She no longer felt anything. The pills blunted her pain, and adding wine warmed her cold body.

The house got dirty - full of empty tuna cans, wine bottles and used plates. Daniel saw Terrence during their piano lessons once a week, but he stopped coming over for dinner. Terrence knew Shelly was in a bad way, and he felt extremely sad for her. But he realized that her current incarnation was who she truly was: broken. He knew he could do nothing for her.

Love couldn't help her. Love, in the end, was what killed her spirit. She clawed and grabbed at love and tried to make it hers, but she never was able to really latch on. And with this newly discovered prospect of eternal aloneness, Shelly Guile gave up on living.

Terrence never told Daniel of the late-night phone calls and rambling answering machine messages left for him by Shelly. He would often wake up to several messages left by Shelly in varying degrees of drunken, maudlin sentimentality. As badly as he wanted to barge in and save her, he had been in this situation before and had only ended up a little worse for wear on the inside. There weren't enough years left for him to rebuild his own mind. He knew he wasn't capable of piecing together Shelly's, either. It was a decision that he'd deeply regret later in life.

Instead, he saw Daniel and made sure to encourage him and adore him and give him pieces of strawberry hard candy for the hour they'd spend together each week.

Daniel was a superior pianist. He inspired Terrence to begin hosting a recital he called May Day. On the first of May, the kids from Jackass Flats would play an electric piano hooked up to an amplifier Terrence bought from John's Pawn. They'd perform from Terrence's front lawn the first year, and in later years at the gymnasium at the old south Hawthorn Baptist Church. Daniel was the star during the first, and only year he performed at the recital.

He played a truncated, simplified version of Beethoven's Fifth. Shelly and a few others, sitting in lawn chairs in Terrence's front lawn, were entranced. Shelly stood and clapped as Daniel finished. The others, not wanting to be impolite, followed suit. Daniel looked out at the small crowd of grown-ups clapping for him, and he felt peculiar. He wanted it to stop. This sort of attention, he decided, wasn't for him. He wanted to be invisible, and from that day forward, he lived his life in stealth and put his musical talents away with his army men.

Eric, on the other hand, lived for it. He too was part of the recital, against his wishes. He was the last to perform. He was to play a hymn selected by his father, but he hadn't even practiced it once. He got up in front of everyone with an evil grin and started pounding on the keys with his fists and elbows.

Eyebrows were raised, and some attendees even put their hands over their ears. Terrence, cursing under his breath, yanked the amp cord out. Eric's crushing of the keys could still be heard, but much quieter.

"Hey, what gives?" Eric said. "I wasn't done." The audience, half-oblivious and half-apathetic, clapped. Had Father Redmond been in attendance, he would have been furious. Mrs. Redmond was there physically but she wasn't listening, as evidenced by her enthusiastic clapping.

Shelly approached Terrence as he was packing up his gear. "Hey, stranger," she said with slurred speech.

Terrence nodded. "How're you doing?" He extended his hand. Shelly winced. "You can do better than that," she said, embracing Terrence. Terrence patted Shelly on her back and chuckled nervously.

"I've missed you," Shelly whispered. "Where have you gone? I need you."

Terrence whispered back. "Are you okay, Shelly?"

Shelly looked into Terrence's eyes. She slowly shook her head no. Her face tensed. Her eyes were hidden by sunglasses. She patted Terrence on the shoulder and gave a heartbroken smile. She walked away and called for Daniel.

"You did good today, Danny," Shelly said to her son from the driver's seat of her Cadillac. "Real good. I'm proud of you."

"I messed up once," Daniel said. He noticed his mom was off somehow, and her driving was slightly impaired, swerving a bit off of her side of the road.

"You couldn't tell," Shelly said. "All that practice paid off, see?"

Daniel nodded.

Shelly drove by Lloyd's old lot. All that remained was the tree stump from the Hawthorn tree Lloyd ordered to be cut down, and a pad of dirt where his trailer once was.

"Looks a lot different," Daniel said.

"Looks a lot better," Shelly said, voice flat. She lit a cigarette - her first in five months. "Come on," she said. "Let's get out and look around."

The two walked around the yard for a while.

"What are we doing, mom?" Daniel asked, half-whining.

"Just getting a look around," Shelly said. "It's a strange feeling when a whole lifetime of memories add up to a whole lot of nothin'," she said, chuckling.

"Are you sad?" Daniel asked.

Shelly paused before answering. "Yeah, I guess I am sad," she finally said. "I'm not sad he's gone, but I'm sad that it could have turned out different."

"But aren't we doing good?" Daniel said.

"I don't mean for us," Shelly said. "I mean for him."

Daniel looked puzzled.

"I hope one day you'll look back at you and me, and it makes you smile," Shelly said. "When I'm gone, I hope I gave you some happy memories."

Daniel now felt his mother's sadness. Shelly dropped her cigarette butt to the ground and stamped out the fire with her high heel shoe.

"Come on," Shelly said, grabbing Daniel's hand. "Let's go home. Ain't nothin' to dwell on here anymore."

As they drove away, Daniel looked straight ahead at the road from the back seat. Shelly threw her pack of cigarettes out of the window.

The last words Daniel heard his mother say were the lyrics of a song. He couldn't tell which song exactly, but Shelly had a lovely singing voice. It was exceptionally beautiful when it was unencumbered by the tightness of sober vocal chords.

Daniel noticed a change in his mother around the time she started seeing her psychiatrist. Known around their household as simply "the doctor," he was a short, fat man with wild hair who had left his position at Missouri State University when his wife divorced him. He sold his house and moved to north

Hawthorn. He was a friend of Father Redmond's, as they belonged to the same local Masonic Lodge. They bonded over their shared hatred of Catholics.

Once Redmond opened the south Hawthorn clinic, he asked his doctor friend to work there full-time, prescribing methadone for the opioid addicts, and looking after drunken vagrants who needed a place to crash for the night. At Redmond's request, he started seeing Shelly. She was his only regular client.

The afternoon after her first appointment, Shelly seemed relieved that she had finally received treatment for this strange tightness in her chest and the heaviness in the crown of her head. By that evening, her whimsy had turned into dopiness. Her eyes were shiny, and the black in them had all but swallowed her hazel irises. Her words ran together like they were soaked in water. However, she was laughing - for the first time in her life, she was laughing, and Daniel thought that was nice.

Daniel heard Shelly on the phone in the middle of the night. "Daddy," she purred, "Come see me. Come tuck me in." Shelly would laugh a wild, loose cackle, followed by a dark tone shift. "No, Harold, I haven't been drinking."

Her tone would then get furious. "No, Redmond, don't you dare hang -" A moment of silence was followed by a loud crash: the phone flying across the room, or other things, such as the time Shelly ripped up her pillow with her bare hands before crying and passing out in a cloud of tiny white feathers.

This was always followed by the running of bath water and humming. Sometimes, Shelly would sing.

On this night, Shelly skipped all of that and went straight to the medicine cabinet, then ran a bath. She poured a glass from the bottle of Merlot she kept under the bathroom sink. She ran hot bath water, singing loudly while the water ran, then hummed when the bath was full.

Daniel fell asleep on the floor while cartoons played on the television. He woke up around midnight and found himself alone, the television lighting up the room. The sound effects bounced off the walls and echoed and made the house sound like an empty fishbowl.

Daniel found his mother in the bathtub face down. He turned his mother over, and her eyes were closed. Her skin had turned a strangely beautiful shade of olive; her eyelids were violet. Her lips were vaguely in the shape of a smile.

Daniel's body froze. His mind and his world were immediately shattered, but there was no time to acknowledge that. He pulled the plug on the water, which had turned a rose-colored tint from the spilled wine. Shelly's body lowered with the water until the tub was drained.

Daniel considered what to do next. He contemplated calling the police or even Terrence. But he looked at his mother - naked, clammy, and an otherworldly skin shade - and thought that she wouldn't want anyone to see her like that. She would want to be seen as beautiful, young, and in control of her own fate.

Daniel grabbed the candle that sat on the edge of the bathtub. It had long been snuffed out, but he re-lit it. He sat it on the floor, under a small stack of washcloths, and he rolled toilet paper from the dispenser down to the flame. He kicked over the decorative kerosene lamp on top of the toilet. It shattered, and golden liquid splashed all over the candle, and all over the washcloths.

He sat in front of the television, staring straight through the screen into the next dimension.

Once he smelled the melting fiberglass tub, he got up from the couch, put some of his mother's photos in his backpack, and rode away on his bike to Eric's house.

He flattened his face on the ride there, letting the breeze dry his cheeks just as his mother had done so many times before - and making his emotions fade along with the sunset. He never told anyone what he saw, or what he did.

Five

Shelly's safe deposit box had only two things in it: a piece of gold-plated costume jewelry from her dead mother, and a folded-up handwritten will that she ripped out from Daniel's school notebook.

No one knew the whereabouts of Daniel's father; he could have drunk himself to death for all anyone knew.

Father Redmond pulled into Terrence's driveway a week after Shelly was buried. He came directly from Shelly's moderately lavish funeral, which Daniel did not attend. The car idled until the clock struck three.

Daniel didn't do much of anything that whole week after finding his mother's body, being stuck in the muck of silent denial. He watched old, familiar tapes featuring Mickey Mouse - retrieved from the remains of the burned parsonage - on Terrence's VCR. When he ate, he ate only store-brand Froot Loops, which happened to be Terrence's breakfast of choice. Daniel stayed silent that entire week, and Terrence didn't press him to talk.

The two sat in Terrence's musty recliner. Daniel had recently hit a growth spurt, and he was getting too heavy to sleep in the embrace of adults. He sat halfway on Terrence's lap, and halfway on the puffy arm of the recliner, picking pieces of rainbow-colored cereal from a Styrofoam cup and crunching them slowly like a grazing cow.

"Boy, you keep eating those, and you'll turn into a Froot Loop," Terrence said, mussing Daniel's white hair.

Daniel shrugged. "I like Froot Loops," he said.

Terrence laughed. "I know you do," he said. "You done ate all of mine."

"Sorry," he said, shrugging again.

Terrence just laughed and shook his head.

Father Redmond's car could be heard outside. They looked at each other when they heard the car door shut.

"Is that him?" Daniel asked.

Terrence picked up Daniel, stood him up next to the recliner, and got up to look through the blinds. "I think so, Danny," he said. "You ready?"

Terrence had been preparing for this day since Shelly's funeral, but his dread never subsided.

Daniel, on the other hand, wrapped himself in the comfort of his solitude - taking over Terrence's bedroom, always keeping the door closed, even in the daytime.

Terrence kept himself busy during the day working around town, and when he came home, he slept on the couch. Daniel only came out of the bedroom to watch television and eat cereal.

Wanting to be alone was nothing new for Daniel. It wasn't all that surprising to the few who knew him that Daniel didn't want to go to his mother's funeral, and everyone agreed that it was probably for the best anyway. As far as Terrence could recall, there were few tears shed by Daniel; just a pair of dry, hazy blue eyes staring at everything really hard.

Father Redmond knocked on the door. His knock seemed melodramatic, pausing just long enough between raps to convey proper sadness. Terrence hugged Daniel's limp body. Daniel didn't hug him back, but leaned his head on Terrence's shoulder and closed his eyes.

For the week that he lived in Terrence's house, Daniel was the center of someone's universe. Daniel now realized that he had taken that for granted, and he wished he could stay.

Once Redmond entered their home and it was clear that there was no turning back, Daniel sauntered toward him with his head down. Redmond lifted his chin gently, and smiled. "Are you ready, son?" He asked. Terrence flinched at the word "Son." Daniel's face was grim.

"Where's Eric?" Daniel asked. Redmond's smile dissipated a bit.

"He's waiting in the car," Redmond said. "Come on, let's go see your new home."

Daniel turned around toward Terrence, who was sitting in his recliner. His grin belied his despair. Daniel raised his hand up in a depressed goodbye-wave. Terrence did the same.

"You be good for the Redmonds, you hear?" Terrence said, voice cracking. "They're good people."

Daniel turned around, his backpack hanging loosely down past his ribcage. He opened the screen door and walked down the steps, descending until he was gone.

Terrence leaned back and looked up at the ceiling. He heard the front door shut, and the motor revved a bit, then faded to silence. He tried his best to sleep.

SIX

Daniel looked around the Swiss villa that the Redmonds now called home. There were boxes scattered amongst the vintage furniture, and the whole house smelled like fresh stucco, sawdust, and mothballs. There was a spiral staircase that went higher than Daniel was comfortable climbing. Eric seemed to enjoy it. He ran up and down the steps with spritely legs - hopping, really - while Mrs. Redmond hummed to herself in the dining room and knit primary-colored doilies to place under antique, nonfunctioning lamps with bases that were all the same shade of transparent amber.

Daniel was a Redmond now, and his heart felt bogged down by musty, clammy anxiety. The memory of this old familiar feeling had faded while he was at Terrence's, until his first night sleeping at the Redmonds' home.

Mrs. Redmond walked by Daniel's room. He was lying in bed silently, staring at the ceiling, wondering how he got there. He paid Mrs. Redmond no mind as she sat at the foot of the bed and stared at Daniel with a vacant smile.

"You must be feeling strange," Mrs. Redmond said.

"What do you mean?" Daniel asked.

"Strange house, strange...circumstances," Mrs. Redmond said. "But there is a dash of good fortune mixed in with all this yucky stuff." She dotted his nose with her leathery fingertip.

Daniel looked around the room and could see what she was getting at. This is everything his mother would have wanted. The bed sheets seemed soft and expensive, and the central air conditioning hummed and made the house seem like a sleeping giant. But there was something off about this new life, and it wasn't just that it was new.

"Let us pray," Mrs. Redmond said, sliding to the floor and kneeling beside the bed. Daniel put his hands in prayer position and closed his eyes. When he opened them, Mrs. Redmond was staring back at him with that same old creepy smile.

"No dear," she said with a chuckle. "We kneel while we pray." Mrs. Redmond patted the carpet. "Come on down here."

Daniel knelt beside Mrs. Redmond, closed his eyes, and pretended to pray at first. But after a few seconds, he really did pray silently. Daniel prayed to be rescued from this house and these people. He prayed that his mother would return and that his father Dwight would take her place in death before he got sober enough to track Daniel down. Daniel asked God why everyone who tried to do good always seemed to be on the brink of death. Mrs. Redmond was right. It was strange.

After Mrs. Redmond mumbled, "Amen," she stood up and pulled the comforter back onto Daniel's bed. "Get some rest dear," she said. Father Redmond entered the room as she left as if he'd been standing there the whole time. This startled Daniel, and he got into bed quickly and put the covers to his face.

"Lights out, boy," Father Redmond said flatly, right before everything went dark.

Daniel awoke at three a.m. to find Eric sleeping next to him. He nudged Eric, and slowly woke him through a series of jolts to his frail upper arm.

"What do you want?" Eric finally asked, mush-mouthed from half-sleep. He was turned away from Daniel.

"What are you doing here?" Daniel asked. "Don't you have your own bed?"

Eric sat up, rubbed his eyes, and looked around. "I thought this was my bed," he mumbled. He then jumped out of bed, and without further explanation left Daniel's room.

Breakfast was another ordeal. The Redmonds held hands around the table and prayed before they ate. But they didn't merely pray; they sang their prayer.

Daniel's left hand was in Father Redmond's, and his right hand was in Eric Redmond's as they sang a hymn in harmony over stacks of pancakes and gravy boats filled with scrambled eggs prepared by the help. Mrs. Redmond's vibrato unnerved him. When they were finished singing, they opened their eyes and looked at each other and said, "Amen," very dutifully. Everyone that is, except Daniel, who just sat there with wide eyes as if he was hypnotized-by-singing. They all stared at Daniel, waiting for him to say it.

Father Redmond coughed.

Daniel mumbled it. "Amen," he said. But he said it differently than they did, with an "Ah," instead of an "Ay." And with that, the Redmonds began their day as if nothing much had changed. Daniel realized he was all alone for the first time, and perhaps forever.

A few days after Daniel's arrival, Eric became ill. The Redmonds avoided western medicine as much as they could, so they let their son stay home from school with a hundred-and-three degree fever. Blisters covered his body.

"Oh dear," Mrs. Redmond said at dinner one evening - a dinner for which Eric was absent. "I fear our son has been...taken over," she said.

This perked Father Redmond's ears. "What do you mean?"

"I mean the skin lesions, the fever, the sleepwalking...I don't know what to make of it."

A few nights prior, the Redmond parents found Eric running around the house in the middle of the night, frantically screaming things like, "You'll never catch me!" and "No! I won't let you!" He waved his hands as he ran behind furniture, swatting away imaginary bats.

This was the beginning stages of Eric's fever, which was the culprit of the night terrors he was experiencing. The superstitious Redmonds, of course, assumed it was spiritual warfare. Redmond even mentioned it before collecting tithes that Sunday.

That Monday, Eric awoke to a bunch of people he recognized from church, holding hands around him with their eyes closed. Father Redmond led them in prayer.

"By the power of Christ," Redmond said, "I release these demons from this boy. His soul belongs to Jesus." Eric opened his left eye a tiny bit; just enough to see a circle of old people holding hands around him and chanting in prayer. He pretended to be asleep until they all left.

Before they filed out one-by-one, Daniel nudged his way into the room. "What's going on?" He asked. "Is he going to be okay?"

Father Redmond, slightly irritated at Daniel's intrusion, said, "Your brother is at war with Satan. Satan will not prevail."

Daniel walked over to Eric, who was still pretending to be asleep. He looked at him - skin pale and covered in sores, his lips chapped and cracked, and his breathing heavy.

"It's chicken pox," Daniel said matter-of-factly.

"What?" Father Redmond said.

"I had 'em too, in second grade," Daniel said. He turned to Eric. "You've never had chicken pox before?" Eric suppressed laughter as best as he could, then immediately feigned sleep once again.

"Have any of you ever had chicken pox before?" Daniel asked the circle of uncomfortable churchgoers. No one said anything.

"It's really contagious," Daniel said.

Father Redmond was bewildered and the small crowd was silent, staring at Daniel as he walked out of Eric's bedroom.

"I wouldn't worry," Daniel said in the doorway. "You can only get chicken pox once."

SPRING FLOATED ON INTO summer and the boys grew closer. Daniel grew to appreciate Eric's eccentricity, just as Eric found patience for Daniel's orderly tendencies.

They met up at lunch to gawk at their fellow students. Eric broke into the most expensive-looking lunch boxes, which were piled up around a lonely bench. Daniel stood guard as Eric stuffed candy and snack cakes into his backpack.

After school, an older boy, Kenneth McAdams, taunted them. He was mean like an angry ape and built like an ogre. They called him Papa Smurf because he looked like an old man even though he was barely a year older than they were. Though, they were never brave enough to call him that to his face.

Kenneth McAdams lived with his three younger cousins - triplet girls, whom Eric and Daniel never bothered trying to tell apart. They were known only as the Toby sisters. Two of the girls followed Daniel and Eric on their walk from the bus, and the third sister lagged behind, always scowling. Daniel took pity upon them and spoke with them, but Eric was annoyed by their presence.

They heard Kenneth before they saw him. "Hey, faggots!" He yelled.

"Papa Smurf," Eric whispered to Daniel with dread in his eyes. He turned to the girls. "Can't you call off your retard brother? I'm getting tired of this."

"He's not our brother," the scowling girl said. "And if you want him off, you'll have to do it yourself."

"He stinks," Eric replied. "At least give him a bath before school." Daniel shushed Eric, seeing Kenneth approach.

Kenneth rushed Eric. Once he caught up with him, Kenneth forced his head under his arm, smashing Eric's nose into his sweaty, clammy armpit.

"I smell, huh faggot?" Kenneth said, grunting as Eric resisted. "Smell it."

Eric howled, feeling suffocated.

"Leave him alone," Daniel said, tired and rolling his eyes. Kenneth released Eric and gave him a shove as he ran away.

"Go to your boyfriend, faggot," Kenneth said. He towered over Daniel as he walked by, and gave his backpack a swift kick, knocking him to the ground.

One of the girls shoved Kenneth. "Stop it!" She cried. "He didn't do nothin' to you!"

Kenneth's face flushed. He picked up the girl by her throat, only managing to lift her onto her toes. Out of nowhere, a rock hit Kenneth's temple and he instantly fell. The girl grabbed her neck and gasped for air. One of the sisters tended to her, and the other stood over Kenneth's unconscious body. Eric and Daniel rushed to her side.

"Is he dead?" She asked.

"Who cares," Eric said, nudging Kenneth with his foot.

"We'll be in trouble," Daniel said. "Wake him up."

The sullen sister bent down and slapped his face repeatedly until Kenneth woke up. His eyelashes fluttered, breaking up the sunlight.

"He's alive," she said. "For now." Kenneth slowly got up, and when he realized where he was, he ran home.

"What did she mean, 'For now?'" Daniel asked Eric as they walked away from the scene.

Eric shrugged. "Who cares? They're all creeps," he said. "Let them kill each other."

It was Eric's streak of psychopathy that both intrigued Daniel and made him afraid. Daniel's emotions went through filter after filter. He never spoke a word that he didn't labor over for a cosmic minute, chronically afraid to upset the delicate balance of things.

Eric, on the other hand, was wild. He didn't know he was wild, but he was more savage than anyone Daniel ever knew. Wilder than Lloyd, and more savage in his anger than Dwight. Eric was not troubled with decency, and that was the difference. It wasn't that he didn't respect social graces - it was more so that he had no patience for them.

Daniel learned from watching hours upon hours of true crime mysteries with his mother that Eric's future would most likely unfold on the evening news. Either Eric Redmond would learn to be human, or he would make the whole world suffer. He saw potential in Eric - flickers of warmth beaming through his reptilian eyes - but he saw that less and less as the boys grew up.

He rarely saw it after the Toby sisters' house burned down. Eric seemed mesmerized by the flames; Daniel never saw Eric's eyes get so wide. Eric was silent the whole time.

They caught the Toby sisters walking with a gas can one evening, marching toward their house like soldiers. Eric was the first to see them across the way, pointing at them without saying a word. The boys were playing pitch-and-catch with a large rock similar to the one Eric chucked at Kenneth's head a few days prior. It was Daniel's idea to play, but Eric had no ball to throw, so he picked up a rock.

"Hey, what are you doing?" Daniel called out to the girls as they walked lock-in-step, weighed down by the dense tin gas can. The sisters were silent. They marched two together with the gas can between them, hand in hand. The sullen sister, who had a swollen left eye, led them.

"What do you need that gas for?" Daniel asked them.

One of the sisters holding the gas can mumbled, "Dad's car." She had a split lip.

"Come play catch with us," Daniel said.

The sullen Toby sister looked at Daniel in his eyes and hissed, "We don't want to play with your stupid rock. Leave us alone."

The Toby sisters got smaller and smaller and the boys watched them as they carried the gas can inside through the back door - marching up the steps gallantly despite the fact that their feet could have easily broken through the rotten wood on account of the extra weight of the gas can.

When the fire started, the boys had long tuckered out, sitting beneath the Hawthorn tree, swatting at cicadas and talking about all the people at school they thought were stupid. Talking with their eyes skyward, they started to smell smoke.

"Do you really think they were just gassing up the old man's car?" Daniel asked Eric with concern in his voice.

"I dunno," Eric said, digging in the dirt with a stick.

"Because...Eric, do you smell something burning?" Daniel asked.

"I can't smell nothin'," Eric said. "I got allergies." He sniffled like his father always did. "But yeah I kinda smell it, I guess."

"Kenneth wasn't at school today," Daniel said. "He didn't get on or off the bus."

Eric looked at Daniel and shrugged. "Maybe he's dead."

"That's not funny," Daniel said.

"I didn't mean it to be," Eric said. "Surprised he hadn't been killed yet, the crazy sumbitch."

The fire grew. Cars and pickup trucks with lights on the dashes and sirens on the cabs piled up. A group of men in plain clothes grabbed buckets and hoses. Among these men was Terrence, who saw Daniel and Eric in the distance.

Tears fell down Daniel's cheeks.

The smoke smell was familiar. It was sour; like something unnatural was burning. "What should we do?" He asked Eric.

"Let's walk away," Eric said after he thought for a minute. "I don't want nothin' to do with this."

He didn't notice Daniel's tears until about fifty steps in. "Why are you crying?" Eric said.

"I'm not sure," Daniel said, wiping his cheeks, not able to stop the flood. "Do you really think he was already dead?"

"I don't know," Eric said, becoming a little agitated.

"I hope so," Daniel said. "It's got to be an awful way to die."

“What does?” Eric asked.

“Burning,” Daniel replied.

Eric grabbed Daniel by the back of his neck and cradled his head on his shoulder for a few steps until Daniel got too dizzy and had to walk upright.

"*If* he's dead," Eric said. "We don't know that he's dead. We don't know anything."

"I hope nobody's dead," Daniel said. Eric nodded in agreement.

Seven

The Toby house fire was quickly forgotten, and the culprits were never pursued. The house was only partially burned, and they never found Kenneth's body. He was listed as a runaway, just as his twin brother Daryl had been so many times before and after. Most people just assumed Kenneth was the one who started the fire, as he had been heard to threaten so many times.

Kenneth McAdams was suspected in several other house fires in Hawthorn that year, though the cops in town didn't bother to investigate burned homes in Jackass Flats.

"Good riddance," one deputy was overheard saying at the Cue 'n Brew one evening after a few too many beers. "I hope that little bastard burns the whole damn neighborhood down before it's over with." He never got a chance to, thanks to the Toby sisters.

At Daniel's music lesson the following week, Terrence prodded Daniel a bit.

"I saw you and your brother there underneath that tree while that house was burning," Terrence said. "You didn't see nothin'?"

"I saw plenty," Daniel said. "It happened right there in front of us."

"I mean, you didn't see how it happened?" Terrence asked.

Daniel shook his head no.

"All right," Terrence said. "I had to ask."

"I heard he isn't dead," Daniel said. "Is that true?"

"Nobody was home," Terrence said. "Nobody was hurt." He gently touched Daniel's shoulder and turned the pages of his music book. He pointed at the top of the page, and Daniel started playing.

Terrence gazed at Daniel. He looked like a haggard old man in an impish body; his eyes were heavy and dark, and his fingers were slightly curled inward.

His lips pressed together and pursed when he struggled to see the notes on the page. Insomnia had taken a slight toll on his vision.

"Stop," Terrence said calmly. He closed the lid over the piano keys, and Daniel's eyes burned with shame.

"I practiced," Daniel pleaded. "I really did practice."

"I'm sure you did," Terrence said. "Let's go get some ice cream."

They sat silently for a while at a picnic table outside the Old Country Drive-In and ate vanilla cones.

"You're not going to make me play?" Daniel asked.

"Nah," Terrence said. "Your heart ain't in it this week. I reckon you could use a break."

"Yeah," Daniel said.

"Just don't let it ruin your dinner," Terrence said.

"Can I have dinner with you?" Daniel asked.

"Is that okay with your family?" Terrence asked.

Daniel rolled his tired eyes. "I dunno," he said.

Terrence drove Daniel back in his sweaty-smelling truck. Daniel avoided looking out of the window. He looked at the dirt on the floor, and he tried to piece together from analyzing various tools and rags on the floor what Terrence's life was like these days. Daniel missed Terrence more than he missed his old life. He missed him as much as he missed his mother.

"How come you didn't take me?" Daniel blurted out.

Terrence sat uncomfortably and kept his eyes on the road.

"Because I thought we were friends and now I don't know," Daniel continued. "I thought we had fun together and I don't have fun with hardly anybody in this stupid town, and it really hurt my feelings when you let me go with them."

Terrence's chest pained him. His face remained stone.

"I can't give you nothin', boy," Terrence finally said after eighteen seconds of silence. "They can give you everything." The words came out like a car backfire.

"I don't need anything," Daniel said. "I just need to be normal and happy."

"Ain't you happy?" Terrence asked, voice breaking a bit.

Daniel looked at Terrence incredulously.

"They would never let me take you," Terrence finally admitted. "Your mama was clear in her will. It's not that simple. We ain't supposed to mix."

"What's the difference? We're in the same truck right now!" Daniel exclaimed angrily. "Everyone can see us!"

Terrence grabbed Daniel's wrists and bent down to whisper. "You know what I mean, boy."

Daniel crossed his arms in an angry pout, but he couldn't keep it together for more than a few seconds before he began to cry.

Terrence reached out to Daniel.

"Please don't cry, Danny," Terrence said. He wiped his tears away with his long, bony index finger. "I ain't fit to raise you."

Daniel sobbed. "Why not?"

"Because..." Terrence didn't know how to finish that sentence. "I'm just not." Terrence put on his blinker and pulled into the church parking lot.

Daniel wiped his remaining tears with his sleeve and put his face back together. "I hate this stupid town," he mumbled. He opened the truck door.

Mrs. Redmond was parked nearby. They observed her talking to herself while looking at her reflection in the rearview mirror. Daniel looked at Terrence, and Terrence looked away in shame.

Daniel slammed the truck door. He got into the back seat of the car, and Mrs. Redmond snapped out of her hallucination.

"Hello, dear. How was your lesson?" Mrs. Redmond said sweetly.

"Fine," Daniel said with his arms crossed.

Mrs. Redmond put the car in reverse and drove away, leaving Terrence alone in the church parking lot.

Terrence looked himself in the eye, in his rearview mirror. He skimmed the tapestry of his life for the origins of his acquiescence to the parishioners of Hawthorn. Terrence remembered a time when he was resolved to burn it all down. Just as quickly as they came, he shook those memories as shameful; as something he must never remember and always work to forget. He had found his place in society somewhere along the line, and was displeased to learn that his position held little power, even over himself.

He wanted to take Daniel with him to another place - if not to look after him, just to get him away from the Redmonds. But this was impossible.

It was around this time that the dreams returned in a variety of narratives. Terrence's sleep became uncomfortable and sweaty, and he woke up every morning with a hangover-of-sorts. His hearing became fuzzy, and his leaning equilibrium jolted his brain with every step.

Terrence stopped smiling at people, even the ones he knew. He stopped showing up for jobs except for right before the electric was due.

He went from the church parking lot straight to the Cue 'n Brew the night Daniel got mad at him. He hadn't drunk a drop of alcohol in over ten years and hadn't been to a neighborhood bar for even longer, as trouble always seemed to follow him inside.

"I'd like to start a tab," Terrence said as he sat at the bar, eye-to-eye with the surly white bartender with a bald head and goatee.

"We don't do tabs here," the bartender lied. "Cash only."

"Fine," Terrence said. "Whiskey neat."

“Hey,” a woman from across the bar slurred at him. “I know you.”

Terrence didn’t even look her way. “I think you’re mistaken, miss,” he said coldly.

This blond woman with an acid-washed face squinted at him. Her pointy chin lowered, making her resemble a witch.

“Nah,” she said. “I know you. You used to teach music.”

“A long time ago,” Terrence said. “I was just an assistant.”

The bartender cleaned glasses while watching this exchange.

“You don’t remember me, huh?” The woman asked sweetly, wobbling as she lit a cigarette.

“No, ma’am,” Terrence said.

“How do you know?” The woman said, her tone shifting toward the belligerent. “You won’t even look me in the eye.”

Terrence could feel burning gazes all across the room. He felt the claustrophobic anxiety of being in a place he was not welcome. He sat for a couple of minutes, gulped his glass of whiskey, and stood up.

"That's it?" The bartender said with a smirk. "You wanted to start a tab for just one drink?"

Terrence tipped his hat at the bartender before he left. He threw a few coins on the bar. They clattered loudly and spun for a few seconds.

The sky was a purplish-pink, and it was starting to get dark.

Terrence's truck was loud, and so he often didn't recognize when things were happening outside of it. He didn't realize he was being followed until he was almost home.

There was a vehicle behind him. It sped up and began flashing its bright lights at him. Terrence turned around to try to get a glimpse of the driver, but the interior was smudged out by white light.

Terrence grappled his gun discreetly and flicked the safety off. He kept his hand on the gun at his side. Meanwhile, the car that had flashed him several times had turned on its high beams and left them on, blinding Terrence. He put his hand over the rearview mirror so he could see where he was driving.

Terrence drove past his house. He drove past the old racetrack where the weeds had grown up, and he parked his car in the place where he took Donna all those years ago. Terrence kept the motor running, and he dried the sweat off his palm on his pants. He took the gun out of the holster.

His headlights shone on the road, illuminating very little. He saw Shelly's Cadillac drive by him. Yes, it was hers. It had to have been - there was no mistaking that rust pattern.

Eight

Missouri summers were brutal - not only in their oppressive heat but also in their unpredictability. The temperatures didn't matter much. Eighty-five degree-days could often feel as if they were one hundred and five degrees.

"It's not the heat, it's the humidity," folks would recite, as if that were some consolation for having to dig ditches or plant crops in the heat of the day, exposing their bodies to the blistering sun, entrenched in the boiling steam rising from the ground.

Cold fronts, as much as they relieved, were also precursors to possible destruction. When the temperatures rose again as they inevitably would, so came the storms. If God saw fit, or perhaps if He added too much of one thing to the recipe, the winds became particularly destructive.

There were several perfect storms brewing in Hawthorn that year, and the tornado at the end of April was the first, if not the worst. The Redmond's had an underground bunker in their backyard, which Father Redmond had constructed for doomsday. It had everything their home had, minus a few amenities.

Eric enjoyed being in the bunker. Not only did it have television where he could watch the destruction unfold live on the local news - which interrupted regular programming as much as the networks could get away with - but the bunker held boxes and cans of preservative-filled junk food, which he was never allowed to eat above ground. This type of food, Father Redmond rationalized, was high in calories and never spoiled.

Most of all, Eric felt sheltered in the bunker. Not from the storm, which he enjoyed, but he felt like he was being kept from the world. In the bunker, Eric thought, he might live here once his dad kicked the bucket. He barely concealed his disappointment when the storm was over, and he had to once again join the rest of the world above ground.

Through sheer coincidence that Father Redmond quietly considered an omen, a tornado spun through Hawthorn the night before a planned family trip to visit Edna Redmond's mother in the retirement home in Springfield.

Edna had not seen her mother for several years. Had that not been the case, Father Redmond would have canceled the trip to fix the missing shingles on their home. Instead, he hired Terrence to do it during their trip.

The eerie quiet of the drive was accentuated by scenes of the aftermath of the storm: centuries-old trees ripped up, their carcasses resting on caved-in homes.

"My, my," Mrs. Redmond muttered under her breath with sadness. "What will these folks do?"

"They'll get through it, mama," Father Redmond said firmly. "We'll help them. God will help them."

Eric looked at Daniel with a goofy face. Daniel did his best to hold back laughter, and he was only partially successful. Father Redmond looked back at both of the boys with a warning.

"Eric, do you have your seatbelt on?" Father Redmond asked, scolding.

"Yeah," Eric said.

"What'd you say, boy?"

"Yes sir," Eric said, rolling his eyes.

The further they drove from Hawthorn, the less dramatic were the scenes of destruction. The sun started to peek out through the clouds, and the only branches on the ground were already dead, culled from the healthy trees by the strong winds from the night before.

They arrived at the retirement home, which resembled a bank or a school. The boys got out first. Daniel opened Mrs. Redmond's door for her.

"Thank you, dear," Mrs. Redmond said, holding a picnic basket and looking elderly herself - her hair pulled back into a bun, her gray roots starting to show underneath her dyed brunette hair. Her face looked dour, a change from her usual blankly pleasant expression. It belied her sweet voice, a practiced and perfected affectation.

Mrs. Redmond stopped in front of the main entrance. She looked back at her husband and the two boys with a patient smile. She batted her eyes at her son, who was the first to meet her there. "Eric," she said in a saccharine voice, nodding the crown of her head gently toward the door.

"Boy," Mr. Redmond scolded, "open the door for your mother." Eric opened the door, and waved his mother inside in a dramatic fashion, patronizing her. Daniel walked beside Mrs. Redmond, but he looked back to see Father Redmond jerking Eric up by his collar, whispering something in his ear. Eric laughed, which turned his father's red face deep crimson.

The family entered the room that held Edna Redmond's mother. It smelled of faint raspberry potpourri and urine. Eric pinched his nostrils. Daniel pulled Eric's hand down to his side before anyone could notice.

Old Mrs. Price blinked her sunken eyes twice. "Edna?" She squalled with a gravelly voice. "Who the hell are these people?"

Edna pulled her wicker purse up to her chest and managed a smile. "Mother, you remember Harold," she said.

"Yeah," she said, looking Father Redmond up and down. "I wasn't talking about him."

"And this is your grandson, Eric," Edna said, gesturing toward the boy.

Old Mrs. Price coughed up a puddle of mucus. She spat into a cup near her bed. "Looks like his father," she said disdainfully. Then she looked at Daniel. "And who are you, young man?"

"Daniel," he said softly.

"You belong to them, too?" She croaked.

Daniel shook his head no, but Father Redmond spoke up before Daniel could. "He does, yes," he said. "We adopted him."

Old Mrs. Price blinked a couple of times. She let out a chortle. "Good luck, kid," she said.

Harold whisked the boys away to the cafeteria and let Edna and her mother visit with each other. Edna pulled a chair close to the bed. She sat with her hands in her lap.

"To what do I owe this visit?" Mrs. Price asked with a gnarly half-grin.

"Nothing, mother," Edna said. "It's been a while, and I wanted to make sure the storm didn't get you."

"What storm?" Mrs. Price asked snappily.

"The tornado, mother," Edna said. "Didn't you hear it?"

"Tornado?" Mrs. Price repeated. "Is your house still there?"

"Yes," Edna said. "But we've moved just outside of town. We built a new house."

"Is that right?" Mrs. Price said. "I guess it's not big enough for an old lady with emphysema."

"Mother, please," Edna said.

"I'll give you credit," Mrs. Price said, "you stuck around longer than I ever could have."

"After all of these years," Edna said, "can't you just be decent to my husband?"

Mrs. Price looked down at her lap. "No," she finally said. "And you know why. I just hope I'm alive long enough to see the kid grow up," Mrs. Price said. "So you can finally leave the rat bastard."

"Mother!" Edna exclaimed in horror.

"In my day, we didn't have the options you girls have now," Mrs. Price said. "We didn't have the option to say 'no,' and we didn't have the option to take care of the problem that came from...that."

"I don't know what you're talking about," Edna said, her voice getting tired.

"I'm talking about men, Edna," Mrs. Price said. "You were a smart girl, and I just knew you'd be independent. That's how I brought you up. But instead, you gave up your good mind to the first con man to call you pretty."

"You're just being cruel for no reason," Edna said in a near-whisper. "You're upset with me for not visiting."

Mrs. Price shook her head no. "I may be cruel, but I have to tell you this while I can. In case you wait another two years to come visit." Her face softened. "I look at you now, and I see nothing behind those eyes. What has he done to you, Edna?"

"Nothing," Edna said. "He loves me."

"If I had the option when I was younger, Edna, I don't know what I would have done with you when I got pregnant," Mrs. Price said. "I suppose it doesn't matter now. But one thing I always tried to do is teach you to not depend on the kindness of men. Men aren't kind unless it gets them what they want. Women are strong by nature. It's the men of this world who tell us different. And for whatever reason, we believe them."

"I didn't come here to hear this," Edna said. "You're making me upset."

"Good!" Mrs. Price said. "I was beginning to think you couldn't feel anything at all."

"Are they feeding you well?" Edna asked in a desperate attempt to change the subject. "You look thin."

"Listen to what I'm telling you," Mrs. Price said. "If you really want to save your soul, get out however you can."

"And do what?" Edna asked, losing her patience. "What do you propose I do with my freedom?"

"Find something or someone you truly love," Mrs. Price said. "And who loves you back."

Edna laughed, her friendly veneer giving way to her mother's cynicism. "What do you know about love? You've never loved anyone."

"No," Mrs. Price conceded. "But you're full of love. You're not like me."

Edna's smile was gone and her eyeballs glistening. She got up, dabbed her eyes with a Kleenex, and walked toward the door.

"I don't say this to hurt you, Edna," Mrs. Price said. "The world is an unfriendly place, but that doesn't mean you can't find shelter from it somewhere."

Edna turned her chin and leered at her mother out of the corner of her eye. "Every place I've ever looked," she said, "has turned me away."

Edna sat in a metal chair outside of Mrs. Price's room, its door wide open. She stared at the wall in front of her. Daniel was the first to notice her from the nearby cafeteria. He watched her eyes. She didn't blink. She did, however, whisper to herself words he couldn't make out.

"Hey," Eric said, getting Daniel's attention back to their game of tic tac toe. "Your turn."

"Did you ever notice that your mom talks to herself?" Daniel asked, looking down at the table in an effort to soften the question.

"Yeah, so? Don't you ever talk to yourself?" Eric said.

"I guess so," Daniel said. "But not like she does."

"My dad says it's the demons," Eric said. "But really she's just got mental problems from when she was younger."

"How do you know?" Daniel asked.

"Why else would someone talk to themselves?" Eric said, chuckling.

"Doesn't she have a doctor?" Daniel asked. "Or someone to talk to?"

Eric shrugged. "None of my business," he said. "Dad said it's the Devil. What's a doctor supposed to do about that?"

In a way, Daniel envied Eric's detachment. On the other hand, it worried him. What would Eric do to help Daniel if he got in a bad way? Eric was his only friend in the world, despite the fact that his very essence disturbed him greatly. Everyone who ever meant anything to him had either died or denied him - except, so far, Eric Redmond.

It seemed the Redmonds all lived separate lives under one roof. They each served a practical purpose in each other's lives, and nothing more. Father Redmond provided the money and discipline. Mrs. Redmond was a female counterpart who stood next to her husband like a breathing statue. Eric completed the family portrait. They appeared to be a family unit, but it seemed more like they were bound together for the sake of their obligation to tradition. Daniel got the feeling he was there to anchor Eric. Father Redmond depended on Daniel to keep Eric's eccentricities in check, at least for appearance's sake. Or maybe, Father Redmond needed a true heir; perhaps it was clear to him that Eric was destined for anarchic, sinful adulthood.

Father Redmond always referred to Daniel as his son, though they barely ever spoke. The things he did say to Daniel were cordial and short, whereas his scolding of Eric was constant and his tone extraordinarily resentful, if somewhat warranted. Harold Redmond seemed to have run out of patience for his son long ago, and if Eric had even a tiny sensitivity chip inside of him - which he didn't appear to - he would have been a gravely wounded little boy. Luckily, Eric had no use for other people, especially his father, who he looked upon with slight disgust every time they happened to be in the same room.

Edna didn't say a word on the drive home, and Harold didn't bother to ask her anything about her visit with her mother. He was distracted by Eric's loud music coming from his Walkman - the gothic new wave music bleeding out of his headphones, causing a tinny echo of reverb that pulsated coldly and crudely when mashed with the cassette tape Father Redmond was playing of his own sermon. The noise became a crudely quiet entity lingering in the background, and Edna Redmond fell asleep and dreamt of quicksand.

In her dream, her husband stood before her, yelling at Edna in panic as her body was slowly swallowed. "Do something!" He said. "Don't just stand there."

"I need a rope," Mrs. Redmond said calmly. "Give me something to latch onto, or I'll die."

Just before her head went under, Harold Redmond's final words were, "I'll tell the boys you love them." The loose sand filled her nasal cavities, and her physical survival instinct caused her mind to short circuit with panic. Her soul was at peace, but she couldn't breathe. It was this choking that woke her up.

She came back above the earth, her seatbelt holding her a little too tightly.

"Eric, turn that down," Father Redmond said. "Or turn it off."

"What?" Eric yelled with a mischievous grin. He winked at Daniel. "Can't hear you, Dad."

Father Redmond's face became flushed. "Yes you did, boy," he said. "You heard what I said. Give it here." He reached back and tried to grab Eric's Walkman from his hand, but Eric giggled and dodged his attempt, holding the Walkman up to the roof. The car swerved, and Mrs. Redmond's temple hit the window. Her head bounced a bit, and she seemed dazed.

"Are you okay, mama?" Harold said, still angry. He looked at Eric in the rearview mirror. "You see what you did, boy?"

"It's not his fault," Edna said faintly. "I just had the strangest dream," she said.

"What was your dream about?" Eric called out from the back.

"Quicksand," she said. "I was in quicksand."

"I heard if you die in your dream," Eric said, "You die in real life, too. Is that true?"

"Of course not," Father Redmond said. "Dreams are dreams. Unless they're from God, they don't mean anything."

"How do you know her dream wasn't from God?" Eric argued.

"Stop talking nonsense," Father Redmond said. "Play your headphones. Quietly this time."

Then, without warning, Edna opened the passenger side door and leaped out of the speeding car.

Her body rolled and tumbled on the blacktop of the barren state highway. The Cadillac behind them squealed its tires and spun, as did Father Redmond's car brakes. No one screamed. They didn't have time to. All three remaining Redmonds sat with their mouths agape and their hearts in their throats.

Father Redmond put the car in park, bowed his head, and began to pray, mumbling phrases and holy platitudes to himself. Eric opened his door and ran to his mother. Daniel followed him.

Eric bent down to his mother's unconscious body and put his fingers under her nose. "She's still alive," he said.

Daniel ran away.

"Where are you going?" Eric screamed.

"Payphone," Daniel yelled back. "Ambulance."

Eric knew better than to move his mother, but he tried to wake her by pinching her hips and gently slapping her face. Edna's eyes slowly opened.

"Mom?" Eric said, eerily calm. "Did that other car hit you?"

"I'm not sure," Edna said. "I didn't feel it if it did." Edna smiled through the pain of broken bones and cuts. "I'm fine," she said.

"You will be," Eric said. "Danny went to call an ambulance."

"I don't care if they come for me," Edna said. "I'm free."

Eric's eyes got wide. "Sure," he said. "You're going to be fine."

"It's just a body, dear," Edna squeaked out. "Bodies die all the time."

"You're not dying," Eric said.

"No," Edna replied. "Maybe not. But I'm free. I'm free now."

As Daniel ran back for the nearest pay phone two miles away, Mrs. Redmond's words haunted his racing thoughts. Hearing Edna's dream of drowning in quicksand brought back an observation he once made about his own mother - that her insides were made of quicksand. They could never be filled.

Tears flew off of Daniel's face as he realized that Edna Redmond, unlike his own mother, came to this sudden realization in a span of a few seconds. Unlike Daniel's own mother, Edna took action to escape the quicksand however she could.

Father Redmond laid his head down on the steering wheel and wept. Eric laid down beside his mother in the middle of the street and held her hand until he saw the flashing neon red and blue lights reflect off the windows of the neighborhood houses, and he heard that piercing siren speed through the thick afternoon air.

Nine

It was too hot to go outside. Eric could never stand the heat. Daniel stayed out often, helping Terrence after school with the chicken farm Father Redmond bought as a tax write-off. Manual labor eased Daniel's mind, and every other penny he earned, he put away in a savings account that no one knew about.

Every day, after sleeping through every class at Esther B.Williams high school, Eric wrote in a notebook for hours - endlessly pontificating about the end of the world and writing cryptic poetry in a journal. On the cover of the notebook, he crudely wrote the word "TWEAKERBABY" with whiteout he swiped from his father's office desk. The diary became an encyclopedia of his fantasies, his fears, and his delusions.

He drew abstract drawings of his classmates as well as objects of his fascination - the chubby Cuban-American girl Marcia Cruz, for whom he had a peculiar hatred that seemed unwarranted and irrational; and of his heroes, like Daryl McAdams, a classmate who it was an open secret he sold dope and his body, everywhere from Hawthorn to Lampe to Springfield to Kansas City.

Eric referred to Daryl as his brother. He was entranced with his aloofness and his fearlessness. Eric's volcanic personality meshed with Daryl's still waters, and they became great friends, neutralizing each other's propensity for catastrophe, if not tragedy.

Daryl McAdams was the fraternal twin brother of Kenneth McAdams, who the Toby sisters attempted to burn to death. Whereas Kenneth was thick both in the head and the body, violently loud, and oafish, Daryl was slender, quiet, and had not a care in the world. Eric looked at Daryl and wondered how he could be so content in such a shitty town - in such a shitty world. He wanted to know Daryl's secrets.

Eric Redmond became obsessed with this world he had created within the pages of the one-dollar spiral notebook he shoplifted from the local general store. His head swirled when he tried to contemplate the complexity of the universe that seemed to thrive on chaos. Writing and drawing seemed to ease his mind. The meth he watched Daryl smoke became a sideshow, or theatre. The visage was a smoky, smelly grungy comedy that propelled Daryl's thoughts to the speed of sound. It's when Eric felt closer to Daryl in spirit. He could relate.

On Adderall, Eric could focus, but with fidgets and odd tics – there was always a trade-off, a sacrifice to be made, for something as simple as sanity. As he became wrapped up with Daryl's energy, Eric Redmond let go of his sanity.

A little more each day, Eric stayed in his room by himself trying to answer questions no one else could or would. And a little more each day, his thoughts were increasingly coming from somewhere else – some strange, hostile place.

Daniel knocked on Eric's bedroom door late one night. When Eric didn't answer, he nudged it open and entered the room carefully. He found Eric in his underwear, his nose deep in the Tweakerbaby notebook. Other notebooks with different colored covers were lying all around him. They also had the "Tweakerbaby" moniker scrawled across them. The room smelled musty, and judging from Eric's greasy, wild hair, he hadn't had a bath in some time.

Eric finally noticed Daniel's presence. "Can't you fucking knock?" He snarled.

"I did knock," Daniel said.

"Oh," Eric said. "What do you want?"

"I don't want anything," Daniel said defensively.

Eric got up and strolled toward Daniel. He faced him, nose to nose.

"I can smell death on you," Eric said, in a tone that resembled his father's when he got angry. "Are you aware that you're dead?" Eric's eyes were furious and full.

Daniel smirked. "I think you might be smelling yourself," he said.

Eric searched deep into Daniel's eyes, looking for something he wasn't quite sure of. He said nothing, and went back to bed, continuing to review his writing.

"What does Tweakerbaby mean?" Daniel asked. Eric didn't acknowledge him.

"Eric?" Daniel called out slightly louder.

Eric, perturbed, looked up at this young man - his brother - who he just accused of being dead. "It's not anything you could ever comprehend, Dead Man," Eric said.

While Daniel and Father Redmond had a silent breakfast of cold cereal, Eric tried to sneak past them.

"Where are you going?" Father Redmond asked.

"The park," Eric said, already halfway out of the door.

"Come here," Father Redmond said in an authoritative tone. Eric slowly made his way to his father, seated at the end of a large dining room table.

"Closer," his father said. Eric stood over Father Redmond.

Redmond motioned for Eric to bend down. He grabbed Eric's hair and smelled it. Eric yelped.

"Go take a shower," he said, releasing his hold on Eric's hair. "Don't ever try to leave this house looking and smelling like that again."

Eric gritted his teeth. "Yes sir," he said.

"And you don't leave unless you tell me where you're going!" Father Redmond called out as Eric stomped up the stairs. Daniel found this a very odd exchange, even by the Redmonds' standards.

Both boys were fifteen, nearing adulthood. Daniel had aspirations of buying Redmond's chicken farm, which made the Redmonds a decent side income. For Daniel, it would be more than enough.

For him, peace and quiet was a foreign concept. He would have liked a wife, but he didn't need one. He just wanted to live and breathe on his own terms. He wanted a little control over his life before he got too old to enjoy it.

Daniel thought he might let Terrence buy a chunk of the farm once the time came. After all, Terrence did most of the morning work. His bitterness about the past aside, Daniel loved Terrence like family. Of all the cruelties of the world around them both, Daniel found their inability to be a family the most absurd and hurtful. As angry as he was inside, he understood a little better with each passing year why Terrence was, in fact, right about the world in which they lived, and why he could only look after Daniel from a distance.

It was Saturday. Daniel worked the farm every day - after school and on the weekends. Terrence was always there with a courteous smile, even as he was wringing a sick chicken's neck, putting it out of its misery. The two kept their distance, stretching out fifteen minutes of small talk over three years.

They sat on the edge of Terrence's truck bed one day, drinking cheap beer and making pleasantries when they spotted a Cadillac driving slowly on the county road across a nearby pasture.

"Hey Terrence," Daniel said. "Remember my mama's old Cadillac?"

"Yeah," Terrence said guiding his eyes toward where Daniel pointed. "Kinda looks like hers, doesn't it?"

"Mmm-hmm," Daniel said. "Whatever happened to that old car anyway?"

"Not sure, Danny," Terrence said. "After she passed, it was gone. Somebody must'a stole it."

"You don't think that's Dwight, do ya'?" Daniel asked. "Surely not. Right?"

Terrence's eyes got wide. He took a swig of his beer.

"Nah," he said. "I find it hard to believe that old car can still run."

"But I think that's it," Daniel said. "I think that's the same car. Look at the rust."

"You reckon we oughta find out?" Terrence said, making no mention of the Cadillac that followed him home from the Cue 'n Brew on that odd night years ago.

"Let's go," Daniel said.

The two men got into Terrence's truck and sped down the quarter-mile gravel drive. They stopped at the road. The Cadillac, which had the driver's side sun visor down, eclipsing the driver's identity, peeled out.

"That's odd," Daniel said.

"Nothin' to worry about," Terrence said. "I don't think that was the same car."

Terrence was lying - the first lie he ever told Daniel, and he wasn't sure why he bothered to protect him after all this time. He wondered if his protection was only delaying the inevitable; if he was actually hurting him. His lie seemed to ease Daniel's mind, but Terrence was worried.

Dwight was an unstable man when he and Shelly had that dramatic confrontation several years back. Terrence knew what drinking and isolation would do to a man's spirit. At his most desperate, a man is capable of just about anything.

This Cadillac, hovering around them like a UFO dropping in and out of their lives over a period of years was an eerie, intrusive thing – but it was most certainly a coincidence. Every time Terrence saw something that reminded him of Shelly, he was haunted by his mother's phobia of white women. He wondered if after all he'd seen for himself, that she was right to be afraid.

Ten

Megan Milstone was basically the opposite of Daniel's mother, Shelly Guile. Megan's beauty was a practical, modest sort. She was a foul-mouthed, unkempt, chainsmoking brat, raised by clean-cut former Mormons with Native blood who were born in the Mountain Time Zone. The Milstone family had converted to Baptism when Megan was twelve. Perhaps predictably, Megan went through different phases from twelve to sixteen: Pagan, Wiccan, and Buddhist. She finally settled down as an indifferent and fatigued agnostic.

Her parents had moved to Hawthorn the previous year, after finding out about Megan's cigarette habit and her satanic heavy metal CD's. They did not explain or confront Megan with their findings. They just moved, and Megan's CD's and cigarettes mysteriously disappeared while the family packed their vehicles for Missouri. She was introduced as a new student on the same day that Marcia Cruz, another Hawthorn transplant, began high school. The two became friends of convenience. It was less a friendship than it was an alliance: two brown outsiders in a school full of snotty white kids who all talked like Barney Fife.

Megan and Marcia didn't have anything in common except an awkward and shallow interest in boys. So they sat outside during lunch period, objectifying the boys playing tag football with their shirts tied around their waists.

One day, Megan looked beyond this crowd of sweaty, sinewy pale skin to focus on a boy who appeared to be doing math homework - Daniel Wright-Redmond.

Daniel's face had thinned out since his years as a seraphic, blonde grade-schooler, but Megan had no yearbook photos to prove he had gone through this phase. He caught her eye not because of his Nordic good looks, but because of how staid he looked compared with the chaotic, sweaty energy of his classmates.

Daniel was not a misfit. He seemed to be well adjusted, and well liked. If he had a mind to be, he could be athletic and goofy with the rest of the boys, and he stood out as their leader. He always picked the teams in gym class, and his answers in class were the only ones that ever seemed to satisfy the history teacher, the macabre bitch Mrs. Danforth.

On this day, during a particularly oblivious moment of Daniel's, Megan took a mental photograph of him. He was pouting and counting to himself with a calculator on his left knee and a notebook on his right, chewing on a pencil in between jeers to his friends on the makeshift football field on which they played.

"Why's he doing homework during recess?" Megan asked Marcia.

"He's got a job after school," Marcia said. "The only boy with a job that's not selling Boy Scout popcorn or dope."

"What's he do?" Megan asked.

"Chicken farmer," Marcia said with a shudder. "But at least his dad's loaded."

"What's his dad do?" Megan asked.

Marcia smirked. "You don't know? He's like this famous preacher."

"Is he on TV?" Megan asked.

"Yeah," Marcia said. "Local TV. But their church is huge."

"Do you go to it?" Megan asked Marcia.

"Everyone goes to it," Marcia said, rolling her eyes. "And so will you, probably."

"So why does he go to public school, if they're so rich?" Megan asked.

"The only private school here is Catholic," Marcia said. "So I guess not everyone goes there. But most do. Why, do you think he's cute?" Marcia said, smiling.

"Maybe, it's hard to tell from this distance," Megan said.

"He is cute," Marcia assured Megan. "But good luck. That family is weird."

"How are they weird?" Megan asked.

"They're religious," Marcia replied. "But Daniel's kind of normal, I guess. He's not blood-related."

Daniel looked up when one of his friends called his name, but his eyes quickly moved to the pair of girls with brown skin, gossiping about him across the playground. When Daniel's eyes met Megan's, his sharp gaze dissolved her tough, eagle-eyed pout into a blushing orb. He quickly looked down at his homework, but it all became a series of unintelligible marks and numbers stacked upon each other - but the world around him made a little more sense.

"Ah, young love!" Marcia said, elbowing Megan and snapping her back to reality.

"Shut up," Megan said. "But do you know-know him?"

"Just come with me to church on Wednesday," Marcia said. "Then you can know-know him."

"Is it Baptist?" Megan asked. "My parents are Baptist."

"It's probably the most Baptist place on Earth," Marcia said.

"They'll be happy that I'm volunteering to go to church on my own, I guess," Megan said.

"So it's a win-win," Marcia said.

When the girls looked ahead, Daniel had escaped back inside. They looked at each other and giggled.

MEGAN GOT OFF THE BUS shortly after three that afternoon and walked by a couple of movers. One of them, a jug-headed Cue 'n Brew regular, said, "Hey, darlin', you live here?" Megan ignored him and went inside. She heard him say from inside, "I got a thing for Mexican chicks, man."

The other mover said, "You're an idiot," and, "She can't be older than fifteen."

Almost immediately, Megan's father, a tall, burly man with deep frown lines, stepped outside. He grabbed the mirror out of the offending mover's hand, and said, "Please hurry up. We are about to start dinner." He took the mirror inside.

Megan began searching for the public access channel that screened Hawthorn Baptist Church sermons twenty-four hours a day. She caught a glimpse of the man who Marcia claimed was Daniel's father - a bald but charismatic man who shouted a lot of nonsense and hid behind rose-colored sunglasses.

Megan's father, still irritated from the perverted mover, said, "Megan, go start your homework."

Megan stood up and handed her father the remote control. Mr. Milstone watched the television for a few minutes, shook his head, and turned it off to help his wife in the kitchen. Megan glimpsed at the movers outside through the glass door. The squirrely mover saw her and waved. She quickly ran up the stairs.

Megan laid on her bed, holding her math book close to her body. She looked up at the ceiling and counted cracks in the wood paneling until she fell asleep.

She had a dream that closely resembled a nightmare, in which the mover - a pasty man in his twenties who had a bright orange t-shirt with a V-shaped sweat stain trickling down to his belly - was put in an electric chair. Someone in the dark of the room flipped the switch, and the mover died after a few dream seconds of jittery, mouth-foaming electrical currents coursing through his crown, down to his toes. She watched him die for several dream seconds, which often resemble hours or days - God's time.

Megan saw herself walking across a checkered floor. She infiltrated white and black squared tiles with scuffed Mary Jane soles, laughing like a sinister witch from an old MGM film. Megan stood over this dead man and straddled his lap, wrapping her legs around his waist. However, before she could defile the singed corpse, her father woke her by calling her downstairs because the Hamburger Helper was finished.

The movers came inside, carrying a piece of wicker living room furniture. The family was gathered around the table, holding hands with heads bowed. There was a crash, followed by a thrash of cursing.

Megan ran into the living room and saw that the mover who had disrespected her with violating eyes and trash talk was bleeding from his hand and standing over a crushed mirror. Megan put her hand over her mouth. The mover was unsure whether she was in horror, or suppressing laughter.

The other mover shook his head. "You dumb idiot," he said and then turned to Megan. "I'm sorry. We'll replace the rug and the mirror and everything."

"Does he need to go to the hospital?" Megan asked in a monotone voice.

"Um," The mover said. "Yeah, probably. But I'll take care of it, don't worry."

The bleeding mover ran outside. Megan's mother ran into the room and put her hand over her mouth. There was no mistaking her horror. "My grandmother's mirror," she said, ready to faint. "It was priceless."

The mover scratched the back of his head and shuffled his feet. "I'm really sorry," he said. "But I've got to get him to the hospital."

Megan's father entered the room. "We understand," he said. "Things happen. You'd better get him to the hospital now."

Megan's mother, holding back emotion, waited for the door to close. She looked at her husband with fury. "I saw you with the mirror," she said. "Where did you put it?"

"I'll replace everything," he said. "What's done is done."

"How did it even happen?" Mrs. Milstone asked.

"I'll make it right," he said, waving her off.

Mr. Milstone sat back down at the kitchen table and outstretched his hands. Megan and her mother looked at each other, and sat down next to him, grabbing each other's hands to pray. After the prayer was finished, Megan's mother and father cleaned up the bloody mess in the living room while Megan picked at her food in the kitchen.

Eleven

In Eric Redmond's mind, the world was on borrowed time.

As a newborn, his eyes flared when his father held him. Eric would gurgle and spit up violently on his father's collar. The longer that the stubborn Harold Redmond held him, the more violently baby Eric reacted to his father's unwillingness to take no for an answer - ear-busting screams, hyperventilation - and on one scary day, the young baby Eric cried so much he lost consciousness briefly. Harold and Eric's spirits seemed to overwhelm each other.

To Harold, this was evidence that his family was under spiritual attack. "This is a test," he told his wife, handing over his vomit-covered son to her as she dabbed his shirt with a towel.

"This is what babies do, dear," Edna Redmond said. "They cry and spit up and several other unsavory things."

Redmond grabbed Edna firmly by her shoulders while she held Eric, who began to cry again. He pointed his finger and whispered with his now-trademark melodrama. "No," he said. "This is a test." That was the last time Harold Redmond ever held his son.

It was this intensity that attracted Edna to Harold. They met at a religious conference in Nashville. Harold was the son of a prominent figure in the Gospel music industry, and Edna's father was able to schedule an audition for his daughter, who he considered to be a great singer.

On the day of the meeting, Edna shuffled into Harold's office with her arms crossed. She gazed in wonder at his walls, which were decorated with framed photos of many of her favorite musical acts with vacant smiles, standing next to Redmond backstage in venues from Branson Missouri to Nashville, to Memphis and Los Angeles.

Redmond observed her starry eyes and colonial-style dress immediately.

"Okay, Edna," Harold said with a poker face.

"Her stage name will be Estelle North," her father corrected.

Edna glanced at her father with bugged eyes, as this was the first time she had ever heard the name.

"Okay, Estelle," Harold said, winking at Edna. "Why don't you stand up and sing for me."

Edna sang a pleasant and unremarkable rendition of "Praise God From Whom All Blessings Flow." She fidgeted her hands and sweat beads formed on her top lip, to her father's dismay. When she finished, Harold gave her a standing ovation.

"Really?" Both father and daughter said in unison.

"You liked it?" Edna asked in half-disbelief.

"Absolutely," Harold said. "Edna, I'd like to talk about our future together over dinner tonight."

"Great," Edna's father said. "Where are we going?" He made darted eye contact with Harold.

Harold leaned back in his chair and grinned. "Have you been to The Texas Cantina?"

"Nope," Edna's father said. "We ain't picky, though, are we Edna?"

"No sir," Edna said with a forced smile.

Harold got out his black book. "What time is best for you?"

"We eat dinner 'round four," Edna's father said.

"Early birds!" Harold said. "Unfortunately, I have a meeting at that time. How's six?"

"That's a little close to Edna's bedtime," Edna's father said, crossing his knee over his leg.

"I see," Harold said. "Well, in that case, I'll give you a call."

"We're wide open tomorrow," Edna's father said.

"Tomorrow's no good," Harold said, busying himself with paperwork. "Good luck to you."

Edna's father stammered a bit. "Not even -"

"I'm a busy man, Mister Price," Harold said. He got up and opened his office door. "Good luck to you."

As Edna walked out of the door, Harold gave her a wink. He extended his hand, and Edna obligingly shook it. He slipped her a small index card, and she kept it hidden in her sweaty palm. She looked confused and closed the door behind her.

Edna's father's scolding could be heard throughout the building. It was her fault he failed at his attempt at a power play, he said. If she had done this or that with her hair, or worn a different dress, or controlled her nerves better, they could both be rich. His throat-scraping whispering was as loud as a scream. As they walked down halls and in and out of elevators, Edna looked straight ahead, utterly nonreactive to her father's hysterical antics.

In the cab on the way back to their hotel, Edna's father fell asleep. When he started snoring, she uncurled the slightly wet business card. It said: *For when your father's not around*, and listed a handwritten phone number on the back, which was somewhat different than the one that was printed as his office number.

"We're leaving town in about four hours," Edna later said to Harold over the phone.

"I only need two," Harold said with a chuckle. "At the most."

EDNA HAD CALLED REDMOND at about four in the morning, and he happened to be awake. They met for breakfast.

"Don't you want anything other than dry toast and tea?" Harold asked Edna for the third time. And for the third time, Edna replied, "No sir, I'm fine."

"I'll get you a Coke," Harold said with a wink. "Bet you've never had a Coke this early."

"I've never had a Coke," Edna said.

"No kidding?" Harold said. He waved down a waitress.

"Daddy says it rots your teeth," Edna said.

"How old are you...Esther?" Harold asked her.

"Edna," she corrected. "I'm twenty-seven."

"Why not Esther?" Harold asked.

"I hate that name," Edna said. "It sounds like an old woman."

"Are you religious, Edna?" Redmond asked, scooping up a yellow slush pile of wet eggs with his toast.

"We're Pentecostal," Edna said.

"We?"

"Me and -"

"-Your daddy," Redmond said, nodding.

"Edna," Redmond continued, "do you want to be a singer? Tell me the truth."

Edna hung her head. "No," she said quietly.

"I see," Harold said. "So why did you call me?"

"I'm not sure," Edna said. "I guess because..." her voice trailed off, and she shrugged.

"I think I know why," Redmond said. Edna perked up.

"I asked you if you're religious," Redmond said. "But do you believe in fate?"

Of all the tricks up Harold Redmond's sleeve, this had to be the oldest. He looked at Edna with mock-intensity.

"I'm not sure what I believe, Mr. Redmond," Edna said with a sudden boldness in her tired voice. "I'm not sure why I'm here, why I called, or why you want to meet with me so bad," Edna continued. "I know I ain't no great singer, so that can't be it. I'm ugly. I've never had a boyfriend. I know you don't want me for that. So I reckon it must be fate or somethin' kin to it, Mr. Redmond, because you're here, and I'm here, and I can't go home with him. I ran it through my mind a thousand times: some way I could tolerate going home with him - some scenario where that would work." Edna looked down at her hands, which were tearing up her napkin into tiny little flakes.

"It's the first time I seen this many lights in one town," she said with a nervous smile. "Maybe I got too haughty or too worldly, and maybe I need Jesus. But as far as I can see, I had Jesus my whole life, and he just stood by and watched all kinds of terrible stuff happen to me. Whatever your reason is for being interested in me," Edna said with resolve, "I don't really care. I'll sleep on your office floor if you take me away from that town, and away from that man."

The waitress came with Edna's Coke.

"Are you sure you don't want to order some real food?" Redmond asked.

Edna took a sip of her soda. "I'll have what you're having," she said. Her eyes widened as the carbonated sugar water rushed down her throat.

"That's the deluxe platter," Redmond said. He looked at the waitress, who was smiling uncomfortably. Then Redmond looked at Edna. "Go on," he prodded.

Edna looked at the waitress, making eye contact. "I'll have the deluxe platter, please," she said.

"Okay," the waitress said, darting her eyes away from this odd couple. "Anything else?"

Edna looked at Redmond. He shrugged, leaving Edna to order for herself. "A muffin," she said. "Blueberry."

It was this sudden discovery of her boldness that allowed Edna an escape from her frightening life, and how Harold Redmond gained a second wife. She took her cues from Redmond's resolve. Harold Redmond was a man who was never wrong.

But as soon as Eric was born, she saw that resolve challenged for the first time. His own flesh and blood – his own creation - seemed to be a mirror for everything Harold Redmond tried to hide about himself. When he looked at Eric, he felt his own rawness and his own weirdness, and Harold knew that he gave his son those qualities.

It was Harold Redmond's inability to comprehend paternal love that made Edna start to doubt the infallibility of her husband.

As he grew up, Eric raised himself. And in a way, he raised Edna, too.

Eric's anarchic ways were self-contained, for a while. But as he became a young man with demands and desires, he became as dangerous as the tornadoes and earthquakes they drilled for during school once per semester.

Eric always suspected that he had superpowers. It's what got him through a childhood rife with anxiety and doubt, a result of being different from everyone around him. As he cultivated the idea of these powers, the powers became stronger, and the illusion became indistinguishable from his reality. He was emboldened by testosterone, and then he became drunk on it.

He wrote, as Daniel discovered while snooping one afternoon, that he was born with a hereditary spiritualism. He referred to it as a disease, or a mutation. His father had some form of it, one journal entry read, but he had become too power-driven; Harold Redmond had become evil at some point, and it was up to Eric to destroy him.

He never shared these thoughts with anyone, and so without context, he simply appeared deranged. His actions became indecipherable.

He would watch his father's TV program - which, by the time the boys had graduated high school, had made the jump from public access to the local

Fox affiliate on Sunday mornings when everyone was either at church or work. Everyone, that is, except those Redmond was really trying to reach: the lost, the fallen, the broken-down and the poor in spirit. His target was the ones who didn't attend church - not because they had to work, but because they chose not to.

When Father Redmond would catch his son watching it and taking notes, he would try to watch with him. Once, when Harold sat next to his son, Eric just hissed at him like an angry alley cat then left the room, tossing the remote control onto his father's lap.

He went with Daryl McAdams often, and stayed overnight with him as often as he was allowed. He'd share with Daryl his plotting and planning, and Daryl would shake his head and laugh. "You're crazy, Tweakerbaby," he'd say, taking the sheets of paper filled with the chicken scratch that Eric jumbled down, pretending to read it.

At first, Eric thought this term "Tweakerbaby" was a term of endearment by his childhood idol. Then he found out that Daryl was just repeating what the other kids called him. Or was it the other way around? His tics and odd mannerisms were a result of his neurological system being jolted continuously by time-release capsules of amphetamines prescribed by the same shady doctor that killed Daniel's mother. He couldn't help it. In this light, the affable Daryl had a streak of cruelty that Eric had never seen before.

Father Redmond took a liking to Daryl, having him over for dinner and palling around with him, to his son's dismay. Daniel was suspicious of Eric's new idol, and he became quietly concerned with Daryl's relationship with Father Redmond. He thought it looked odd.

Once, Daniel found Daryl and Father Redmond in the garage, counting money together and jabbering nonstop about nonsense. They didn't come inside the house until three in the morning, and a sleepless Daniel found Daryl smoking a cigarette on the couch at 7 am. Eric came in behind Daniel, shirtless and yawning. He seemed surprised to see Daryl.

"What are you doing here?" Eric asked Daryl. "You can't smoke in here."

"Sorry," Daryl said. "I came to drive you to school."

"You got your license back?" Eric asked somewhat excitedly.

"No," Daryl said.

"What's that smell?" Father Redmond called out from upstairs. "Boy, you had better not be smoking in here again," he said, talking to Eric, who scowled at Daryl.

"S-Sorry, Mr. Redmond," Daryl called out.

"Daryl?" Redmond said, his voice changing to a higher pitch. "I didn't know you were still here."

"When were you here?" Eric asked.

"He was here on church business," Redmond said. "After school job, isn't that right, boy?"

"Yessir," Daryl said. He turned to Eric. "Ready for school?"

Eric and Daryl left in Daryl's Bonneville. Daryl drove off the beaten path.

"Where are you going?" Eric asked. "School's the other way."

"We ain't going to school," Daryl said, his eyes hidden by dark sunglasses.

"We'll get in trouble," Eric said. "Daddy will wring my neck."

"Don't worry about it," Daryl said. "I'll get us excused."

"How?" Eric asked.

"Don't worry about it, I said," Daryl snapped. "Just trust me. I wouldn't get you into trouble."

Daryl slammed on the gas pedal. He was going like a fireball onto the highway.

"Where are we going?" Eric said again, lighting a cigarette.

"You wanna make some money?" Daryl finally asked, looking at Eric's face in the rearview mirror.

"Depends," Eric said. "What do I have to do?"

"Not much," Daryl said. "Consider this your training day."

Eric would have done anything Daryl said. He looked at Daryl as a demigod. Eric didn't know that he was searching for his father in every person he came across until he came across Daryl.

Daryl was a chain-smoking delinquent with a perfect face and a piss poor vocabulary. He hustled just about every vice imaginable, and he figured one day he'd get rich off of it if he lived long enough.

To most people, the rumors around Daryl seemed part of an exaggerated idea. He was a character you saw on TV, not someone that existed in real life. While Eric envisioned everyone around him dying or dead, he chose to believe Daryl was very much alive. It was a dangerous game, as Daryl was more fractured than Eric would ever be. The difference between the two boys was the difference between a pet rock and a lump of coal.

This boy Eric, who was raised by the most prominent hustler in southern Missouri –Father Redmond, was infatuated with his protégée.

They met through Eric's sheer will. Daryl spoke to no one in school, but everyone talked to Daryl. Eric saw something in him that, truth be told, everybody saw. Eric wanted to be Daryl.

He was content to take notes on him from afar, just saying hello and observing, but the day Daryl saved Eric's life changed everything.

A fat jock was chasing Eric down the hall in full view of indifferent teachers, for giving a love letter to his girlfriend - a cheerleader who refused to acknowledge him. The wiry Eric could have easily outrun this jock except he tripped over his own shoelaces, and smashed his nose against the floor. As the jock was about to lay his hands on Eric, they both heard a click sound, followed by Daryl's bass voice.

"Leave the kid alone, dude," Daryl said. Eric looked up and saw a switchblade knife across the bully's throat. "Go throw a football around with your faggot buddies."

"You're gonna cut my throat in the middle of school? Yeah right, McAdams," the jock said with a quivering voice.

“Never know what I might do,” Daryl said.

Daryl shoved himself between the two boys and elbowed the jock in the stomach. The jock stumbled backward, gasping for breath.

Daryl extended his hand to Eric. Fluorescent lights formed a halo around his head. Daryl folded his knife and gestured with his fingers.

"Come on up, kid," Daryl said. "I washed my hands, don’t worry." Eric grabbed Daryl's calloused hands, and Daryl lifted Eric back to Earth.

Daryl brushed some dirt off of Eric's shoulder. "There," he said, chewing a wad of bubble gum. "Good as new."

Eric just stood there with a stupid look on his face.

"Well," Daryl said after a pause, "see ya' ‘round, kid."

"Wait," Eric said. He extended his hand again, not knowing if this would be his last chance to meet his hero properly. "I'm Eric," he said.

Daryl shook his hand and grinned. "I know who you are," he said.

"Thanks for..." Eric nodded at the jock, who was in the background gasping for breath and plotting his revenge.

"...For that," Eric said.

"It was nothin'," Daryl said.

"No," Eric said, "he would have kicked my ass. And then my dad would kick my ass for getting my ass kicked."

"No shit?" Daryl said. "That sucks."

"Yeah."

"You know, a scrawny guy like you needs to be scrappy," Daryl said. "No offense."

Eric nodded. "Got any tips?"

Daryl thought for a second. "I guess the main thing to remember," he said, "is just to get so mad, you make them believe you. You could be a tiny little guy - even smaller than you - and if you look mean enough, nobody will fuck with you."

Daryl started walking toward his locker. Eric followed him. "Oh, and don't mack on other guys' girlfriends," Daryl said.

Eric followed Daryl all the way outside. "Where you headed anyway?" Eric said.

"To my car," Daryl said. "You smoke?"

"Smoke what?" Eric asked. Daryl smiled and put on his shades.

"You're my kind of people, Eric," Daryl said. "I can tell."

THE WINDOW WAS DOWN, and the breeze was hot. "You wanna hit this baddie?" Daryl asked, passing a fiberglass cigarette with a wad of green grass on the end of it.

Eric quickly rolled up his window and took the baddie between his fingers. "If you're not going to talk about what we're doing, can we at least listen to the radio?" He asked.

"Of course," Daryl said. "I'm not some kind of fass-ist." Daryl turned on the radio to the classic rock station.

"You mean fascist," Eric said, lighting the one-hitter and taking in the smoke.

"Whatever," Daryl said. "Fash-ist," he repeated.

They stopped in every small town between Hawthorn and Kansas City. On the first two stops, Eric was told to stay in the car.

"Why?" Eric said. "I thought I was training."

"These guys get skittish around new people," Daryl said. "I won't be long."

Once Daryl was inside, Eric took out his phone, which bulged out of his pocket. He opened it and dialed Daniel's phone, which was never on. "I'm with Daryl right now," Eric said in a voicemail message. "I don't know where we are. So if I don't come home...um...call the police I guess, because I've probably been murdered." He closed the phone and put it away, double checking the ringer, making sure it was all the way up.

It was a testament to how scared Eric felt that he even called Daniel, who he referred to as a dead man during one of his manic episodes. It was a moment of clarity brought on by sobering anxiety. He wasn't sure, even if Daniel got his message, that he would call him back - or at least call the police had Eric failed to come home.

Daniel was preoccupied with his own happiness, as he had recently become engaged to Megan. They were juniors in high school, and it was a quieter kind of insanity that they experienced together, but it worked. Daniel knew he wanted to marry Megan when he saw her on the playground. In Daniel, Megan saw stability and beauty, and her decision to say yes to his proposal came from an unexpectedly logical place.

The ring was procured from Wal-Mart, and it turned Megan's brown finger a weird shade of green, but she convinced herself that it was beautiful.

"When I get on full-time at the farm, I'll buy you a real one," Daniel said.

"I love it," Megan lied.

That night, Megan and Daniel lost their virginity. They were the only couple in history, they thought, who lost their virginity to each other.

They thought it was magical, but only because they couldn't see themselves, just each other. They both kept their shirts on - Daniel was especially shy about his body. The sex consisted of Daniel thrashing himself clumsily into Megan's body for a few painful seconds.

Megan laid in a wet spot for a few minutes before getting the bravery to check, and it was what she feared: blood. She immediately started to cry.

Daniel stroked her hair. "What's wrong?" He asked frantically. "Are you still in pain?"

Megan shook her head no and raised the covers to let Daniel see the mess they made.

"Are you okay?" Daniel asked with panic.

Megan nodded yes and continued to cry.

"I'm sorry, it's so embarrassing," she said, wiping her tears.

"No," Daniel said, comforting her. "No one will know."

He held her for a few silent seconds. "That's...normal, right?" He asked. "I mean, should we get you to a doctor?"

Megan exhaled sharply and rolled over. "Yes, it's normal." She stood up and put on her underwear. "Christ, didn't you have sex-ed?"

"No," Daniel said. "My dad teaches it at the college, and he said I'm not ready yet."

Megan laughed, wiped her remaining tears, bent down and kissed Daniel's head. "This is what I'm marrying into," she said. "Can't wait."

Megan grabbed her backpack and headed for the door.

"Where are you going?" Daniel asked.

"My mom goes nuts if I'm late for dinner," Megan said. "And I have to shower when I get home, so I don't smell like you."

Daniel laid in bed until the morning, getting a few minutes of shallow sleep.

He got up, put his clothes on, and met Terrence outside. He stumbled into his truck.

"Damn, boy, what happened to you?" Terrence asked. "You look like shit run over twice."

"I don't want to talk about it," Daniel said.

"Usually when people say that, they're begging to get it drawn out of them," Terrence said. "We got twenty minutes. Give me the twenty-minute version." He put his truck into gear and started driving.

"I asked Megan to marry me, and she said yes," Daniel said.

Terrence was surprised and silent. "Okay," he said. "Before I scold you, I'll ask you why you look like somebody shot your dog."

"We did it last night," Daniel said. "And it was weird."

"How was it weird?" Terrence asked.

"She bled, for one thing," Daniel said. "And I got scared and said something stupid, and I think she's mad at me."

"If it was her first time," Terrence said, "that's pretty normal."

"Okay."

"Now I want to know what the devil got into you, thinking you can propose marriage at sixteen years old," Terrence said sternly. "Ain't nobody knows what the hell they want or who they are at sixteen. And you better hope she don't get in a family way."

"I've always known who I am," Daniel said. "I been the same since the day I was born."

"That's what you think," Terrence said. "Come to me in ten years. You don't know shit, boy."

"Well, it's done," Daniel said, crossing his arms. "And I was going to ask you to be my best man but not if that's how you feel."

"Of course I will," Terrence said, his heart warming quickly. "I just don't want to see you get hurt."

"If I get hurt, I get hurt," Daniel said. "You or nobody else can stop that."

"That's true," Terrence said. He chuckled to himself. "That's true. You're smarter than I give you credit for."

The two sat side by side in the truck in silence for ten minutes.

"Say," Terrence finally said, "How come you didn't ask your brother to be your best man?" He looked over at Daniel, and he was asleep. Terrence got out of the truck and started work, leaving Daniel to sleep.

Eric was halfway to Kansas City when Daniel proposed to his girlfriend. He was nervous, though the marijuana he smoked helped him some.

In Springfield, they wandered downtown. "What are we looking for?" Eric asked.

"Not what," Daryl said, "But who."

"Okay," Eric said. "Who?"

"I'll tell you later."

They heard a sultry, soprano voice call out. "Hey, farm boy!"

Daryl turned around to see a square-jawed lady in a pink wig strutting bowl legged toward them. Daryl embraced this lady, who wore a jean jacket and a leopard print halter-top. Her lipstick smudged on the few remaining brown teeth she had up front. Daryl kissed her on the cheek, and the lady kissed both of Daryl's cheeks like Eric saw them do on the European TV channels at home.

"Who's your cute friend?" This toothless lady asked in a whiny vocal fry.

"Sasha," Daryl said, "this is my best friend, Eric."

"Hi," Eric said, waving nervously.

Sasha sashayed over to Eric and kissed both of his cheeks. "You can do better than that, honey," she said, hugging him as he stood there, stiff as a board.

"What's wrong, sweetie?" Sasha asked. "Never met a tranny before?"

"Um," Eric stuttered, "I don't guess I have. What's a tranny?"

Daryl and Sasha laughed.

"Isn't he adorable?" Sasha said. She turned to Daryl. "Where'd you find him? Study hall?"

Daryl scratched the back of his head and laughed. "Sorta, yeah," he said.

"How darling," Sasha said. "Do you have my shit?"

"You know I do," Daryl said with a shit-eating grin. "It's why I'm here."

"Fabulous," Sasha said. "Step into my office."

Daryl and Sasha went to a nearby alley between an Anarchist bookstore and a Christian Scientist Reading Room.

Eric heard them in the alley, chitchatting in hushed whispers and flicking lighters. He observed a man in the Reading Room, straightening the bookshelf and then dusting it.

The man caught Eric looking at him. He smiled and waved. Eric waved back. The man opened the door, which rung a bell. "Can I help you, young man?" He asked warmly. "Are you lost?"

"Uh, no," Eric called out with a shaky voice. "Thank you."

"What the fuck?" Eric heard Sasha say from the alley.

Sasha stumbled out, teeth chattering and eyes wild. Her lipstick was smeared all over her face, and her skirt was undone. "Who are you talking to?"

Daryl ran and grabbed Eric by the arm. "Let's go," he said. "This bitch is nuts when she's geeking."

Eric and Daryl speed walked to the car, got in and drove off, leaving Sasha there with the Christian Scientist, who quickly went back inside and pulled the blinds down.

They drove past the Wal-Mart and Olive Garden. "Do you need anything?" Daryl asked Eric. "I'll buy you a soda or something."

"No," Eric said. "I'm all right."

"You sure?" Daryl asked. "You hungry or anything?"

"No," Eric said. "Are we going to Kansas City?"

"Nah," Daryl said. "I gotta get back home." Eric let out a subtle sigh of relief.

"Well," Daryl said, correcting himself, "I gotta make a stop when we get back into town. Actually, I need you for that."

"For what?" Eric asked.

"Just this thing. It's no big deal," Daryl said, not looking at Eric, using the car cigarette lighter on his Marlboro Red. He handed the pack to Eric, but he waved them away.

"You okay?" Daryl asked.

"I guess," Eric said. "But I still don't know exactly what all this is for."

"Come on, Tweakerbaby," Daryl said. "It ain't a big mystery."

"Just tell me," Eric said. "And don't call me that."

"Pardon me, Eric," Daryl said, putting a vaguely European emphasis on his name. "Life is all about hustling. This is wisdom, is what this is," he said pointedly, using his cigarette like a sixth finger as he spoke with his hands. "I'm teaching you real shit."

"I still don't get it," Eric said. "And I'm not sure I want to."

"Well, I guess we'll see," Daryl said. "Just don't be a little bitch about it."

"What are you talking about?" Eric said.

"You'll see," Daryl said, getting impatient. "And if you can't hang with it, we'll know what you're made of, and it's still all good." He smiled and looked at Eric. "No worries," he said.

As they got off the highway and into Hawthorn, Daryl turned off his lights. "So, here's the deal," Daryl said. "This guy just wants to watch."

"Watch what?" Eric asked.

"Here," Daryl said, handing Eric a half-capsule full of peach dust, which Eric couldn't see. "Take this."

"What is it?" Eric asked.

"It's a crushed xanny, dude," Daryl said. Put it under your tongue or up your nose or something. "Takes the edge off."

Eric wanted to cry but held it together. "Why won't you tell me shit?" Eric said. "You're being weird."

"Look, man," Daryl said. "You wanted to know what I'm about. This is what I'm about. Secrets and lies, and making money off of secrets and lies."

"Just tell me what we're about to do," Eric said, rolling his eyes. "Stop talking like you're in a fuckin' mafia movie." He stuck the small cylinder capsule in his nostril and sniffed.

"There ya go, buddy," Daryl said. "Let's do this."

Daryl pulled up to a ranch-style home with dead shrubbery.

"Isn't this our math teacher's house?" Eric asked, spotty eyed and spacey.

"Yup," Daryl said. "Just be cool."

Eric knew he shouldn't have been there, and there were many questions as to why he was. But the dust lodged in his nasal cavity - which quickly dissolved inside the mucous membranes close to his brain - was stopping the questions from forming entirely. His periphery went dark, and a dark vignette formed with a big black tunnel surrounding everything.

"You all right?" Daryl said. "That space dust got you good, huh?"

Eric could only nod.

"Half hour tops," Daryl said. "I'll get you home safe and sound, I promise."

Daryl opened his door and got out. Eric sat in the car, looking at the stars through the windshield above the bristling leaves that belonged to the Hawthorn trees.

Eric felt a jolt of the cool breeze from the open car door. "Come on, man," Daryl said, holding the latch. "Let's get this shit over with."

Eric and Daryl walked side-by-side. "I'll call you Mason," Daryl said. "You call me Paul."

"Why?" Eric asked.

"Just trust me," Daryl said.

Eric saw his math teacher, Mr. Black, peer out of his blinds. They heard the deadbolt unlock. Daryl just walked through the door like he owned the place, holding Eric's hand, basically dragging him inside.

"Hello, boys," Mr. Black said. "Have a seat." Eric sat on the edge of the floral loveseat, across from Daryl.

"Not there," Mr. Black said. He pointed to Daryl. "Sit next to your big brother."

Eric got up and sat next to Daryl. Daryl inched closer so that their legs touched.

"So, how was your day?" Mr. Black said, sticking his hand in his right pocket.

"It was good," Daryl said. "We had gym class today."

"Both of you?" Mr. Black said.

"Yeah," Daryl said. "We like to take gym together."

"That's sweet," Mr. Black said. He looked at Eric. "What's your name, young man?"

Eric looked at Daryl, who mouthed at him silently.

"Mason," Eric said, almost whispering. Mr. Black's pocketed hand started moving.

"What's your favorite subject, Mason?" Mr. Black asked.

"I don't have one," Eric said.

"Why not?" Mr. Black asked.

"Because I hate school," Eric said. "They're a bunch of rednecks."

"Do they pick on you?" Mr. Black asked.

Eric nodded his head yes.

"Doesn't your brother take up for you?" Mr. Black asked.

"Yeah," Eric said.

"Yes, sir," Mr. Black said sternly.

"Yes, sir," Eric repeated quietly.

Mr. Black smiled. "Good boy," he said. "Are you close with your brother?" Mr. Black asked.

"Yes, sir," Eric said.

Mr. Black moaned lightly.

"Do you share a bed?" Mr. Black asked.

"Of course," Daryl said. "Mason is a good cuddler."

"Show me," Mr. Black said.

Daryl put his arm around Eric and pulled his head into his musty chest. Daryl stroked Eric's hair. Eric shivered.

"How's that feel?" Mr. Black asked, almost panting. "Do you feel safe, Mason?"

"Yes, sir," Eric said.

"Does Paul smell good?" Mr. Black asked. "What does he smell like?"

"He smells like my dad's cologne," Eric said.

"Do you ever give your brother kisses?" Mr. Black asked.

"Just relax and breathe," Mr. Black said softly. He grunted and thrust, and rubbed Eric's backside gently. "You're doing fine," Mr. Black said. "It won't take long."

Soon, Mr. Black entered Eric wholly; applying pressure and ignoring Eric's cries, nerve sensations overpowering his sense of hearing. Mr. Black finally groaned and collapsed on top of Eric, the greasy sweat from his gut rubbing off on Eric's lower back.

He pulled himself out of Eric's body slowly. "He's bleeding a little bit," Daryl whispered. "Can you get a washcloth or something?"

"Mason," Mr. Black said, "Do you need the shower?"

Eric laid on his stomach, sobbing into his hands.

"I think we'd better go," Daryl said. "You owe me for this, dude."

"Do you have my stuff?" Mr. Black asked. Daryl picked up his jeans off the floor, dug into his pocket, and handed Mr. Black a small Ziploc bag with white crystals inside.

"Come on, man," Daryl said, wiping Eric's tears. "You're gonna be fine."

Mr. Black approached Eric, his naked ass in the air.

"No," Daryl said. "Don't touch him."

Daryl wiped Eric's backside with the rag. Eric felt the sting of cold water against his raw skin. He jerked up.

"It's okay," Daryl said. "It's me. You're okay."

Eric and Daryl drove away in silence. Eric didn't blink for the entire drive; he just looked ahead, showing the whites of eyes.

Daryl drove to his house. "Come on," he said. "You can stay with me tonight."

They laid in bed together that night, Eric unable to stop his tears, and Daryl doing his best to comfort him until he fell asleep.

Twelve

The first time Terrence Haight experienced fear was when he was seven years old. His parents, Marianne and Martin, had scrounged up enough money to take a weekend trip to Arkansas to visit Martin's parents, and to see that giant statue of Jesus. It was the first time Terrence had ever left Hawthorn except to go to the supermarket with his mother in Lampe when the local grocer was out of butter or milk.

Guided by the gothic intrigue of the bridge that stretched across the Mississippi river, Terrence for the first time daydreamed about what life might be like other places. Places where he didn't know anybody and sure as hell wasn't related to them. Places other than Hawthorn - a town that decided that running the one so-called "nigger family" out of town, a family that had been there longer than most - would somehow upset the delicate temperament of God. So, it was easier to let the Haights be and to grandfather them in.

It was God who let them be, Marianne often argued to the boys. No one else but God.

It wasn't until Father Redmond took Terrence under his wing with Shelly as a reference that the townsfolk started tipping their hats to him, or holding the door open for him at the grocery store when he had too many bags to carry. Some even called him Terry to his dismay. Still, the camaraderie brought him the warm reprieve of safety - at least in the physical sense. And yet, some part of Terrence silently revolted against it.

He had concluded shortly after he lost his mind and grew a brand new one that everybody had a place in this world, and the world was far from fair. Instead of fighting the powers that kept him from the purest form of happiness, he negotiated with them - and with God, too.

We ought not be vengeful toward those who keep us down, he thought. They're doing the best they can with what they know. And if there was a God, Terrence figured, he must just be learning as he goes, a lot like all the others.

The problem with Terrence, as his mother Marianne would often remind him, was that he looked at those sinewy white boys playing football on the playground as a young man, and saw himself out there – as one of them. The world, however, whose mundane evolution unfolded on the edge of that playground and beyond it, saw him as a novelty. To them, he was someone you could strike up a conversation with if you wanted to do a good deed, or had time to kill.

His muscles grew, just like those white boys. He spoke that Missouri twang just like those white boys. He knew how to play football, just like those white boys. But for some reason he could never be bothered to figure out, he never once played with them. He sat out and watched, feeling an extreme pull of gravity around his shoes every time the thought of joining the game crossed his mind.

The drive back from Arkansas was a quiet one. The windows stayed down, and Terrence could smell the sugary fragrance of honeysuckle in some counties, and persimmon trees in others. The fallen persimmon had no doubt rotted, but from the safe distance of a moving car, those rotten fruits still smelled sweet.

Terrence was living. He felt the humid breeze - a perfect mixture of moist heat and crisp coolness that hinted at autumn. As they drove closer to Hawthorn, he could hear the dry flies bleating, and though he was too caught up in the sensations of sundown to look at road signs, he knew he was close to home.

When Martin pulled over for some gas, Marianne gently protested. "We got enough to get home, baby," she said. "Let's just go home."

"Nah," Martin said. "You know how I am." Martin, a man fraught with anxiety, couldn't let a gas tank fall below a quarter-full. He kissed his wife on the cheek and headed toward the attendant.

"Excuse me, "Sir?" Martin called out through the half-open service window, behind which sat a fat man in a white t-shirt. "I was hopin' you could get me some gas." Martin took off his hat and held it near his crotch. "'Course, I'd be more than happy to do it my—"

"We closed, man," the fat white man said coldly, looking at Martin dead in his eyes. He shut the window and the curtain. Martin flinched.

He walked toward his car as Marianne was getting ready to light another cigarette, fidgeting with it, growing impatient. She was probably daydreaming, wrapped up in her own fantasies as she always did in stressful situations, but Terrence heard and saw the whole exchange.

Martin closed the door and put on his seatbelt. Marianne looked at him.

"I thought you was getting gas?" Marianne said. "They closed or something?"

"Yeah," Martin said. "They closed."

"Mmm-hmm," Marianne said skeptically as she lit her cigarette. "Let's get on home, then."

Suddenly, there was a tap on the glass. Marianne jumped and shrieked. Martin gripped his gun, concealed between the seat and the door.

"No, Martin," Marianne said out of the corner of her mouth. "Don't do that."

"It's okay," the man said. He looked like a younger, thinner version of the hateful old man that turned away Martin. "I'm sorry about him," he yelled through the glass.

Martin cracked open the window. "I just need a little gas to get home."

The man nodded and took off his hat. "I know. Let me get it for you," he said. "On the house."

"That's very kind of you, sir," Martin said.

"You ain't kind, mister," Terrence said from the back. Martin and Marianne gasped. The attendant looked at Terrence and smiled.

"Well of course I am," the attendant said. "Why would you think that way, young man?"

"Your eyes are mean," Terrence said. "They mean just like your daddy's eyes."

Martin reached back and grabbed Terrence's leg. The attendant laughed. "I been told some form of that once or twice," he said. He looked at Martin and Marianne. "Cute kid ya' got there," he said.

"Thank you, sir," Martin said. "He's a hand full."

"That just means that someday he might be somebody important. Could be president one day," the attendant laughed. "You never know!"

"Well, I appreciate your kindness," Martin said. "We best be on our way."

"Yeah, I filled you up there," the attendant said. "You folks drive safe."

"Bye," Marianne said faintly, in semi-disbelief.

Terrence didn't reflect on that moment until those later years when he was able to put his mind back together. The details varied slightly every time he tried to recall it, but the feelings it invoked always stayed the same, and they never dampened with time.

It was an encounter in which he first experienced two life-defining emotions, almost simultaneously. He felt the traumatic, violent danger of simply being who you are. But he also felt the summery sensation of kindness. This tortured him even more. That he could be grateful to simply not be spat upon was shameful to an adult Terrence. He considered it a strange form of entertainment for the universe to impress on its own creations. A sick joke.

But as his feet grew out of his boyhood loafers and people in his world got more polite, the anger that was responsible for the McAdams' cotton field fire had quelled itself with a blanket of tepid understanding - which, in the end, proved to be the most dangerous thing of all. He understood, as an Other. But they had the luxury not to bother with trying to understand anything - even themselves.

He knew he could never stand up to be Daniel's father, though he insisted on trying and simply discarded the official title. When Daniel asked him to be his best man as if it should never have even been a question, those conflicting emotions came back.

He knew, however, in a mental flash of a million scary scenarios, that even if it ended up getting him thrown away like a rotten raisin in a bowl of porridge, or whispered on, or killed, that it was the right thing to do.

He had to do right by this boy, and nobody - not even the goddamn universe - was right all the time.

However, Terrence was somewhat relieved that Daniel and Megan decided on having a courthouse ceremony. Neither was the type for fanfare or frills. Daniel and Megan would end up being the sort of couple who would split the grocery list, then met at the checkout counter to save time. They decided to do the pragmatic thing and make it legal, then throw a party later - much later; so long that maybe nobody cared anymore and they'd just cancel the whole damn thing and meet up with the family at the steakhouse and have buffet apple cobbler as the wedding cake.

The three walked through the courthouse in attire that was unbefitting for the old ladies in the Collectors' office. Megan was wearing low-waisted jeans and an over-sized t-shirt that belonged to Daniel. Terrence and Daniel arrived in their work clothes, smelling to high heaven of the ammonia from the chicken barns, and with fine feathers lodged in the threads of their coveralls.

Waiting their turn, Megan went to get a root beer. As she bent over to retrieve it from the bottom of the soda machine, she heard a catcalling whistle. Megan rose up with a rumpled nose, scanning the room for someone to punch in the groin. She settled on Dwight Wright, who was there for his latest DWI. He grinned and laughed.

"Just kiddin' darlin;" he said. He walked closer to her, and Megan's skin crawled. He was close enough for Megan to smell the liquor on his breath. "What you in for?" Dwight slurred. "Angel faced girl like you ought not get into too much trouble," he said.

"I'm getting married," Megan said at full volume.

"Here?" Dwight said. "I guess this place ain't just for bad stuff. I forget that."

"Sure," Megan said condescendingly. "Well, I better get back in line."

"Make sure he treats ya' right," Dwight said with a wink.

Megan chuckled courteously. "Don't you worry about that mister," she said as she walked away. "He's probably the one in trouble."

Dwight laughed and waved, then looked at his citation with crossed eyes. Megan stood out of the way and watched Dwight stumble up the stairs to his courtroom.

Daniel sauntered behind her, and was too close when Megan turned around. She jumped and grabbed her upper chest in panic. "Oh, Jesus!" She said. "You scared me."

"You okay?" Daniel said. "We can wait if you're too nervous or I mean if you just want to think things over or - "

Megan grabbed his face. "Honey?" She said. "I love you to death, but you babble when you're nervous. You ever notice that?"

"Sorry," Daniel said. "I guess that'd be grounds for calling it off," he said, shuffling his feet.

"No," Megan said, grabbing his arm and leaning on his shoulder as they walked. "It's one of those husband-wife things. I fix you, and you fix the toilet when it breaks."

"Fair enough," Daniel said, stroking Megan's hair. He stood in front of her and grabbed her shoulders, making doe-eyed adoring glares at her. His rough fingertip traced the soft skin of her cheekbones and chin. "You have never looked more beautiful than you do right now," he said.

Megan grabbed his hand and placed it on her heart. "It's because it's the first time I have been truly happy."

Daniel's eyes, nose and lips smashed together - the precursor to an ugly cry.

"Also," Megan said, "you smell like a dead possum rotting in a trash can." Daniel went from near-tears to laughter.

"We gotta get you a shower before the honeymoon," Megan said, guiding him to the appropriate office.

"What had you so shook up?" Daniel asked.

"There was this weird guy talking to me by the soda machine," Megan said. "I think he was flirting or something, but he was drunk and it was weird."

"Want me to beat him up?" Daniel asked, half-jokingly.

"Yeah, I'd love to end up on the news on my wedding night because the groom beat up a drunken hobo," Megan said.

As the threesome exited the courthouse, Dwight Wright tripped over his feet right in front of them, somehow more intoxicated than when he entered the courtroom. Terrence leaped to his side. "Here man," he said. "Let me help you up."

He pulled up Dwight until he was steady enough to stand. Terrence looked at Dwight and froze, recognizing him for the first time.

"That's the guy that was being creepy," Megan whispered to Daniel. Daniel locked eyes with Dwight and felt an electric shock. He grabbed Megan and raced toward the exit.

"Come on," Daniel said. "Now."

"What's wrong?" Megan asked. "This is weird. Who is that?"

"Please stop talking," Daniel said quietly. "I'll tell you later."

Dwight shook his head. "What're you doing here, nigger?" He said to Terrence, his eyes barely open.

Terrence leaned in closer. "You call me that again," he whispered, "and Ima' feed you to the pigs."

"You listen here," Dwight said, barely lucid. "You will never, ever be his father. I'm his father," Dwight said.

"No," Terrence said. "You ain't shit. You stay away from him. Or you'll have to deal with me."

"I'll deal with you, nigger," Dwight said, raising his voice. "You'd better watch your damn mouth and be careful what you wish for."

"I got something for you," Terrence said quietly. "You come around, threatening me, come around that boy, following us. I'm tired of your shit, and I ain't gonna take it no more." Terrence walked away.

"Dammit, you'd better -" Dwight's voice went from raised to screeching and splitting through damaged vocal chords.

"Get your shit together, man," Terrence said, walking toward the exit. "That sauce is gonna kill you."

Thirteen

The problem with Eric wasn't that he was too bold, or too stubborn. The problem with Eric was that he was too many people at once.

All of his life was spent jumping up and down, looking for a counterpart to keep him steady. For a while, it was Daniel Wright. But as the world spun faster, and the clock bell tower kept ringing, and Eric's testosterone got the best of him, and his mind went off the beaten path, his selfhood became tangled up in Daryl McAdams.

The truth of the matter was that Eric Redmond wasn't tough at all. He was dangerous but soft. His heart and mind were malleable. His troubles stemmed from the fact that he was the only one that didn't know it.

After a while of being intoxicated by Eric's energy, people grew tired of it. Wonderment turned to pity. That's when he became truly dangerous - when he felt most alone.

The morning after his sour encounter with Daryl and Mr. Black, Father Redmond beat his backside with a belt for not coming home the night before.

Eric didn't feel physical pain, though. He felt his soul break into a million pieces, bent over his father's fleshy lap, his face pressed up against his khaki slacks. Tears fell, but they consisted of something direr than blood, and more bitter than salt. They came from the deepest well within him; a place he never knew existed.

After a few whacks, Father Redmond jerked his knees to get Eric off of him. "That's all, boy," he said quietly. But Eric stayed put. He let the tears fall, and he clasped his father's slacks.

"Didn't you hear me?" Father Redmond said, dizzy from over activity. "What's the matter with you? Did I hit you too hard?"

"No," Eric whispered. "Just give me a minute."

"Why?" His father asked.

"Please," Eric said, choking on tears. "Just a minute."

Father Redmond awkwardly placed his hand on Eric's head. Eric allowed himself to sob, and Redmond obliged him, stiffly stroking his hair.

"Dad?" Eric asked.

"What," Redmond replied softly.

"Do you really believe in God?" Eric asked.

Father Redmond didn't know what to say. He just stroked his son's hair, as if it was the first time he'd ever been soft with his son.

"Am I bad?" Eric asked after a few moments of silence.

"We're all born bad, son," Father Redmond said. "That's why we ask forgiveness."

Eric didn't say another word. He curled up on his father's lap until the tears stopped. When he got up, his father had fallen asleep. Eric wiped his wet cheeks, sniffed a couple of times, and went upstairs to his room.

After a long nap, he called Daryl.

"Who's this," Daryl said, half-asleep. "Tweakerbaby?"

"Yeah," Eric said. "You working tonight?"

"Every night," Daryl said.

"Come pick me up before you do," Eric said. "I need to make some money."

"Okay."

"And you still owe me half from last night," Eric said assertively.

"I know, I know," Daryl said. "It got a little weird, huh?"

"Just be here tonight," Eric said.

"Okay," Daryl said.

"SO, WHAT DO YOU NEED money for, anyway?" Daryl asked Eric as he settled into the passenger seat of his Bonneville.

"I'm moving away," Eric said.

"Oh yeah?" Daryl said, flicking cigarette ash out of his window. "Where to?"

"I don't know," Eric said. "But it sure as shit ain't gonna be anywhere near here."

"Right on," Daryl said. "I been thinking of moving, too."

"Where?" Eric asked.

"Either Atlanta or Houston," Daryl said. "Haven't decided yet. A lotta' hustling going on in those cities."

"Maybe I can come with you," Eric said.

"Maybe," Daryl said. "We'll see."

Daryl parked the car in an empty parking lot. He pulled out a glass pipe. "You ever hit this before?" He asked.

"Nope," Eric said.

"Your nickname is Tweakerbaby, and you ain't never tweaked before?" Daryl asked. "You fuckin' poser," he said, playfully punching Eric's arm. "Watch me."

Daryl flicked his lighter and slowly moved it toward the glass pipe gripped firmly between his teeth. He held the lighter on the bulb until it glowed brightly. He inhaled ghostly white vapor, and then he looked at Eric with bulging eyes, holding his breath.

He held up one finger...

Then two fingers...

And on the third finger, he exhaled and promptly coughed.

"And that's how you do it," Daryl said. Eric reached for the pipe. "Careful," Daryl said. "It's hot as Hell."

After Eric hit the pipe, he looked straight ahead and let the spots take over his eyes.

"How do you feel?" Daryl asked.

"Amazing," Eric said. "Everything is, like, fast and pretty, you know?"

"I know," Daryl said. "But you ought not do it every day. Don't be like these losers in town."

"Why not," Eric said. "I'll probably never do better than them."

"Nah," Daryl said. "That's bullshit."

"So what are we doing here?" Eric asked. "What now?"

"Now," Daryl said, "we wait."

A few minutes later, Jose Cruz pulled up in a beat-up old pickup.

"That's Marcia Cruz's cousin," Eric said.

"Yup," Daryl said, putting white crystals on a black plastic rectangular scale, then scooping them into a tiny plastic bag. He handed it to Eric.

"You want me to do it?" Eric asked.

"You want the money?" Daryl replied. "Just get in his passenger side door, give him the dope, and take the money."

Eric opened the truck door with jittery hands. He got in.

"Who are you?" Jose asked.

"I'm Eric," he said.

"I know you," Jose said. "Son of the preacher."

Eric nodded.

"My cousin, Marcia, she talks about you all the time," Jose said.

"She hates me," Eric said.

Jose laughed. "She likes you, little dude," Jose said. "Trust me."

Eric smiled crookedly.

"So you got my shit or what?" Jose asked.

"Yeah," Eric said, handing over a half-dollar sized baggie of white crystals.

Jose held up the baggie, eye-level, after looking over both shoulders. Then he tossed a small stack of money into Eric's lap.

"I drive a truck," Jose said. "I just use it to stay awake. I ain't no junkie."

"Okay," Eric said. He started to get out of the truck.

"Tell your dad I'll see him on Sunday," Jose said. "Bright and early with the family."

"Okay," Eric said. "I'll tell him."

Daryl waited in the car, chuckling to himself as Eric came back with a strip of sweat above his brow.

Daryl took the money and counted it quickly. He looked over at Jose and nodded. Jose rolled out of the parking lot, waving as his truck pitter-pattered. Daryl handed Eric a wad of cash.

"What's this?" Eric said.

"It's your split," Daryl said.

"You just pay me for handing people dope?" Eric asked.

"For now," Daryl said. "'Til you get the hang of the business. And you just met your first regular client."

The two drove off.

"Jose said Marcia likes me," Eric said. "You figure that's true?"

"Everybody knows that, man," Daryl said. "Shit, even I know that, and I'm oblivious as fuck."

"So should I stop being mean to her?" Eric asked.

"No," Daryl said. "She probably likes it."

Eric called his father from Daryl's house to get permission to stay over. He hung up the old rotary phone and turned to Daryl.

"I want to look tougher," Eric said. "If I'm gonna really hustle, I need to look tougher."

"Well, what're you thinkin'?" Daryl asked.

"A tattoo," Eric said. "On my face."

Daryl tussled Eric's greasy, shaggy hair. "Let's start here," Daryl said. "I'll get the clippers; you get a bucket to sit on."

Mrs. McAdams came out to greet the boys with two tall glasses of lemonade. "You boys know how to cut hair?" She asked sweetly, setting down the tray.

"Nope," Daryl said, a cigarette hanging out of his mouth. "I know how to shave hair, though."

"Daryl, put out that cancer stick," Mrs. McAdams moaned. "You're too young for that."

"Yes ma'am," Daryl said, throwing the butt down and stepping on it with his sandaled heel.

"Make sure you pick that up and put it in the trash when you're done," she said. "And try to get this hair up as best as you can. It smothers the grass."

"Yeah, especially this hair," Daryl said. "When's the last time you washed your hair, Tweakerbaby?"

"Couldn't tell 'ya," Eric said.

"You boys," Mrs. McAdams said. "You're just such...boys." She sighed and went inside.

"You get along with your folks?" Eric asked.

"Sure, I guess," Daryl said. "We all just kind of go our own way. As long as they don't have to bail me out of jail, we get along fine. What about you?"

"No," Eric said.

"I figured as such," Daryl said.

"Why's that?" Eric asked.

"Because your dad's a preacher," Daryl said. "And you're a demon."

"I suppose you're right," Eric said. "My mom's in an institution. I don't really talk to her anymore."

"That sucks," Daryl said. "What for?"

"She's just crazy, I guess," Eric said. "I don't know what you call it."

"Well," Daryl said, "that sucks," he repeated, not knowing what else to say. He stopped the electric clippers, which were being powered by an extension cord. "All done," Daryl said. "You're a new man."

Eric walked to the sliding glass door to look at his reflection. He ran his fingers over his prickly scalp. "Wow," he said. "Feels nice."

"You like it?" Daryl asked.

"It'll take some getting used to," Eric said, "but I feel like a different person. That's the point of getting your haircut, right?"

"It's why my mom's a blonde," Daryl said, picking up his cigarette butt and lighting it again.

That night, Daryl and Eric slept side-by-side on Daryl's twin mattress.

"You sure you don't want me on the floor?" Eric asked.

"I hate sleeping alone," Daryl said. "Plus, if I have one of my episodes you'll be right there."

"What episodes?" Eric asked.

"Oh," Daryl said, "it's nothing, really. Just seizures. I shake, and my eyes roll back, and I pass out."

"That sounds like the opposite of nothing," Eric said. "What do I do if you start doing it?"

"Um," Daryl said, "I guess just hold my arms down or something. Sometimes, if you wake me up in the middle of it, I'll stop doing it. But it's gotta be timed right."

"Just don't sleep naked," Eric said.

"Wouldn't dream of it," Daryl said. "You ain't my type."

"You can get a lot of drugs and stuff right?" Eric asked.

"Pretty much anything," Daryl said.

"What about stuff to make someone pass out?" Eric inquired.

"I'm not into date rape drugs or nothin' like that," Daryl said. "That's where I draw the line."

"It's not for that," Eric said.

"How much you need?" Daryl asked.

"Whatever a normal dose of it is," Eric said, "I want three times that much."

"Fine," Daryl said. "Just don't ever tell me what it's for. You swear you're not trying to rape anybody?"

"I swear," Eric said.

"I'll have it A-S-A-P," Daryl said.

"Can you get it tomorrow?" Asked Eric.

"Yes, your majesty," Daryl said. "Now get some fuckin' sleep. I can't skip tomorrow. I got a final, and I have to at least get a D on it." He turned off the light.

"Goodnight, Daryl," Eric said.

"Goodnight, buddy," Daryl said. He kissed his own hand and placed it on Eric's forehead.

Graduation day was approaching, but that wasn't what excited Daniel. The day after graduation was the wedding ceremony of he and Megan. No one knew, except for Terrence. Daniel wanted to wait for the right time to tell Father Redmond because he couldn't predict his reaction.

Time snuck up on Daniel, and so he didn't let him know until Redmond walked into tissue paper streamers.

"What in the Devil?" Redmond said, swatting away the paper like a swarm of gnats. "Danny, what did you do to the house?"

"Oh, right," Daniel said, halfway down the stairs in his cap and gown. "Me and Megan got married last week, and we didn't want a party at first, but now she does so I put all this together and sort of forgot to tell you. I'm sorry."

Father Redmond crept up the stairs with a constipated look on his face. He leaned into Daniel and embraced him, Daniel's face against his squishy torso. "Why didn't you tell me?" Redmond said. "We could have put it on TV."

"I don't think anybody cares about a dumb wedding," Daniel said.

"Nonsense," Redmond said with gusto. "You're a Redmond."

Eric and Daryl didn't speak much that day. At the end of the day, Daryl discreetly handed Eric a bottle of pills.

"What's this?" Eric asked.

"What you asked for, dummy," Daryl said. "You don't even remember, do you?"

It dawned on Eric that he had asked Daryl to score for him. "I remember," he said, "But I forgot my money."

"'Course you did," Daryl said. "But I know you're good for it."

"You coming over tonight?" Eric asked.

"You mean revisit the scene of the crime? Nah," Daryl said. "I gotta go to a party."

"A party where?" Eric asked.

"I don't know, somebody Vanessa knows," Daryl said. "College kids."

"Oh," Eric said, disappointed.

"Chin up," Daryl said. "It's just a work thing. Don't worry about it."

"I hate parties," Eric said. "But you could have asked."

"Yeah, I could have," Daryl said, shutting his locker. "Good luck with your thing tonight."

ERIC WALKED INTO THE same streamers as Father Redmond had earlier. "What the hell?" He asked.

Daniel peeked his head into the room. "You coming tonight?"

"Coming to what?" Eric asked.

"I'm getting married," Daniel said.

"If it's going to be here, I guess I'll have to be," Eric said.

Daniel followed Eric up to his room.

"Get out, dead man," Eric said.

"What's up with you?" Daniel said.

"What are you talking about?" Eric asked, averting his eyes to a guitar catalog.

Daniel sat down on Eric's bed and made firm eye contact. "I mean the last two years," he said. "You keep calling me 'Dead Man,' and acting really weird, and I want to know why right now."

"Why do you care?" Eric asked.

"Because we probably won't see each other after today," Daniel said. "And you're my brother, and I want to know."

Eric sat up straight. "Okay," he said. "You want to know why I hate you?"

"Yes."

"You sure you want to know?" Eric asked.

"Why start sparing my feelings now?" Daniel asked.

Eric laughed bitterly with a twisted grin. "*Your* feelings?" Eric asked. "With your stupid wedding and your perfect life after you took my dad away from me? You hang out with fucking normies and jocks, while I sit here going crazy from loneliness. You kiss my father's ass, and he gave you a farm. I'm nothing but myself, and it's gotten me nowhere. That's why I call you a dead man: because you're dead. At some point, you stopped being you and started being someone I don't want to know. The real you is dead. You suffocated him. He choked on bullshit."

"I didn't do anything with your father," Daniel said. "Anyway, you hate your dad,"

"I'm a teenage boy! Of course I hate my dad!" Eric said. "Don't you hate yours?"

This had Daniel stumped.

"I never wanted to take anything away from you, Eric," Daniel said. "I love you."

"Everyone calls me crazy," Eric said. "They call me Tweakerbaby. I don't know how that even got started. If I knew how to be normal like you, I would. But you know what I think? I think I'm actually the only sane person in this whole goddamn town."

"I don't know what to say," Daniel said. "I'm sorry."

"I hate you," Eric said. "Get out of my room."

Eric's words stayed with Daniel for longer than they should have. He did often wonder where his biological dad was or if he was even alive or what, but he never let that question linger. If Daniel knew where Dwight was at that moment, he'd blow a gasket.

Dwight was inside of Terrence's house, waiting for him to come home after work. He had jimmied the front lock with his suspended driver's license.

Dwight walked around Terrence's tidy but dilapidated home, looking at the artifacts from his life. He looked at a dusty old picture in a plastic, metallic-colored frame of Terrence and Marianne together at Terrence's graduation. He placed it softly back on the shelf.

Dwight looked inside the refrigerator, and found nothing but a stack of bologna and expired milk. He sat in the chair Terrence had once held a very small Daniel all those years ago, waiting for the Redmonds to come and take him away. Dwight leaned back and fell asleep.

The setting sun bled out through the blinds, which were contorted and bent from a cat Terrence watched for one of his girlfriends about twenty years ago. It shot a red heat through Dwight's eyelids, which woke him slightly, but it was the sound of Terrence's voice that woke him completely.

"What are you doing here, Dwight?" Terrence's voice boomed.

Dwight jumped up. His chin immediately started to quiver. "I'm here to kill you, nigger," he said before bursting into tears.

"You got a gun?" Terrence asked.

Dwight, hunched over and emotional, slowly grabbed it from his pocket. Terrence swiftly took it from him and kicked Dwight in the shin. Dwight fell and grabbed his leg, wailing in pain.

Terrence held the gun out and pointed it at Dwight, with his finger on the trigger.

"I'm not gonna kill you, Dwight," Terrence said. "And the reason is, if you kill me, nothing happens to you. But if I kill you," Terrence said, "they'd just kill me anyway."

"I think that's fair," Dwight said, still in tears but exhaling in relief.

"Get up," Terrence growled. "Easy. There, yes. On the couch. Hands to your sides. Stop crying."

"Can I please just leave?" Dwight asked.

"Hell no," Terrence said. "We gonna settle this once and for all." Terrence sat in his recliner.

"Now, let me explain something to you," Terrence said.

Dwight sobbed quietly.

"Everybody in this town knows you ain't right in the head," Terrence said. "I know it, you know it..." Terrence pointed to the north. "And *he* knows it. You ain't fit to raise him, and as far as I'm concerned, you did him a favor by runnin' off."

"Shut up," Dwight said.

"No, you shut up," Terrence said. "What don't you get? You are in my house. I have your gun. Pointed at you."

"I loved him," Dwight said.

"You loved that bottle," Terrence replied.

"What do you know, nigger?" Dwight said. "What you know about raisin' a boy?"

"What I know is if you call me 'nigger' one more time I'm gonna put it right between your eyes," Terrence said. "And let 'em come for me."

"They will, too."

"Let 'em," Terrence said with resolve in his voice. "And what do you know about it, you big fuckin' baby? I wish I had your chances in life. I'd be a millionaire by now. Not no snot-nosed, skinny ass drunk who can't pull a gun out of his shorts without bursting into tears. You even know how to use this thing?"

"You'd better shut up," Dwight said.

Terrence fired a shot into the ceiling. Dwight yelped and covered his face with his hands.

"If you tell me to shut up one more time," Terrence said, "I'm gonna watch you fill in that hole I just shot, while I hold this gun to your balls."

"I'll shove that gun up your ass," Dwight said. Before even a second of silence passed, Terrence had put a bullet in the top of his foot. Dwight wailed and rocked back and forth, untying his laces.

"Don't touch it," Terrence said. "You only gonna make it worse."

"You fuckin' shot my foot!" Dwight yelled.

"You're damn right I did," Terrence said. "Be grateful I didn't aim for those balls, boy."

Just then, there was a pounding on the door. Dwight forced his lower face into a twisted smile.

"You done did it now," Dwight said. "Shoot me," he said. "I deserve it, I know. But they gon' kill you, no matter what happens to me. They been out there the whole time."

The pounding on the door got more severe. Terrence shot Dwight in the gut.

Dwight wailed. "Hurry up, motherfuckers!" He yelled.

"They might take me," Terrence said, "But I'm gonna enjoy makin' it painful for you before I send you back to Hell. You drunk piece of shit."

The sun was almost set. The sheriff was outside. He pulled a cigarette out of his shirt pocket and lit it. "Hold up," he said from the other side of the door.

"Terrence, this is Officer Grady," he said. "Just open the door. Stop shooting the little feller."

"I'll make you a deal," Terrence called out. "If I spare this slug's life, you send me to jail. I drop the gun, and you don't shoot."

"Fair enough," Officer Grady said through the door.

"No!" Dwight screamed. "That's not the deal we made! He shot me in the guts! I'm as good as dead, anyways!"

"Shut up, Dwight," Officer Grady said, rolling his eyes. "Terrence, let me in. Let Dwight go."

Terrence put his face on the door. "All right," he said, sweaty and exhausted, "I'm gonna open the door."

"Drop the gun first," Grady said.

"He's gonna grab it if I do," Terrence said.

"He ain't gonna do shit," Sherriff Grady said. "He woulda' already done it."

Terrence had a choice to make: Shoot Dwight dead, and end his and Daniel's suffering, or trust Grady not to shoot him and go to jail for however long it took to get rid of the charges - even though it was Dwight's gun, and Terrence's house. As he usually did, Terrence did what he thought was right.

He sat the gun on the kitchen table. He looked over at Dwight, whose eyes flared anger. Dwight charged at him. Terrence reached back for the gun, but Dwight limped quickly. His life depended on it.

Dwight stood there with the gun, his hands shaking and his color-drained face soaked with tears and sweat.

"You took them from me," Dwight said, shivering. "You took my life from me."

"No," Terrence said, "You gave them to me."

Dwight let out a painful cry and pulled the trigger. He watched Terrence fall on the floor. Dwight went silent. The pounding on the door began again.

"Dwight!" Grady shouted. "What did you do, Dwight?"

"I killed him!" Dwight said. "I killed the nigger. Ain't nothin' you can do about it!"

SIRENS CALLED FROM a distance.

It was about twenty minutes before Terrence died that Daniel realized his best man wasn't going to show up. Eric stood in for Terrence during the ceremony, which took place in the Redmond's backyard. There were videographers there. After the events of the night unfolded and Father Redmond had a few days to digest them, he ordered all copies of the wedding video destroyed.

It was a dismal evening. Daniel and Megan had lost interest in being there after it was clear Terrence wasn't going to show up.

Megan adjusted the bosom of her white dress - poorly tailored from her own mother's wedding dress, with the same corsage of artificial blue roses Mrs.

Redmond wore during her wedding. She was there, too, along with her minders from the hospital. She didn't speak to Redmond, even when he approached her.

"Hello, darling," Mr. Redmond said. "How've you been?"

Mrs. Redmond didn't even look up.

Father Redmond sent his wife divorce papers about a month after he had her committed - somehow expediting the usually arduous process of getting a court order. She signed them as soon as her psychiatrist explained what they were in a delicate whisper. Accompanied by two nurses with Haldol syringes and two lawyers whose faces she barely recognized, the stone-faced doctor broke the news to her.

"Mrs. Redmond," he said, "I have some difficult news."

"What?" Mrs. Redmond asked. "What could it possibly be, now?"

"Your husband has sent some documents," the doctor said, grasping for the right words, "wishing to end your marriage."

"Divorce papers?" Mrs. Redmond asked.

"Yes," her psychiatrist said.

Mrs. Redmond held out her hand. "Give 'em to me," she said. "And a pen." She signed them without hesitation, only pausing to ask where to sign and to focus her eyes on the X.

"Do you want to hear the terms, first?" Her psychiatrist asked her.

"No," she said. "There's no fighting with him." She signed it energetically, writing her first name in pretty cursive, and mangling her last name, letting the tail of the 'D' slide off the pages.

Mrs. Redmond sat there, looking pale and vacant.

"How are you feeling?" Her psychiatrist asked.

Mrs. Redmond looked into his eyes and smiled. "I feel free," she said. "Really free this time."

She maintained her defiance at Daniel's wedding. She wanted to attend to get closure and to say goodbye to her wretched family, who she felt she barely knew.

Father Redmond looked down at his grumpy ex-wife at Daniel's wedding - frail in body, but with a mental hardiness he always knew was there lurking underneath her sweet, dumb disposition. He shook his head at his ex-wife, and then shook the hands of her medical minders.

"Thank you for taking care of her," he said. The nurses nodded, unsure what to make of this strange man. His speech was slightly slurred, Mrs. Redmond noticed. She fantasized about his death often, and maybe, she thought, he had turned into an alcoholic. He certainly had the gut for it.

But in fact, Father Redmond was drinking iced tea with lemon all night. His neurotically restrained nature would never permit him to drink alcohol. He couldn't even drink from the same punch bowl as other people.

"Hey," Daniel said, "have you noticed Dad acting weird?"

"Yep," Eric said. "Consider it a wedding gift." Daniel looked at Megan with one eyebrow raised.

"What does that mean?" Megan pondered out loud.

"The less we know, the better," Daniel said. He pulled a flask out of his suit jacket and poured some heat into his glass, and his wife's.

As the party went on, Father Redmond got more and more intoxicated, and Eric disappeared.

The party wound down, and Daniel and Megan got into the new Cadillac Megan's father bought for her. Mr. Milstone kissed Megan on her head and shook Daniel's hand. Mrs. Milstone waved. Daniel's family was nowhere to be found. He started the engine, and drove away, escaping into the night.

On their way to the freeway to start their life together, they were halted by a line of emergency vehicles - an ambulance, a Highway Patrol car, and the Fire Department. Daniel had a bad feeling.

"Should we go back?" Megan asked.

Daniel bit his bottom lip and stared at the light. It turned from red to green. He accelerated through it. Megan held his hand on her lap and turned on the radio.

Eric rode his bike to Daryl's house. His crying mother came to the door.

"What's the matter?" Eric asked.

"I'm sorry, Eric," Mrs. McAdams said, handing Eric a sheet of paper. "Daryl left us this note. Did you know he was leaving?"

"Where did he go?" Eric asked, opening the note, checking for Daryl's sloppy handwriting but not reading it.

"He says he went to Atlanta," Mrs. McAdams said. "He said he'd call us when he gets there."

Eric became furious immediately.

Mrs. McAdams said, "I don't know what we're going to do with that boy," she said. "He's not even supposed to be driving!"

Eric drove his bike back toward his house as slowly as he could. The closer he got to his house, the tighter his chest felt. About halfway through his journey, Eric ditched the bike and started walking. He wondered if his dad was dead, and he wondered if killing him made Eric a bad person. He prayed, but to whom, he didn't exactly know.

He heard sirens. Thinking they were for him, he laid in a nearby field full of cotton and stared up at the moon to try to calm himself down. It was full, and it lit up the sky, the light fading into black just before it reached the hills.

But the sirens weren't for him.

As soon as Grady was finally able to knock open the dead-bolted door with help from the Highway Department, they were greeted by Dwight with his guts dripping out, standing over Terrence's body, and holding the gun to his head.

"Dwight, don't do nothin' else stupid!" Grady said.

"I done fucked myself," Dwight said, his swollen eyes nothing but slits. "I should have just killed him myself. You can't trust nobody!" Dwight screeched and hit himself in the face with the gun two times.

"Dwight, listen to me," Grady said. "We can get you some help, son."

"Ain't nobody can help me but the Good Lord," Dwight said. "Say a prayer for me, y'all. You dumb motherfuckers."

"We'll pray," Grady said. "Let's pray together." As officers from the Highway Department rushed to him, Dwight opened his mouth to scream, but his voice was raw, and he couldn't make a noise. He pulled the trigger, and his brain splattered all over Terrence's kitchen table.

The person who Terrence planned to call after he killed Dwight, Father Redmond, was comatose on the toilet, in the bathroom connected to his foyer while the party went on outside. One nurse with a small bladder had knocked on the door to the minute, every minute, with no response.

Finally, she tapped her coworker on the shoulder. "I think there's someone locked in there," She said to him. "I think it might be that drunk pastor."

"Let me try," Mrs. Redmond said. "This knob always stuck." She opened the door, and Redmond was sitting there with his pants down. The opened door unleashed the smell of shit and bile, the latter of which was foaming out of Redmond's mouth.

The remaining partygoers gasped. Mrs. Redmond covered her mouth and nose from the smell, but also to hide her wicked smile.

People rushed to Redmond, pushing her aside. She sat on the couch and turned on the TV. Redmond's head leaned against the bottom of the medicine cabinet over the toilet. The male nurse cleared the bathroom, pulled up Redmond's pants, and called yet another ambulance from Lampe to the outskirts of Hawthorn.

The female nurse sat with Mrs. Redmond, unsure what to make of her reaction.

"Are you okay?" The nurse asked Mrs. Redmond, stroking her shoulder.

Mrs. Redmond knocked her hand away. "Why wouldn't I be?"

If the nurse hadn't been with her the entire evening, she'd have thought Mrs. Redmond was responsible. Her reaction disturbed the nurse greatly, but she sat there watching a nature program with Mrs. Redmond, reminding herself that she was unwell and that everyone reacts differently to stress.

As Father Redmond was rolled out of the house on a stretcher, Mrs. Redmond let out a deliriously happy cackle.

"We'd better get her home," the male nurse said. "We have a lot to tell the boss when we get back."

Mrs. Redmond could see her ex-husband's gut rising and falling slightly as he was carted out of the door. "He ain't even dead," she said. "I can see him breathing, for God's sake."

Several thoughtful party guests cleaned up the house after the night's events ended. One unlucky party guest cleaned up the foyer bathroom.

By three in the morning, the house was clean. The bathroom no longer smelled demonic, and the kitchen freezer was packed with leftovers. One of the party guests, the Sunday worship leader, complimented the decorating while she snooped around the house with her friend, pretending to clean.

The 9-1-1 dispatcher decided not to send police to the Redmond residence that night because they were all tied up at Terrence's. So when the paramedics and party guests left and the house was emptied out, it would stay that way for the first time since it was built.

It looked spooky and grand from the highway, where the spotlights in the driveway stayed on because no one at the party that night knew how to turn them off.

People often asked, "Who lives there?"

The newly-built house was so ostentatious, so vast, and so unlike any other home nearby that to the unfamiliar, it resembled an ancient castle full of history and ghosts.

"I think that preacher from Hawthorn lives there," was the usual reply. "Or, at least he used to."

Part Two

Zero

Hawthorn entered the new millennium slowly and clumsily, but eventually all of it - including the one-time eyesore Jackass Flats - grew into something palatable and civilized. The town had a superficial sheen that could fool a tourist into spending money at the River's Edge Winery or having brunch at the Smoked Chicken, a quaint cafe that overlooked the White River.

Those rusty trailers were long gone now, replaced by double and triple-wide modular homes with concrete foundations to hide the wheels. Just about everyone ate well, and those who still lived in the dregs were never seen by the wide-eyed world that existed above ground.

Seasons got shorter and shorter and seemed to blend into one another. Missouri was never known for its forgiving weather, but now there were tornados in January and cold snaps in the tail end of summer, which used to be the hottest part of the year.

Armadillos migrated from Texas and Arkansas, getting splattered along I-55; at first they were a novelty, but everyone eventually got used to them.

Church sermons capitalized on this, with more emphasis on the End of Days than ever before, and people were scared. People started building doomsday shelters in the backyard, and you saw more Rebel flags than ever before, after the terrorist attacks in New York City.

Things were quieter than ever, and the young people who stuck around Hawthorn to have families never had it so good, but people were never more afraid.

Adding to the list of Others, which always included people of color, queers, and Satanic cults looming about eating babies was technology, which advanced stupendously in those first few years. If you had shown Stephen Shrine a typical device Hawthorn residents now used to communicate with each other, he would have cast them out, fearing witchcraft.

Hawthorn citizens always reveled in their simplicity. They were the last people in the Western hemisphere to own smartphones and computers, but eventually they did and relied on them like everybody else in the civilized world.

But even as church services featured giant projected movie screens that came down from the heavens to display hymnal lyrics, old folks lamented, "We don't even use paper programs, anymore."

Perhaps they were afraid, at least in part, for personal reasons. Small-town gossip - once locked away within the confines of back porches and bonfires and informal dinner parties - could now be seen by everybody on internet message boards. Secrets were harder to keep. People stopped talking to each other, stopped knowing each other, and stopped caring. No longer burdened by the need to go out and discover new people like they did in the city, everyone became an Other to everyone else. People kept to themselves more than ever, their isolation serving as a security blanket under which small townsfolk were slowly sliding off their rockers without even noticing.

In that way, Hawthorn became a part of the twenty-first century. People got colder, more distant, and less concerned with each other. They became fixated on what they didn't like about each other and used these things as reasons to stop leaving the house. And when they did venture out, things got more volatile. There were more car crashes, more rage, more social anxiety, and one killing - the first one since Terrence Haight died. It was a little girl, killed by a gun misfire.

Usually when tragedy struck the townspeople would come together whether they liked each other or not. They'd bake pies and casseroles and deliver them in person. But nobody knew this little girl or her family beyond what they saw on the news after she died. The family was from some state down south, and since they didn't belong to a church, they had no real friends in town.

There was no coming together with strangers; strangers were strangers for a reason. After it was discovered that the parents of the deceased were opiate addicts, people stopped even pretending to care. When they heard that detail, they shook their heads and mostly said, "What a shame, but not a surprise," and went on with their insular lives.

It was an odd time, even for a strange place such as Hawthorn. With all of the changes, however, some things remained the same: the clock kept ticking, things kept moving in a circle, the days were still numbered, and nobody knew the day or the hour.

One

Following a vast swarm of Magi cicadas, Eric Redmond returned to Jackass Flats. The peculiar little insects were everywhere. This was normal for this time of year in Missouri, except for the sheer magnitude of them. For a couple of months that year, the one small talk topic that always came up among people in line at the grocery store wasn't the odd weather - and in Missouri, the weather was always bizarre - it was "those damn locusts."

Male cicadas could be heard bleating for mates in waves. The annual May Day recital had to be held indoors that year because no one could listen to the electric piano over the obscene noise made by the bugs, who had waited almost twenty years to announce their arrival.

Farmers were worried. Usually, cicadas posed no threat to crops, but the glass-shattering loudness of the bugs meant that females would soon be laying eggs. Enough eggs laid on plants could kill crops, and judging from the menacing waves of screaming, the locusts would be active as hell.

"Those damn dry flies," they'd say as they walked out of their houses at four in the morning, the cicadas' music reverberating in the darkness.

When Eric rode into Hawthorn in the back seat of a big black SUV, the noise was the second thing he noticed, after the smell. He leaned in to make conversation with the driver for the first time since their journey began. "You smell that?" Eric asked. "My dad used to say it smelled like money."

"What is it?" The driver asked, grimacing.

"It's shit," Eric said, leaning back and putting sunglasses on. "Cow shit, chicken shit, you name it."

The SUV parked in the empty lot of Hawthorn Baptist Church. Eric got out and marveled at the new construction with disgust.

"It's worse in person than it is on TV," Eric told the driver as he opened the door for him. "Don't you think?"

"I've never seen it on TV," the driver replied. "But it's nothing special."

Eric handed him a twenty-dollar bill. "I like you," he said. "This should take about half an hour. Then we'll eat."

The driver handed Eric his multi-colored backpack. He put on a similarly colored flat bill hat to go with his dark sunglasses. Eric put in a piece of chewing gum, slapped the bag over his shoulder, took a breath, and went inside.

Inside, everything was gilded in gold - even the urinals in the men's room. The smell of the building was familiar. It smelled of pungent potpourri and vinyl. It smelled like the Swiss villa did when Eric was a boy. It smelled like it felt: artificial.

He walked past the cardboard cutout of Father Redmond, which was behind a table stacked with a doomsday prep kit the church was selling via a 1-800 number. Eric approached the receptionist, seated at a mirrored desk in the middle of the vast gold lobby. At first glance, he thought he was looking at Daniel's mother until he remembered that she died. She had the same burnt ginger hair, same pale skin, and same slight frame. Same syrupy smile.

Eric looked around, then grinned at the receptionist. "Subtle scheme you got here," he said. "I feel like I'm in a funhouse." The receptionist's smile faded quickly.

"Can I help you, sir?" The receptionist asked coldly.

"I'm here to see Redmond," Eric said, smacking his gum.

"Do you have an appointment?" The receptionist asked while reaching for the phone.

"He's my dad," Eric said. "I don't need an appointment. At least I would hope not."

The receptionist said nothing else to Eric but spoke on the phone in a hushed tone. She clicked the phone back down. "Someone will be in to get you in a moment," she said. "Would you like some water?"

"Got anything stronger?" Eric asked with a smirk.

"Just coffee," the receptionist said, typing. "But it's decaf."

"No communion wine stashed away under the desk?" Eric asked, leaning over the desk.

"I'm afraid not," the receptionist replied, monotone.

Eric leaned on the tall, silver barricade surrounding the receptionist, never bothering to remove his sunglasses or hat. He began to get anxious. A strip of sweat started to form under the lid of his cap. Just as his nerves began to fail him, a blandly handsome man in a suit approached Eric with a warm smile.

"Mr. Redmond," the man said, extending his hand.

"Call me Eric," he replied, shaking this man's hand. "And you are?"

"I'm Mr. Thomas," the man said with glassy eyes. "Would you like a tour?"

"Let me guess," Eric said, "he's all tied up at the moment."

"I'm afraid so," Mr. Thomas said. "He's actually doing an interview with CNN."

"Mr. Thomas, I would love a tour," Eric said, rolling his eyes behind black shades. "But my driver is sitting outside all alone. Can he come too?"

"Your driver?" Mr. Thomas said, mulling it over.

"He's a big fan," Eric said.

Mr. Thomas retrieved a walkie-talkie from his pants, seemingly from nowhere, and spoke in a coded language, almost military-style. Eric heard the word, "Affirmative," over the crackle of the radio.

"Splendid," Eric said, getting out his phone to call his driver.

"If you don't mind," Mr. Thomas said, "no photographs."

"No problem," Eric said. He then directed his attention to his phone. "Hey man," he said into the phone, "Why don't you come in for a tour? Yes, a tour of the church."

Eric put his phone to sleep shortly after that and smiled at Mr. Thomas. "He'll be here in a minute," he said.

Mr. Thomas looked at his watch.

Eric chuckled. "You're not in any hurry, are you Mr. Thomas?" He asked.

"No, of course not," Mr. Thomas said. "CNN should be wrapping up soon," he said while flashing a quick smile.

Eric snapped a bubble of gum with his molars. "Exciting," he replied, deadpan.

Eric and his driver sat next to each other in the hall across from Redmond's office, both staring at a painting of a muscular, toga-wearing, angel-winged Father Redmond lifting the Earth toward the sky with the help of angels, as sniveling demons looked up from below with forked tongues and pitchforks.

The driver tilted his head. "Who is this guy in the painting?"

Eric said, "My father."

"No shit?" Asked the driver, chuckling to himself.

"I didn't catch your name," Eric said.

"It's better that you don't know," the driver said. "Just in case something happens."

"Right," Eric said.

"You can call me Driver," he said. "I don't mind."

Father Redmond finally shuffled out of his office with two assistants: Mr. Thomas, and a pant-suited, smiling woman.

"Son," Redmond said warmly, reaching his arms out. Eric sat and glared at him for a second, puzzled. He got up after a while and limply hugged his father.

Redmond's office belied the rest of the building in its decor. It had wooden paneling, which gave it a lodge-y vibe. Framed pictures of the staff were everywhere, as well as photos of Redmond with various members of the GOP, both local and federal.

"You running for office?" Eric asked, gazing at the photos in barely concealed horror.

"I'm mayor of Hawthorn now," Redmond said, straightening his tie. "I sent the newspaper clippings to your doctor."

"I didn't get them," Eric said, voice deepening.

"Who's this?" Redmond asked, extending his hand to the man accompanying Eric. The man shook Redmond's hand while staring sternly into his eyes.

"That's my driver," Eric said.

"I see," Redmond said, patronizing and miming a sense of being impressed. "Your art must be flying off the shelves."

"It is," Eric said.

"That's great," Redmond said. "Really it is."

Eric gave his father a smirk and plopped down in a chair in front of his desk. He started digging through his backpack, while Redmond and Driver stared at each other uneasily. Eric practically threw down a wad of paperwork on Redmond's desk.

"What's this?" Redmond asked, putting on his glasses.

"I need you to sign it," Eric said.

"Uh-huh," Redmond uttered, examining the words through the creases. "But I asked you what it is."

"Read it if you have to," Eric said. "I have time."

Redmond exhaled slowly through his teeth and flipped through the pages. He shook his head.

"You want to leave the hospital?" Redmond asked. "But you're doing so well."

"How would you know?" Eric asked. "I haven't heard from you in years."

"Well, that's what happens when," Redmond looked up at Driver, who was tightening his jaw, "things happen you can't easily shake."

"Mmm," Eric said. "What's that mean?"

"It means," Redmond said, generating a low growl, "that you got off easy, boy." Driver took a step forward. Eric looked back at him, then looked at Redmond and laughed silently. Redmond tried to appear unfazed, but he started to shake.

"Look, man," Eric said in a baritone whine, "just sign it. Why do you always have to do things the hard way?"

"There is security here," Redmond said. "Lots of it."

"Is CNN still in the building?" Eric asked. Driver reached back and fastened one of the three deadbolts Redmond put on his office door.

Driver reached into his jacket, and Redmond yelped and leaped under his desk. Eric and his driver laughed. Driver pulled out an ink pen, clicked it, and placed it next to the wad of papers on Redmond's desk.

"So paranoid," Eric said. "Just sign the fucking thing so I can leave."

Redmond sat at his desk; jaw chattering, left eye twitching.

"Sure," Redmond said, trying to appear calm. "It's been ten years. Can't stay in the loony bin forever." He signed it.

"Glad you see it my way," Eric said. He jerked the papers out from under Redmond's pen and put them in his backpack.

Eric got up, and the Driver unlocked the deadbolt.

"This all could have been taken care of with a phone call, you know," Redmond said, lower jaw twitching. "You shouldn't have made a special trip."

"I'm here to buy a house," Eric said. "Are you still at the villa?"

"I sold that to Daniel, along with the farm," Redmond said, coming down off of adrenaline.

"Isn't that nice?" Eric said. "Danny took over the family farm."

A moment of silence between them.

Redmond checked his watch. "Well, I have a meeting to attend," he said. "It was good to see you."

"Good to see you too, pops," Eric said, snapping his gum.

Redmond nodded. "Will you being joining the family for church on Sunday?"

Eric chuckled. "I got plans Sunday," he said.

Eric and Driver left the office, bristly walking past Mr. Thomas. Redmond came out of the door a jangled mess. Eric heard Mr. Thomas whisper to Redmond, "Are you okay, Father?"

Driver and Eric walked across a barren parking lot to the black SUV. The hot leather of the seat stuck to Eric's arm. "Good God man, turn on the A/C," he said.

"Where to now?" Driver asked.

"Well," Eric said, trailing off while looking out of the window. "I guess the villa, to see my brother."

DANIEL AND MEGAN SETTLED into the villa as comfortably as they settled into each other. Neither was interested in the anarchic spiral that life tended to spin down into when you weren't paying attention. They were equal partners in quiet living.

Daniel supported Megan while she finished nursing school, and before Megan went to work, she had two children - blonde, smiling cherubic blobs.

Their lives seemed effortless; Jackass Flats looked upon them like royalty, even though their home was damn near Lampe - outside the grime of south Hawthorn.

Out of respect, the family appeared at church every Sunday morning, though both by now had slid into beige agnosticism. Megan found the services full of theatrics and bluster. She understood why people were transfixed on her father-in-law, but she was never that impressed by Daniel's family.

After a few years, their quiet life became silent, with wordless dinners and noiseless sex. Megan started picking up extra shifts at work just to be surrounded by the messiness of life. The suffocating silence of her life at home was no longer a refuge, but something to endure until she fell asleep.

Daniel was oblivious. After a life of endless racket, the darkness of a cocoon was something to savor. He prayed at night, mainly to give thanks that life was no longer a constant, continuous prick of razor-sharp anxiety. He had made it, despite the best efforts of the universe.

He was unsettled when Megan went to work, and when she drank too much wine, and when she got impatient with her children. Daniel saw that there were now murmurs of his mother, Shelly, in some of Megan's behavior. Those whispers came to the surface at very inopportune times. Sometimes the tension in Daniel's chest kept him up at night.

Daniel and Megan had their first real fight after ten years of marriage. It was around the time Eric Redmond returned to Hawthorn, lending credence to the whispering of superstitious rumors and conspiracy theories that classified Eric as evil amongst the citizens of the town who raised him.

"I don't want to go on vacation with your father," Megan said, swiveling her glass of red wine. "I'm sorry, honey, but I just don't."

"Yeah, well," Daniel said, picking at his TV dinner, "we all do things we don't want to do, sometimes."

"Excuse me?" Megan said, her brow crashing down over her chocolate eyes.

"Please don't," Daniel said, pleading and shaking his head. "Please don't do that. There's no way out of this, and you're making this awkward for me if you refuse to go. My father loves you."

Megan sighed. "Isn't there something we could come up with? Some excuse?"

"What is the matter with you?" Daniel asked.

"Your father is a pig," Megan said. "He looks at me like he wants to eat me."

Daniel stood and kissed the top of Megan's head. "I won't let him eat you."

"Branson isn't much of a vacation," Megan said as Daniel scraped his tray into the garbage disposal in the kitchen. "It's about an hour away, if that."

"It's the closest to a vacation he'll ever take," Daniel said through the door. "Plus, he's paying."

"Oh, now the puzzle is complete," Megan said.

The doorbell rang. Daniel looked out of the French glass door and saw his brother on the other side of it. Daniel froze for a second. Megan took notice.

"Who is it?" Megan asked.

Daniel didn't answer. He just opened the door and whisked himself outside.

"Eric?" Daniel said, looking at his brother for the first time in ten years. "What are you doing here?"

"No hug?" Eric asked. Daniel did a half-chuckle, half sigh, and limply embraced Eric. Daniel's guard went down somewhat.

"Come in," Daniel said to Eric. "Meet my family."

Eric shook hands with Megan and glared at their children with tense, wide eyes.

"So," Daniel said to Eric, "what's up?"

"I'm buying a house here in town, and I was wondering if I could stay here for a couple of days," Eric said sheepishly.

Daniel looked at Megan.

"I don't see why not," Megan said.

Eric went to the SUV to fetch his things, while Daniel and Megan quietly bickered.

"What did you just do?" Daniel asked Megan in a furious whisper.

"He's your brother," Megan said. "Plus, we'll be gone. Who cares?"

"My brother is...complicated," Daniel said. "I'm not comfortable with this."

"Just consider it a free house-sitter," Megan said.

"I just think it's weird that I haven't heard from or seen him in years," Daniel said, "and after a two-minute conversation we're just going to let him have free reign over the house."

"Didn't you say he grew up in this house?" Megan said. "I think you're being a little ridiculous. He probably considers this his house, too."

"That's even worse!" Daniel said, forgetting to whisper. They saw Eric standing there, sunglasses and hat still on, holding a sleeping bag.

"I hope I'm not intruding," Eric said, a frown beginning to form.

"No," Daniel and Megan said in unison. "Not at all," Megan said.

Daniel approached his brother and embraced him. Eric's frail arms were trapped underneath Daniel's farm-honed muscles. "I'm glad you're here," Daniel said in Eric's ear.

"I should have my own place by the time you're back," Eric said, uneasy.

"Don't worry about it," Daniel said. "No rush."

Daniel and Megan's two children, Marianne and Martin, came running into the foyer. They chased each other around Eric's knees. Eric raised his belongings up in fright at the sight of these two kids.

"Guys," Daniel said, in a well-practiced paternal voice. "Say hello to your Uncle Eric."

"Hi," the little girl said sheepishly and with a giggle.

"Hello to your Uncle Eric," the boy said as he rolled his eyes. This struck Eric, and it forced a smile on his face.

"Hi, kids," Eric said quietly.

Daniel and Megan laughed.

"He's not much on kids," Daniel said.

"Is that right?" Megan asked with a wide smile.

"Is it that obvious?" Eric said, chuckling nervously.

"Not even when he was a kid himself," Daniel said, slapping Eric's back.

"It's okay," Daniel said. "I wasn't much on kids either, until we had these little swamp creatures," Daniel said as Megan play-slapped him.

Everyone stood in a circle in uncomfortable silence. Daniel caught a glimpse of the black SUV outside, and Eric's driver, who was talking on a cell phone.

"Who's your friend?" Daniel asked.

Eric looked over his shoulder. He had forgotten. "Oh, that's my driver."

"Will he be staying too?" Megan asked.

"No," Eric said. "I'll be sending him back to St. Louis once my bags are in."

Daniel's eyes got wide. "I see," he said. "Fancy."

"It's not like that," Eric said. "I don't have a car or a license. Remember?"

"Right," Daniel said.

THE FAMILY LEFT, AND Eric and Driver broke into the liquor cabinet.

"Thanks for staying," Eric said.

"Thanks for the booze," Driver said. He lifted his glass, and Eric tapped his against it.

"Actually," Eric said, "I'll pay you to stay the weekend if you want."

"I'm not that kind of driver," Driver said.

"What do you mean?" Eric asked.

"I've got to get back," Driver said. "I have other jobs."

"Oh, I forgot," Eric said.

"Don't you have one of those apps?" Driver asked.

"I do," Eric said. "But none of those app drivers around here."

"Well," Driver said, "Before I get too drunk to drive, is there anywhere else you need to go? Any other people you need me to help you intimidate?"

"Nope," Eric said, "Drink up." He held his phone up, a glowing rectangle. "Do you have any service? I don't."

Driver looked at his phone. "Nope." He took another sip. "Is this where you're from?"

"This very house," Eric said.

"It's a nice house," Driver said.

"Only if you didn't have to grow up in it," Eric said.

"Was it that bad?" Driver said. "At least you grew up with money. I didn't."

"Money from milking hillbillies out of their moonshine money in the name of Jesus," Eric said, swirling a glass of whiskey under his nose. He plopped down on the faux-leather sofa, his bony knees bouncing a bit.

"If you hate it so bad," Driver asked, "why are you here?"

"A new project I'm working on," Eric said flatly.

"Ah," Driver said, "I should have known, judging from your work."

"You know my work?" Eric asked.

"Don't sound so surprised," Driver said. "Italian muscle has brains, too."

Eric shrugged. "I don't want to talk about work," he said, gulping down the rest of the whiskey.

"I don't blame you," Driver said. "I don't really buy that, anyway."

"Buy what?" Eric asked.

"You're not here for work," Driver said. "And you don't need money." He squinted at Eric, who was grinning. "Which leaves one other possibility."

"And what's that?" Eric asked, eyelids restful.

"Revenge."

"I hired you, didn't I?" Eric asked.

"I guess it wasn't a great big mystery," Driver said. "The real mystery is, revenge for what?"

Eric got up and fiddled behind the bar. He poured himself another glass of whiskey. "A few more drinks, and I'm sure all will be revealed."

And it was. Eric and Driver got drunk, and Eric talked more to Driver that night than he had spoken to anyone in the past ten years. He told him what happened after he poisoned his father's iced tea.

Eric was clever, but he was no criminal mastermind. The emergency room told Father Redmond, after they pumped his stomach, that he had been drugged with Rohypnol, a hypnotic drug that date rapists use to ply their prey. It was also used by Daryl McAdams, to sedate himself before especially unappealing gigs.

Eric told Driver everything: That in the grips of solitude-induced psychosis, he imagined his brother Daniel was dead, and that his father was the Antichrist.

"It's amazing what your mind will come up with when you're lonely and need to pass the time," Eric said.

"But he didn't die," Driver said.

"No," Eric said. "And in fact, he sat on the fact that he knew that I did it for a while."

"So then what happened?"

"Well, one day," Eric said, "one random, ordinary, stupid day, a bunch of guys in blue hospital scrubs came into my room with a gurney and wheeled me away."

"Your room here?" Driver asked. "They came here?"

Eric nodded yes. He pursed his lips, slightly biting on the bottom one.

"You don't seem all that crazy to me," Driver said.

"Thank you," Eric said. "I've gotten pretty good at hiding it."

"Why hide it?" Driver asked.

"It's what adults do," Eric said, letting his crown rest on the back of the couch.

"So you stayed in the hospital for over ten years," Driver said. "That's a long time."

"I know," Eric said.

"How'd he pull that off?" Driver asked. "Did he donate a wing to the hospital or something?"

"Or something," Eric said. "He started a phony rehab program run by a bastard crazier than I was. It was kind of like AA, and by the time I was strapped and ready to go, it was conveniently expanded into a private clinic. My dad's got a lot of sway in St. Louis. And if there's a racket to be run, he's all about it."

"How'd you find me?" Driver asked.

"I have a lot of sway, too," Eric said.

"Here's what I don't get," Driver said. "You tried to kill your old man, but you're the one who's back for revenge."

"I didn't say I was here for revenge," Eric said. "You did."

"Okay," Driver said. "Then why are you here?"

"I'm here to finally destroy the Antichrist," Eric said.

Driver analyzed Eric's face for signs of phoniness. "This story is crazy."

"You asked," Eric said. He tipped his glass up, drank the rest of the whiskey, and made a pained face. He wiped his mouth with his sleeve.

Eric got up and headed toward the stairs. "If you don't mind," he said, "Please be gone when I wake up."

"You got it, boss," Driver said.

Armed with the peace of mind that he would soon be avenged, Eric slept in his childhood bedroom; sleep so deep and restful, he thought he might not wake up.

The alcohol managed to blunt his REM cycle only so much. He was on massive dosages of mood stabilizers and antipsychotic medications, but he hadn't taken any of his meds since he left the hospital. They stifled his creativity and increased his appetite, both side effects he had managed to resist though it took almost every ounce of waking energy he had. He walked around for ten years starving himself, writing and painting, scrambling to find the resources to do so by rifling through dark corners and subconscious filing cabinets with his family on his mind the whole time.

He went to meetings every day in the hospital - group therapy, Alcoholics Anonymous - and spilled his guts more readily than any other patient, mostly because his stories were fiction. He used the context of getting better to create his own world; as kindling for re-starting the fire that had driven him to write his Tweakerbaby diaries, which he eventually got a local press to publish. He received notification of their publication on his twenty-first birthday.

Against all the odds, he became a renowned artist, using his free afternoons away from the hospital to enchant local investors, business owners, and gallery owners into showcasing his work and eventually lending him the money to open his own art studio in downtown St. Louis, where real estate was still cheap.

His father was an invisible hand in all of this, knowing that a happy and prosperous Eric Redmond reflected well on him as a father, in spite of all that had transpired. The best-case scenario was for Eric to have an outlet for his hatred five hours away and within the confines of a padded room. It was a relief to Father Redmond.

Substantial anonymous donations poured in when Eric became interested in pursuing an artistic career, and Father Redmond called hospital staff every day during the studio's renovation and soft opening, making sure his son was relatively happy and preoccupied. Eric believed he had done it on his own, because that's what he wanted to believe.

After an average day of managing his gallery or making public appearances at bookstores or art classrooms, he laid his head on a hospital cot, usually with a snoring mental patient in another bed just feet away.

The drugs he was on made him constantly sleepy, but it was always a comatose, dreamless sleep that seemed to do little to energize him. When he finally got out of the hospital and threw out his pills, his rapid-eye movements went into overdrive after days of staying awake, and he dreamed ten years worth of dreams in one night.

The Hawthorn tree outside Eric's window that he used to climb down when he ran away at night was now dead. He heard a hissing noise and got out of his bed to investigate as it became louder and refused to be ignored. Draped over the jagged edges of the tree branch was a serpent, moving and bobbing its head, extending itself until its tongue could touch the other side of the glass. The sky lit up with a couple of flashes of white light, cracking open with loud, echoing trashes. And the rain started.

It hit the window and slid down the glass - translucent at first, but darkening as minutes went by. When the lightning caught it, Eric could see that the rain was blood red and slimy and thick, colored like chocolate syrup. After a few minutes of its torrential downpour, the copper smell of it started to seep through the vents and the whole world around him smelled like death soon enough.

He heard a voice: "Hey! Hey! Down here!"

He looked down and saw Terrence Haight, who he only knew as the Black man his father hired to pick up dead chickens. His clothes and face were soaked in blood, and he had a bullet hole in his head.

Eric said nothing but he stared at this man, waiting and watching as more people gathered around: Daniel's mother and father, various people from the hospital, a few puffy white roosters walking around, their feathers peppered with drops of blood.

They all looked like zombies from the old B-movies he used to watch with Daryl, and they all just stared up at Eric, waiting on him to let them inside. He looked at the tree once more, and an owl had joined the serpent on a neighboring branch, staring into the window, unfazed by the blood raining down upon them. Eric's face was pressed against the glass when the first pebble was thrown, jarring him away from it.

He looked down to see a growing angry mob of the undead of Hawthorn in tattered, bloody clothes and dirty, rotting faces. "Open the door, boy!" Terrence yelled. "We ain't dead yet." Another rock flew through the window, breaking a baseball-sized hole in it. Eric ran out of the room, into the nearest bathroom.

He ran cold bathwater, but what came out was a torrent of rust-colored blood, the smell quickly filling the room. He yelled in shock, turned off the water, and turned it back on. More blood. Eric got naked and got into the bath, hoping to freeze himself awake by submerging himself under whatever was coming out of the faucet.

After he submerged himself under the tub-full of warm blood, he re-entered this dimension - choking on cold water, his fingers pruney, his genitals and nipples shrunken from the cold air on his wet skin.

He crawled out of the bathtub and promptly vomited into the toilet. He was awake and alive, and it was now morning. All was quiet.

He walked down the stairs and found things pretty well where he had left them the night before. He wrapped his naked body in an afghan and went on the hunt for coffee.

After a ten-minute search for the television remote control, he clicked on the local news. Stale, electronic trumpets blasted the news theme music, slightly worsening Eric's headache. He saw a beautiful woman doing a special report. She looked familiar. He then saw her name tagged at the bottom of the screen: Marcia Cruz.

"Huh," Eric said to himself. "She always wanted to be famous."

Gone was the chunky, awkward girl with Coke-bottle glasses that he despised as a child, replaced by a woman with striking hazel eyes and a husky voice.

After the surprise wore off, he started to pay attention to what Marcia was saying in such a solemn tone. His head was still a bit foggy, but he thought he heard his last name once or twice. He turned the volume up. He saw cell phone footage of Daniel's maroon SUV, crushed and wrinkled on the side of Highway 60.

He dropped his coffee mug on the floor as a gallery of photographs showed his father, his sister-in-law, and the darkened silhouettes of two unnamed children.

Eric felt their ghosts immediately. A frantic, stinging series of jabs went up and down his spine like a xylophone. And here he was, standing in the house that molded his psyche so crudely; a fully stitched-together man, his wounds taunted by hasty, vindictive spirits.

His eyes froze open for two days. His medication was collecting dust on the bottom guest bathroom towel rack, as Eric hadn't decided whether to start taking his medication. Without it, he wouldn't sleep, and he would ascend into a sort of psychic hereafter, where every noise and word was jagged poetry. Everything hit his ears like the moans of a plague of dry flies.

After a couple of days, he could see auras.

After a week, he could hear The Devil.

What began as liberation from chemical servitude, transformed into a different sort of mental prison. He could see everything around him just fine; the problems began when he could see what lied beneath.

So Eric Redmond retreated to his old bedroom. He took a shower first, and without drying off or putting on his boxers, he walked stark naked into an empty race car bed. He closed his eyes but didn't sleep. He draped the comforter over his head to soak in his own humid breath, leaving his feet bare.

For the first time in Eric Redmond's life, he prayed sincerely, projecting his anguished cries toward the window as he looked at the moon. And when he was done crying, he slept - cleansing the stubborn grime from his consciousness, and disarming the explosiveness of an emotional buildup from spending a lifetime being toe-deep in Purgatory.

He awoke an uncertain time later with Daniel sleeping next to him.

Daniel had a bandaged right eye, and his arm was in a sling. He had cuts on his swollen lip, which made him look like a very pale fish. He was wearing the same t-shirt and jeans from the day Eric arrived.

Eric got up, wrapping the comforter around his waist, and headed downstairs.

"What'sa matter?" Eric said to Daniel over his plate of scrambled eggs. "Ain't you hungry?"

Daniel said nothing, but he picked up his fork and picked holes in the foamy yellow.

The silence was a comfort to them both.

"You know," Eric said gently, "If I'm in your way, I could -"

Daniel jerked his head up instinctively. "No," he said with barely-contained urgency. "No, you're welcome to stay."

"I'm afraid," Eric said, beginning to make an awkward statement, but reconsidering. Daniel widened his eyes and nodded, waiting for Eric to spit it out.

"I'm afraid I'll just be in the way," Eric finally said.

Daniel put down his fork and dabbed his corner mouth with a paper towel Eric had symmetrically placed near his plate. He stared at Eric for a second, in shock at his own feelings.

"Please stay," Daniel said in a weepy whisper. He picked up his plate, said, "Excuse me," and left the table.

Two

As news of the tragedy trickled into the trenches of Hawthorn, people confirmed amongst themselves their worst suspicions about a "Redmond family curse." It was a curse they had brought upon themselves, most offered.

Father Redmond was crushed not by the impact of a semi-truck, but by his lack of humility. His hubris had gotten the best of him, and in the townsfolk's minds, they could finally envision that gaudy new church of his crumbling down to the ground, like the tower of Babel. Ivory dust would fall over the concrete painted parking lot - a site that once was composed of bland gray gravel, red brick, and the pure prayers of the simple, hardworking Hawthorn denizens who had made the Redmond family rich and famous.

Father Redmond had lost his way, and Hawthorn wasn't thrilled with his openness to Terrence, the town's only Black man. He employed him and in effect attempted to normalize Terrence's Blackness, and though he was the last surviving African-American citizen of Hawthorn, people in town quietly feared his acceptance might lead to more people of color feeling comfortable enough to make Hawthorn their home. It became impolite to voice this concern as years went by, but the fear was still there all the same. When Terrence died, most people took a second to ponder what that meant. The guilt they felt may have crept around their throats for a minute – stuffy and constricting – but it came from out of nowhere, and was quickly choked down.

It was Father Redmond who led the charge of finding Terrence's remains - which they eventually did, about a year after his death. His bones, along with Dwight Wright's, were found in a silo outside of town. Redmond paid for the necessary tests himself to confirm the remains as belonging to the two men, and for a proper burial next to his parents in the old Hawthorn cemetery on the hill.

The funeral was quite beautiful. It was a military service, and it was a pricey affair despite the fact that few people in town showed up to pay their respects.

The crowd consisted mostly of Terrence's relatives from Georgia, a few fledgling local reporters breaking a cold case story from a respectable distance, and Donna, who had heard about Terrence's death via social media and made the drive from her home in Connecticut.

Daniel wept. There laid before him the final remnants of boyhood wisdom - now slipped through his fingers and fallen to earth, despite his constant, desperate grasping for them. His boyhood was a box of bones.

Dwight was in a dull brass urn, short and squat and pitiful looking. Daniel wondered if Dwight ever had a soul, where it went - and if it was there with him the whole time, how it got to be so rotten. He wondered if any part of Dwight lived in him. If his own daddy didn't have a soul, did Daniel? His face contorted when he finally failed in concealing his weeping. He was embarrassed.

Megan grabbed Daniel's hand and didn't let go until he, along with a few men from the Fire Department at which Terrence volunteered, had to perform pallbearer duties at the end of the service.

Terrence laid in a majestic tomb. At the funeral home, when asked which casket he'd prefer, Father Redmond replied flatly, "Nothing less than what you would bury Jesus Christ himself." This raised an eyebrow from the funeral parlor director; most likely in disapproval because he knew whom the casket was for despite pretending he didn't.

Distrust toward the Redmonds from the people of Hawthorn quietly grew shortly after the service was over, and the good memories that set an intrusive haze over their true thoughts evaporated under a vengeful sun.

As far as Eric, they had always suspected him of being a "devil-child"; there were rumors that he was the illegitimate spawn of Father Redmond and a sex worker, though some refused to voice this rumor as it seemed especially careless to speak on with no proof. He was easy to hate with his black, greasy hair and his deep-set eyes with heavy lids. His antisocial behavior was the opposite of God-like, and his predilection for kinship with "white trash" like Daryl McAdams, though it was in line with Father Redmond's mission statement, was unseemly.

It was no coincidence that most of the Redmond family was killed at the same time that Eric had returned to town after ten years - not to mention in the company of a hired thug from St. Louis.

Even Daniel didn't escape the stratosphere of Hawthorn's rumor mill. As the sole survivor of a terrible accident, there must be some dark magic protecting him, they thought.

It was strange to see the tide turning against them. For years, Daniel felt protected under the thick garb of the surname Redmond. After his family died, it became clear that he was only insulated, not protected, from the opinions of others.

The deceased's bodies weren't even cold when Eric and Daniel were beginning to be hounded by the local press. Knocks on doors and ringing landline phones and shouting filled the stale household air, which was tainted by the stench of a stopped-up garbage disposal and overflowing trashcans. Gone were the coldly pleasant odors of plaster and potpourri that Edna Redmond was always diligent about replacing weekly.

Eric snuck outside one morning at four o'clock to smoke a cigarette when he found Daniel directly to his right, smashing the exquisite gold-plated doorbell with a claw hammer. Eric noticed the slowly evaporating tears on his cheeks, and quietly took one step backward to go back inside. Through the garage - where he eventually found peace enough to enjoy his cigarette - Eric heard in a faint but savage tone, a series of grunts and truncated wailing, as if Daniel was trying to hold back the bile in his throat.

Television was softly banned. Daniel even went so far as to turn them backward with the screens facing the wall.

"Daddy used to call TV's the Devil's Eye," Eric casually observed, standing behind the kitchen counter, eating ice cream right out of the carton and watching Daniel rearrange the entertainment center.

"That's rich," Daniel said with a slight scoff. "He would know, I guess."

"That was before you came along," Eric said.

Daniel leaned against the sharp edges of the entertainment center and bowed his head. Eric's gummy chewing of ice cream slowed. He gave Daniel a silent moment so that he could regain feeling in his tongue enough to speak.

"Are you okay?" Eric said, swirling his tongue against the roof of his mouth.

Daniel's head rose slowly, and he turned toward Eric. He blinked rapidly, struggling to hold himself together. "Let's not talk about your dad for a while, okay?" He said. His face was tense, suppressing an agitated frown.

Eric dropped his spoon into the ice cream carton. "Okay," he said, as Daniel exited the room.

Three

"If he could see this now," Eric observed, "he'd shit his pants." He was gnawing on a granola bar; since going back on his meds, he was always eating something.

Outside, there were rumblings of cars and constant clacking of feet on the front courtyard that belonged to members of the press, both local and national.

After Father Redmond's death, it was silent around the house for days. Occasionally, Daniel would hear Eric run bath water upstairs. Eric would occasionally hear Daniel's cries through classical music blasting out of the speakers placed in the corners of every room in the house. Sometimes this served as a passive-aggressive reminder to Eric to not sleep until noon; or perhaps, a call for Eric to keep Daniel company - which he sometimes did, though the two didn't speak much.

They both enjoyed the silence. It was so quiet, they heard jets and crop-dusters go overhead during meals.

Eric once glanced at Daniel, frown lines becoming pronounced at something he was reading - always just so earnest, Daniel Wright - and it reminded him of something.

"You used to make that face when you were afraid you were going to get in trouble," Eric said.

"I was never in trouble," Daniel replied with a smirk.

"That's true," Eric said. "Which always confused me so much."

"What's that?" Daniel asked.

Eric shrugged.

"I guess I was never in trouble," Daniel said, "because I was always afraid of being in trouble. Funny how that works."

"What's it like to be afraid of the stuff outside your head?" Eric asked, laid back on the sofa with his arms crossed, eyes toward the ceiling. "I was always afraid of myself."

"I'd imagine it's not much different," Daniel said.

The two shared the responsibility of the burial and funeral arrangements. Daniel called the nursing home that housed Edna Redmond. When he shared the news of Harold Redmond's death with a staff member, he was told that he'd be called back when Mrs. Redmond felt ready.

And he was called back - just not by his adoptive mother. It was by the same staff member who, with a shaky voice, quietly muttered, "Mrs. Redmond will only attend services, she says, if there's a parade."

"A parade?"

"Yes," the fragile man told Daniel. "She wants to know if there will be a parade."

"I don't get it."

"She anticipated that answer," the staff member replied with an exhausted sigh.

Daniel heard the wrinkling of paper on the other end of the line.

"In other words," the staff member said, reciting from notes, "Mrs. Redmond wishes to express her gratitude to the Good Lord that she has outlived her husband, and sends her best to you boys."

"Got it."

"She also wants to know," the staff member continued after picking up another note, "if you boys are getting along."

Daniel blinked twice and said nothing.

"Mr. Redmond?" The staff member said, likely hoping for a disconnected line.

"Yes, we are," Daniel said. "And remind her that my last name isn't Redmond."

Eric offered to pay for a lavish funeral service for Megan and the boys, but Daniel declined. "Her family is handling that," he said, somewhat coldly. It was to be a separate affair, and Daniel never gave any additional details.

One afternoon when Daniel wasn't home, Eric just assumed that the funeral was happening. He searched on his rarely touched, rarely charged smartphone for the obituaries, just to make sure he wasn't once again losing his mind.

There it was, all laid out: Megan Wright; Martin Wright; Marianne Wright - all no longer on Earth.

After Redmond's funeral, reporters seemed to follow the brothers home. At first, Daniel and Eric humored them, until their questions became too intrusive.

It was when a smiling reporter began asking Eric about his dead father shouting in the Branson Landing Marriott hotel hallway at 11 p.m. the night before the accident that the world outside the villa started swirling, and it was no longer safe. The brothers stopped opening the door when knocked upon.

After a while, no one bothered to knock, except KYKX reporter Marcia Cruz. She beat on the door with the force of a police officer holding a warrant. Her knocking was relentless.

Eric jerked open the door mid-curse word, his face angry, until he laid eyes upon Marcia, who was more beautiful in person than she was on television. Her pillowy, bright red lips pursed a bit before relaxing into a warm grin.

"Long time no see," Eric said to Marcia after an extended few seconds.

"Hi," Marcia said. "I'm Marcia Cruz with -"

"I know who you are," Eric said, showing his teeth in a smile.

"And you are?" Marcia asked.

"Don't you already know that?" Eric asked Marcia.

"This is the Redmond residence, correct?" She asked.

"Correct."

"I'm sorry to hear about your recent loss," Marcia said, glaring at an open document on her phone.

"Don't be," Eric said, catching Marcia's attention.

"You must be Eric," Marcia said.

"You must be psychic," Eric retorted.

"Nope, just a halfway decent memory," Marcia said, smiling. "Can I come in?"

“Sure,” Eric said with a beaming smile.

Marcia took a step forward but was halted by Eric, who suddenly looked stern, and crossed his arms.

"Off the record," Eric said, tensing his biceps and his nostrils simultaneously.

Marcia chuckled nervously. "But-"

"Nope," Eric said, shaking his head confidently with his eyes closed. "Off the record."

"That's as good as it gets, huh?" Marcia asked.

"We haven't opened this door in the past week without slamming it in someone's face," Eric said. "And I quite enjoy doing it. So you tell me."

"Loud and clear," Marcia said with slightly bugged eyes.

Marcia sat at the kitchen counter, folded her hands, and smiled.

"So," Eric said, "you grew up."

"So did you," Marcia said. "I'm a big fan of your work."

"Are you really?" Eric said, skeptical. "It's okay if you're not."

"No, I really am," Marcia said sweetly.

Eric leaned on the counter. "Do you want some hot cocoa?"

Marcia looked perplexed. "Um, sure?" She said.

"I'm off of coffee," Eric said, "So I drink cocoa."

"That's a lot of sugar," Marcia said.

"Would you prefer tea?"

"Tea would be lovely."

Daniel heard the sounds of a conversation happening in the other room just as he was about to fall asleep. He stomped drowsily down the stairs to see Eric and Marcia talking.

"Hi," Daniel said to Marcia. "Who are you?"

"Hi," Marcia said. "I'm -"

"You remember Marcia Cruz, from school?" Eric said. "She was in my grade."

Daniel tensed his lips. "No, I'm afraid I don't, sorry."

"It's okay," Marcia said. "You must have a lot on your mind."

"I do," Daniel said. "But I also have a pretty good memory."

"I was friends with your..." Marcia trailed off.

"My wife?" Daniel asked.

"Yes," Marcia said, almost whispering. "I was a friend of Megan's."

Daniel nodded. "Why are you here?"

Marcia looked at Eric. "Danny," Eric said, "She is a reporter, but I knew her from -"

"I'm sorry, Miss," Daniel said. "But I hope you'll understand that we require privacy right now."

"Of course," Marcia said. "I was just catching up with your brother."

Daniel looked at Eric with a death stare as he went upstairs. "Okay," he said. He gave an obligatory smile to Marcia and disappeared, back to the second floor.

"How's he doing?" Marcia asked, leaning into Eric's direction and reverting to a whisper.

"About as well as anybody would," Eric said. "Under the circumstances."

Marcia looked down.

"So," Eric said, "Reporter."

"Yeah," Marcia said. "Not exactly an actress like I wanted, but close enough."

"Well, if it makes you feel any better, you do have screen presence," Eric said with a wink.

Marcia laughed. "Are you flirting with me?" She asked.

"I know I'm bad at it," Eric said. "I'm trying."

"I always thought you were gay," Marcia said.

"No more than most people are," Eric said. "Maybe a little."

Marcia laughed again, brushing some of her black bobbed hair behind her ear.

"Are you working on anything right now?" Marcia asked, eager to change the subject.

Eric took a breath. "Not really," he said. "I've been kind of distracted."

Marcia looked over her shoulder at the television, which was facing the wall. "Is that why you did that to the TV?"

"No," Eric said, "Daniel did that."

"Why?" Marcia asked.

"Well," Eric said, "it's been kind of a zoo around here lately...no offense."

"None taken."

"He just doesn't want to add to the noise," Eric said. "I think the news kind of gets to him."

"I figured he'd be used to it," Marcia said, "considering who his family is."

"You never get used to it," Eric said. "The trauma of seeing yourself in print and on television never lets up...again, no offense."

"No," Marcia said. "I get it."

Marcia was just warm enough to keep the conversation going. As she looked at Eric, she tried to see the good in him, and she did see some.

His twitching, his oral fixation, his childish giggling – Eric Redmond was as weird as he had always been, but he had grown into it. It suited him. He had a gentle soul, but mean eyes. She related to him now.

It had been fifteen years since his schoolyard taunts made her fantasize about killing boys. This anger had bloomed within her, planted by boys like Eric Redmond, and Marcia became a woman who knew better than to show her intensity to anyone she considered weaker than her. She had no use for love in the conventional sense of the word. Love gets you killed, every time.

And so she learned to use love as a weapon. She would claim self-defense as a pre-emptive strike, but through the years she would wonder, sometimes aloud, if she had become cruel and jaded.

"What would that mean, if you were?" A therapist once asked her.

"I guess it wouldn't mean anything," Marcia said. "Depending on what I wanted out of life."

MARCIA LED ERIC REDMOND to his own bed. He shivered, and she grinned as she took him inside of her. Eric noticed she had lipstick on her teeth, and that made him less nervous. She liked the way he grabbed her buttocks, finessing old stretch marks earned in her teenage years.

She closed her eyes and tried to picture someone else, but couldn't, and so she stopped trying and gave herself to him. He looked powerless and boyish underneath her, his hint of double chin protruding under his sharp jaw. He looked pleading and grateful.

He looked at her like she might destroy him, and the thought of that gave him a thrill. She towered over him, his hips fighting back against hers while he grabbed her wrists and pulled her into him.

They finished – sweaty, empty, and laying beside each other at arm's length.

"Do you mind if I smoke?" Marcia croaked, her forearms covering her breasts by holding the bed sheet up to her chin.

"Only if you open the window," Eric said, "And let me bum one."

Marcia lit two cigarettes at once and gave one of them to Eric. She took it upon herself to grab the incense burner and put it between them to use as an ashtray, after she opened the window.

"So I don't know anything," Eric said after moments of silence. "If that's why you stayed."

"Well, it's why I came," Marcia said, "but not why I stayed. I figured you didn't know anything after being here for a few minutes."

"Well, then, what do you know?" Eric said, propping his head up with his hand.

Marcia turned to him and smirked.

"What?" Eric asked.

"Nothing," Marcia said. "It's just strange that you live with your brother, his whole family just died, and you don't even know the details."

"Well," Eric said, "our family is strange."

Marcia licked her lips, thought carefully for a moment, and told Eric what she knew.

In talking to the hotel staff for her report, Marcia learned that there were noise complaints. Considering that the Redmond family booked the entire top floor, she explained to Eric, they must have been causing quite a ruckus.

"They were fighting?" Eric asked.

"Apparently," Marcia said with a half-shrug.

Eric's face started to lose what little color it held.

"About what?" Eric asked.

"No one is exactly sure," Marcia said. "It's what I came here to find out."

"You must have some idea," Eric prodded.

All anyone knew, Marcia explained, was that there was something inappropriate between Megan and Father Redmond.

"They had sex?" Eric asked, slightly disgusted.

"I doubt it," Marcia replied. "But the police ended up getting involved."

"What?" Eric asked, bewildered.

"I find it hard to believe you didn't know any of this," Marcia said.

"I didn't," Eric said. "What else do you know?"

"I don't know anything for sure," Marcia said. "But putting two and two together wouldn't be too hard."

Eric exhaled cigarette smoke in an extended sigh. "Jesus," he muttered to himself.

"So, wait," Eric said after a pause. "You don't think Danny had anything to do with..."

Eric's face dropped.

"It's quite a leap," Marcia said. "But you said it yourself: your family is strange."

Eric smashed the cigarette into the floor of the incense holder and leaped out of bed, wrapping a blanket around his waist.

"I'd better go," Marcia said. "I'll leave my card here, in case."

"No need," Eric said. "I can't speak on the record about this, at all. Ever."

"In case you need to talk to someone," she said. "Off the record. As friends."

Eric smiled. "Right," he said. "Sorry. And thanks."

"No problem," Marcia said. She had the comforter wrapped around her breasts and waist. Marcia bent down and playfully lifted Eric's chin with her index finger. She placed her lips on his.

Her lips still gently pressed against his, she cooed, "Can I use your shower?"

ERIC NEVER SPOKE ABOUT what he learned to Daniel, even when the police came to the house and asked them both questions. Eric played dumb and answered questions like an honest person would. After all of this, he told himself, he couldn't let his father's sins take down his brother. The Redmond curse has caused enough damage, he thought, and it ends with him.

Eric also knew that he could only hold this weight on his shoulders for so long. He didn't feel the need to mourn his father, and knew that he could be of limited help to Daniel.

For Eric, love and hate existed extremely close together, and every encounter always broke off dramatically. People in his orbit weren't able to drift slowly away, as they did for most. Eric had a compulsion to detonate a bomb – a bomb he always managed to absentmindedly leave sitting in the hidden folds of the object of his affection's soul.

Heaven only existed for Eric Redmond so he could feel the thrill of standing at the edge of Hell - the blistering heat roasting the tips of his toes before backing away from it, always in the nick of time.

Four

What was initially supposed to be a two-night stay at Eric's childhood home became two months, and then a year.

Daniel and Eric wallowed out the living room furniture, never sleeping in their own beds. They were afraid of being alone with themselves, and their scary thoughts. Quiet moments were never tranquil with another person in the room, even if no one spoke. The noisy myth of camaraderie was enough to soothe both men's jangly nerves.

Marcia came around a few more times - and each time, Eric became enraptured by her presence. Every time Marcia left Eric, it was a little harder for him to take. Seeing her face at the front door and deciding to open it became an exercise in masochism. It was after they had sex when Eric Redmond was filled with something he swore off as a young boy: love.

Her body was turned away from his. She checked her messages on her phone underneath musty bed sheets, letting her skin devour his caress, but otherwise paying him no mind. Eric rubbed Marcia's arm and her backside with a soft sweetness. She would only let out a gentle "Mmm," as tacit approval.

Eric turned away from Marcia and looked at the ceiling.

"I only want love when I can't have it," Eric said, gazing upward. "Oncc it's there, showing itself, I disappear."

Marcia turned to face Eric and placed her chin on her hand.

"I can relate," she said.

"I'm trying to work on it," Eric said. He grabbed Marcia's hand. "It's getting easier."

Marcia laid her head on Eric's chest. "Maybe someday we'll be like other people," she said.

The two fell asleep as the noonday sun prism'd through the window shams, and the cold air return hummed hypnotically.

When Eric woke, Marcia was gone.

His gut told him she was gone for good. He closed his eyes and silently prayed for a couple of seconds that she might come back. "If not," he said to God, "no hard feelings."

Eric would explore this sadness. He'd consider it a gift.

HALLOWEEN WAS LIKE Christmas to Eric Redmond, a former Goth nerd and chronic nihilist. It was the anti-holiday. And so when he saw on social media a town Halloween party was happening, he decided to attend. Getting his brother to go would be a chore, but not impossible.

After reasoning with Daniel that they hadn't left the house in months, Eric managed to convince his reluctant brother to take him.

This was no small feat: Just days prior, someone had vandalized Daniel's work truck with the word, "Killer," in big white letters. Upon seeing this, Daniel's face got red, and he scowled but said nothing as he scrubbed it off with a horsehair brush and soapy water.

"Probably just some dumb kids," Eric said.

Daniel didn't even acknowledge Eric under the Hawthorn tree, smoking a cigarette, sitting in a swing Daniel built for his son.

It was more upsetting for Daniel because though people stared at him when he was at the Dollar General store or gas station, no one ever said anything to him about the rumors.

In fact, people were as polite as ever, offering a smile with his change and saying with extra sweetness, "Have a nice day." It was when intoxicated people in the middle of the night let loose their runaway thoughts that the town's suspicions were plastered on the Redmond's property, and made real to him for the first time. It disturbed him to ponder what lied beneath those smiles and displays of courtesy.

It reminded Daniel that he'd never really escape the black cloud over him as long as he stayed in Hawthorn. He often fantasized about leaving but was too despondent to go through with it.

"When you left, what gave you the nerve to stay gone?" Daniel asked Eric during a quiet afternoon of lounging around.

"I was born with a lot of it," Eric said, holding a crossword puzzle over his head, propping it on his bent knee when he needed to write in it. "And the legal documents keeping me away didn't hurt."

"But I just hated it so much that I was determined. I hated the hospital too, but I made it work for me. I guess the reason I stayed gone was that there wasn't anything for me here," Eric said. "So why stay?"

"And now?" Daniel asked. "You've been here for a while."

"That's because you're here," Eric said. "I realize now that's probably enough for me to stick around, I suppose."

The Hawthorn Halloween party took place in the middle of town, at the old Shrine mansion, which was converted into an event space. There were kids there, throwing rocks at each other and running around the carriage house in the backyard. Eric stepped out of the passenger side of Daniel's work truck.

"Aren't you coming?" Eric said through the window to Daniel, who was sitting at the wheel, eyes straight ahead, frowning.

"I have to make a phone call," he said.

"I'm going to sit by the fire," Eric said. "Come find me."

The sun lowered itself behind the tall jagged tree line. The light bled through the pointed branches of trees that were near death, but the rays' reach was diminishing by the minute. Eric sat beside a blond woman, who smiled at him without showing any teeth.

Eric nodded at her, tipping his baseball cap. "How you doin'," he said.

"Cold," The woman said with a shiver. "It was supposed to be warmer today."

"Never can tell, can you?" Eric said, analyzing his surroundings. He saw two other blonde women in the distance, holding red Solo cups in both hands. When these two women sat next to the woman Eric was talking to, a memory struck his brain like lightning. These were the Toby sisters all grown up.

"You look familiar," one of the sisters said. Eric just grinned like an idiot, like a deer in headlights.

"This is going to sound crazy," said the sister to Eric's left, "but are you famous?" Eric nodded his head no. She leaned right to whisper in her sister's ear, which caused her to cackle. She threw her head back and laughed with a slack-jawed howl. She looked at Eric's nervous disposition and clammed up.

"Aren't you going to get something to drink?" She asked.

"No," Eric said. "I gave it up."

The middle sister laughed again. "They aren't serving alcohol," she said. "There are kids here."

Eric could feel the tinge of a panic attack in his toes. The chunky red flames stood tall, the sisters' bodies hidden behind the red glowing fire, which illuminated their faces. The heat of the fire combined with the heat from inside of him caused Eric to sweat. He got up and walked around.

He observed woods at the edge of the property. Eric stood at the outer rim of the forest, wondering whether to wander into the sea of trees.

Eric always had a less-than-stellar sense of direction, and Daniel was undoubtedly pouting in his truck, waiting for his brother to tire of socializing with the poor souls of Hawthorn.

Eric stopped thinking, and just put one foot in front of the other, crossing the line from the boisterous crowd, into the silent forest. Just then, a small child dressed as a devil ran past him, the breeze from the child's spritely body nicking Eric's slacks. This young devil carried a tree branch as tall as he was, chasing a girl wearing a princess costume. She smiled proudly as she laughed and ran from the boy, with her mother's lipstick smeared on her face and teeth.

The children ventured a yard into the woods, but the girl stopped. Instead of capturing his playmate after catching up with her, the devil stood beside her.

"What's wrong?" The devil asked the princess.

"I don't think we're supposed to be in here," she said.

"Who says?" The devil asked incredulously.

The princess turned in the opposite direction. "It's too spooky in there," she said, before running away in the opposite direction. The devil followed her, tossing the branch like a baseball bat.

Eric walked into the woods in a straight line, his heart beating rapidly and his need to be away from people propelling his every step. He saw garter snakes slithering under leaves, but he wasn't afraid.

His father told him long ago that the only good snake was a dead snake. "Just ask Adam," he would say. Later on, it would be Daniel who told him that those kinds of snakes wouldn't hurt you; it's the cat-eyed serpents you had to watch out for.

"How in the world do you get close enough to a snake to see his eyes?" Eric asked.

"Garter snakes just want to be left alone," Daniel said. "So leave 'em be. Every other breed? Just run away. But they still won't hurt ya.""

After a few minutes, Eric looked behind him and could see no trace of humans - just a cacophony of dying trees with seasonally appropriate, neon-colored leaves. Ahead, he saw barren land, incandescent with moonlight, which was broken up by rows of tall gray tree trunks. He found this strange, as it was nearing dusk. His heart beat faster.

Eric stood between two large Hawthorn trees on the edge of the woods and peered out at the old McAdams' farm, which had just been harvested for beans. Golden stalks laid smashed into the dirt. Beside the field was a dirt road, with beautiful green hills in the distance.

Eric remembered the old creek that served as the unofficial north-south border, and he wanted to see if it had dried up. His heart pounded furiously and offbeat, and his mind was unnerved. The water might soothe him, he thought.

He heard waves of cicadas, which was damn near impossible in the fall. Eric kept walking, his feet full of static as if they were asleep. By the time he got to the creek, which looked to be about four feet deep, his feet were numb. He looked up, and the sky was pink. He felt warm droplets on his face that he assumed was sweat until he saw a dark figure with broad shoulders on the other side of the ditch bank. Upon further inspection, his plaid shirt had red raindrops on it.

"Are you okay?" Eric called out to this man with a bowed head.

Eric heard an owl hoot. The cicadas had quieted down.

The man raised his head up. Eric recognized him as the Black man that served as his father's groundskeeper. It was Terrence Haight, though Eric could never remember his name.

"About as okay as you are, I reckon," Terrence said with sadness in his voice.

"What's your name?" Eric asked.

"Neither of us has a name," he said. "But my name when I was on Earth was Terrence."

Eric should have been freaking out. Instead, he was calm.

"I'm Eric," he said.

"I know who you are, son," Terrence said. "But you ain't Eric no more."

"I don't get it," Eric said. He slapped his face with both hands as tears started to form in his eyes.

"Don't do that. You ain't asleep. You're dead, boy," Terrence said. "We don't have need for names no more."

Eric was silent. It was still raining blood. Terrence walked down the embankment without fear - almost floating. He reached his hands out for Eric's. "Come on," Terrence said. "It's time."

Eric walked down the embankment to meet him. The ground was spongy like a cheap bed mattress, but it held his feet down so he wouldn't fall.

"Is it cold?" Eric asked Terrence.

Terrence grinned. "Better than a warm bath," he said. "There ain't nothing like it."

Eric descended into the ditch until he was face-to-face with Terrence, and Terrence grabbed his hands as they stood in the bloody water. His submerged feet and kneecaps felt strange; kind of like they had melted. Eric looked down to make sure his feet were still there, but he couldn't quite see through the murky ditch water. His heart beat slowed down. He could no longer hear it between his ears.

"So this is it?" Eric asked. "This is the hereafter?"

"Naw," Terrence said. "This is the end of the beginning. Wouldn't do no good to try to explain it in words."

Terrence closed his eyes and began to speak in a language that was inhuman - quietly at first, but getting more forceful. Eric realized he was praying, so he closed his eyes as well.

Terrence quit speaking for a second. The rain stopped, and bugs and birds stopped chirping. Suddenly, Terrence violently dragged Eric under the water.

Eric looked up and saw that above the water there was a bright light slowly expanding, turning the pink sky white. Water Moccasins slithered above them, minding their own business. Lighting bugs and dragonflies landed on the surface of the water.

The light was growing, but Eric and Terrence seemed to be getting further away from it - sinking into darkness.

Eric felt his emotions and his physical pain and his all-too-human concerns with time melt away, and he felt nothing but warmth encasing his body, his skin, his eyes, his insides. He never felt so peaceful.

He said goodbye to Daniel and himself. The warmth and the darkness and the peace he felt - and had longed for his entire life - stuck with him, and he knew that this relief he now felt was infinite.

This is what it's like to die, Eric thought to himself. He looked at Terrence, his unkempt hair floating in the water. Terrence nodded as if he heard Eric's thoughts and was affirming it.

Eric gave up the ghost gladly, offering it up to whoever now laid claim to it.

Part Three

Zero

Hawthorn Baptist Church survived a few years after Harold Redmond's death, under the half-ass tutelage of Mr. Thomas: a grinning psychopath with too many teeth, and who had the sheen of a used car salesman. A handsome man with a smooth sermon delivery, Mr. Thomas led the congregation through the transition.

In the process, he ran away with the congregation, milking it like a politician until he reached the next rung on the ladder: national television syndication, and a corporate television headquarters in Kansas City.

Toby McAdams became mayor of Hawthorn, bringing the town into its twilight years. But The Redmonds were spoken about years after their reign was over. Legends in death, Daniel carried the burden with him as he had always done.

To Daniel's shock, the apocalypse Eric had predicted in his journals came true - at least in part. An earthquake devasted Missouri a few years after the Redmonds' death. It had always been a sick joke amongst the Hawthorn locals that California (or "Babylon") would be the first to go due to God's wrath, but the New Madrid fault line proved to be a real son of a bitch. Many towns in the area were devastated, but perhaps none as severely as Hawthorn.

The Swiss villa that had housed the Redmond family for decades was half-gone, but the vines crawling up the shingles were evidence of neglect long before it became rubble. The triple-wide mobile homes, which had replaced those shambolic trailers, were, strangely, the least damaged homes in town, which made Jackass Flats officially the "nice part of town," if only briefly. The highway was closed around Hawthorn, both north and southbound lanes, for months. The town was starving and became more insular than ever.

Whereas before technology had a sanitizing effect on the bond of the townsfolk, making them impersonal and taking away the grit of their daily lives;

wiping everything out made the town vibrant again, despite them having hungry bellies and bagged eyes.

It took a few years, but things unfolded relatively neatly after the dust settled and the earth calmed down. There were storms but no one to blame for them. As the world evolved, culture became a more solitary experience to pursue. The people of the world got more distant from each other, though they communicated more than ever. But for Daniel, the last remaining Redmond, he stayed to himself and stayed quiet, living his life about like everyone else used to do before it all got ruined.

Shortly before the earthquake, Daniel managed to sell off his chicken farm to Marcia Cruz's cousin Jose, who had been a hired hand since he came back from New York City to live with his parents. Daniel had become a quiet, guarded man after a lifetime of loss – among the dead were his mother, his brother, his wife, his children, and Terrence, who he considered his real father and who was ripped from his life by the bigotry and mental incompetence of his flesh-and-blood father.

The irony of Daniel's life became too much to deal with in any sort of healthy way, so he did the only thing he knew how to do: grin and bear it, for crying had no practical use anymore. He was a grown man, after all, and self-pity gave way to a numbing coldness. However, he came to trust Jose.

Jose was a hard worker - many in town recommended him to Daniel because he was "One of those hard-working Mexicans," even though he was Cuban. If he could have afforded it, Daniel would have just signed over the farm to Jose.

Daniel hated the carnage of farming chickens. Chickens with deformities and distorted beaks, the increasing number of chickens that got down in their legs and couldn't walk due to rapid weight gain – he even found a couple of chickens with three legs over the years. They all must be killed because they couldn't be sold.

Eric hated it worse than anyone, which was funny considering his affinity for slasher films.

Daniel liked Jose's attitude. He had respect for the birds but accepted their circumstances. He didn't want the grit and the death, but he was strong enough to compartmentalize it and keep his friendly demeanor. Jose had also known hardship, and Daniel admired his tenacity in getting through it. He tried to learn from Jose.

Jose was a single man, which in a place like Hawthorn, made him stick out almost as much as his brown skin. He was small-framed but masculine, and most people in town assumed he was queer, but no one cared that much because he kept to himself.

Daniel kept Terrence's house after he was confirmed dead. He remodeled it and considered renting it out, but no one in town suited him as a renter. Jose was content in his one-room house in Jackass Flats. So Daniel moved into Terrence's old house, keeping a few of his things in place - such as the recliner they sat upon watching television on so many nights when Daniel was a child, feeling the rumbling of Terrence's snoring on his back as he leaned upon him. It was a house that was the size of the living room of the villa, but it felt more like home than any place he had ever lived.

In a dusty corner of the utility room, Daniel found Terrence's electric piano; the piano Eric Redmond had disrespected on the final May Day festival. Daniel plugged it in and began to peck on the keys. Pretty soon, he was playing the hymnals Terrence taught him, and that Father Redmond had instructed him to learn.

Daniel imagined Terrence peering over his shoulder, his lap holding young Daniel high enough to reach the keys, yet too high to reach the pedals. He pictured Terrence nodding in approval and muttering an occasional "Mmm-hmm."

It was at that moment that Daniel began to mourn - sincerely mourn. His heart sunk into a vortex within his chest, and he felt a loss that sucked him into some sort of foul ether. He was pulled into a past he longed for; a history that fragmented his soul countless times.

One

When news of Eric Redmond's death reached the ears of Hawthorn residents, there wasn't much of a reaction. He was mentioned on cable news and a few niche websites - articles that called him "a provocative artist," and "a rising force of nature in the art world," but after a few days of dull mourning by internet commenters and fellow artists, the only mention of Eric's death was in the implication that it was an omen before the earthquake that killed so many true Hawthornites - people who had stuck around their whole lives, cultivating their little corner of the world into something less than evil. Eric was an outsider, and news of his death made as much noise in town as would a housewife beating a dirty rug on a rock.

Once again, it was up to Daniel to plan the funeral. The man from the funeral parlor greeted him like an old friend and looked at him with sadness. Daniel, with hollowed-out eyes and a polite half-grin, just pointed to a pine box and said, "Knowing my brother, that's what he would have wanted."

"Would he perhaps prefer cremation?" The funeral director asked. "It's cheaper."

Daniel pondered on that for a second. "No," he said. "He hated fire."

Mr. Perry, the funeral director, just nodded. "I know you're good for it," he said. "I'll get around to sending an invoice eventually. You go home and get some rest."

Daniel got out his wallet. "No, I'll just pay you in cash," he said. "I'm not so good at remembering to check the mail these days."

Mr. Perry put his hand on Daniel's shoulder. "It's on me, Danny," he said. "Don't worry about it." He then gave Daniel a light hug, patted him on the back, and led him to the exit. "Take care of yourself, you hear?" He said, before closing the door.

Two

Eric's funeral was a non-event. He laid in the pine box, his face covered by rough plywood that was lightly coated with finish paint.

The funeral service was held in the remnants of the villa. The house was beautifully decayed. Stringy, dark green vines had taken over the concrete foundation, as well as a few of the chipped and weather-faded gargoyle statues and water fountains.

The acreage that held the attendees was safely nestled in the vast bosom of the willowy green circular Hawthorn and Oak Trees. It was an island of lush green grass that foreshadowed those summers that were lousy with cicadas.

The gazebo, still intact, was cleared of cobwebs, and the ghost town of hornets' nests that fossilized in the corners of the ceiling was scraped off with ice scrapers procured from the local gas station off the highway. A picture of Eric taken before the antipsychotic medication-induced weight gain was prominently displayed near the casket, in a distressed golden frame purchased from the local secondhand store.

There were dozens of mourners, but no one cried.

Marcia sat respectably far away from the front, crossing her legs and holding her lips in such a way that it was clear she was diligently attempting to turn them into a funeral-appropriate scowl.

Only Daniel sat in the front row - along with Edna, who sat in a wheelchair next to him with her face sullen and her hands folded in her lap. Daniel looked around and observed that even though every seat was filled, it was clear that few attendees were local.

Many mourners had odd hairstyles and grungy clothing. Some were androgynous hard-looking city-folk. Some looked beautiful - and therefore, out of place - as if they might be famous. Though, if they were, Daniel couldn't recognize them. He even saw Daryl McAdams toward the back of the crowd, who despite all odds looked healthy. He wore a designer pea coat, had all of his teeth, and an expensive haircut.

It was at this moment that Daniel, gazing at the crowd who was there to mourn the loss of his brother, realized that Eric belonged to no one in particular – not Daniel, not anyone, and by Eric's choice. He belonged to the world; a world that, as it turned out, was lucky to have him.

Daniel felt empty. He suddenly wished that he saw what these people saw in his brother that he so dearly loved, but whom he could never quite figure out.

The burial was brief and low-key. No one sang, by Eric's unspoken request. His pine box was let down into the ground as Mr. Thomas recited the Lord's Prayer. Marcia stood by Daniel and grabbed his hand. He looked at her, and tears welled up in her eyes.

"I just...feel bad," Marcia said in a whisper. It was all she could manage to say. Daniel just nodded and squeezed Marcia's hand a little tighter.

Marcia walked with Daniel across the lawn as he pushed Edna to his truck.

Finally, Marcia got the gumption to speak. "So what's next?" She asked.

"No idea," Daniel said. "And I guess I'm okay with that, for once."

Marcia leaned in and hugged Daniel's neck as he lightly touched the small of her back.

"It was good to see you," Marcia said. "Sorry about the circumstances, though."

Marcia walked away and turned back around after a couple of steps. "Just so you know, I could have loved him," she said through tears.

Daniel said softly, "Then why didn't you?"

Marcia's face contorted into an ugly cry. She shrugged her shoulders, and silently mouthed the words, "I don't know."

Daniel began loading Edna into his pickup, lifting her legs up. "Grab on, mama."

He got her into the truck and closed the door. He looked into the distance, and Marcia was still standing there, silently sobbing, looking clear through the ground with a thousand-yard stare.

Daniel walked over to Marcia and hugged her tightly. "He knew how you felt," he said. "And he knew he was hard to love."

"I did grow to love him," Marcia said in a raspy, weary voice. "In my way."

"So did I," Daniel said, still touching her arm. "And he knew that." Daniel kissed her on the temple and walked away.

"Take care of yourself, Daniel," Marcia called out with a sturdy cadence. "Let me know if you need anything."

"Just remember him the way you loved him," Daniel said, halfway into his truck. "That's what he deserves, you know?"

Marcia nodded, suppressing sobs.

"We're all going to be okay," Daniel said. "If anyone knows that firsthand, it's me."

Daniel drove away. In the rearview mirror, he saw Marcia dabbing her eyes with a handkerchief and checking her reflection in her compact mirror.

"Who was that Mexican woman?" Edna asked. "Is she your girlfriend?"

"No, mama," Daniel said. "Just someone who Eric and I went to school with."

"Nothing I hate worse than a funeral," Edna said, exhaling tiredly.

"Especially when it's your son, I imagine," Daniel replied.

"Yes," Edna said. "Even though he wasn't mine, he was still mine."

"What do you mean?" Daniel asked.

"You mean your bastard step-father never told you?" She asked. "I've been barren my whole life. Ain't nothin' work down there."

Daniel shook his head no.

"I never got a straight answer from him," Edna said. "But there were rumors."

Daniel, trying his best to keep his eyes on the road, said calmly but shakily, "What rumors?"

"Maybe this isn't the time or the place," Edna said. "I'll explain it to you later."

"No, mama," Daniel said with frustration, "You need to tell me now."

"Why?" She asked.

"Because it's just us two, mama," Daniel said. "We're the only ones left. Let's not keep lying to each other."

Edna sighed. Daniel gave her a moment to collect her thoughts.

"Your father always wanted kids," she began. "I did love him," she insisted. "I did."

"So?"

"So," Edna said, "after I finally told him the truth...you know, that I couldn't have kids? He damn near strung me up like they used to do them little Black boys."

"So why'd you stay?" Daniel asked.

"Oh, please," Edna said dismissively. "A preacher's wife leaving her husband in the damn Bible Belt? In Hawthorn? Never could have happened."

"Why not?" Daniel asked.

"I might as well sew a red letter on the tits of my dress," Edna said. "I'd never live it down."

"Anyway," Edna continued, "one day, the son of a bitch comes in strung out on something and tells me he knocked up a street-walker," she said, exasperatedly shaking her head. "And he has the gall to say he did it on purpose!"

"I just don't get why you stayed," Daniel said.

"Because you didn't know me back then," Edna said. "You did, but not really. They fed me pills; I was off in space half the time, and quiet as a church mouse. Plus living with him was better than the alternative."

"Which was?" Daniel asked.

"My own father," Edna said. "And that ain't worth getting into, so let's not."

"I have to say, mama," Daniel said, gazing at the yellow line in the middle of the road, "I suddenly feel like I don't know who you are."

Edna shrugged. "That's okay," she said. "I've never really known anyone I've loved. It's not necessary to know the ones you love if you really think about it. And sometimes," she continued, "it's for the best."

"For the best?" Daniel asked in near-disbelief.

"Mmm-hmm," Edna said, nodding with confidence. "To survive."

"But that's so sad," Daniel said, putting the truck in park.

"Yeah," Edna said. "It's also just life. You of all people should know that."

Edna kissed Daniel's cheek.

"All that matters is that we love, dear," she said with the first warm smile she had given to anyone in years.

"Now get me out of this damn truck," Edna said. "It smells like chicken shit."

Three

Time had whittled away Daniel's energy over the next few years. It happened slowly and quietly as he sat alone each night in Terrence's old smelly recliner, watching a projection television he swore he'd never buy after the small-scale media scandal of his dead family.

As Daniel forced his mind into numbness while watching a mix of home improvement shows and Terrence's stories he taped and Daniel had backed up into The Cloud, he gave up the last of his personhood to the universe. He had surrendered. The tangible world became his own lion's den in which he knew better than to dare set foot, ever again.

He had buried Edna. At that point in his life filled with loss, it felt more like a chore than a grievance. It was a reason to get out of bed for a week or two - making arrangements, notifying the people in her address book the nursing home provided him - most of whom had forgotten who Edna was, or politely gave their condolences before excusing themselves from attending her funeral service.

Days and nights melted into each other for Daniel. He had the Redmonds' money and no desire to travel, or date, or sleep regularly. The electric piano he displayed prominently in the living room collected a fair amount of dust.

In a fit of boredom - the type of stressful boredom that makes grown men want to crawl out of their skin just to escape themselves - he flipped the piano power switch on and hit the Middle C. It dinged pleasantly, and it cleared a little of the fog from Daniel's pupils. He decided to try to play a song. The only song he remembered was the unofficial Hawthorn Baptist Church hymnal, "God Be With You 'Til We Meet Again."

He felt a bead of sweat start to break through his brow. Memories of Terrence - chopping down that old Hawthorn tree, and wiping profuse sweat from his friendly face - all came flooding back at once. Daniel didn't cry. Instead, he smiled.

Though he caved on buying a television, he refused to budge on getting proper internet – just relying on his mobile hotspot on the rare occasion that he needed it. *People are too connected*, he thought aloud when he couldn't sleep at night. *But they connect at all the wrong places.*

It wasn't anywhere near the first of May, but Daniel decided to have one last May Day festival on Valentine's Day - a day chosen because he thought more people might show up. He couldn't bring himself to change the name, though. That was Terrence's.

So all through Jackass Flats, to the Wal-Marts and Whole Foods Markets of north Hawthorn, flyers were stapled to everything they would stick to - telephone poles, trees, and even Daniel's front door. He paid Jose a little extra to make the flyers, which featured neon pink musical notes piercing through a crimson heart.

"Don't you think that's a little...severe?" Daniel asked Jose, standing behind him while Jose leaned back from his laptop.

"Definitely," Jose said. "That's the point. It'll get their attention."

"Can you put a smiley face or something up-top?" Daniel asked.

"I could," Jose said, "if that's your thing." He shrugged.

Daniel sighed. "Whatever you think," he said. "This is the last time I'm doing this. Let's do it right."

"Anything else you want?" Jose asked.

"Just make sure people know it's free," Daniel replied.

THE FINAL MAY DAY FESTIVAL happened on a windy day that wouldn't have been so bone-chilling if the breeze had been more cooperative. Daniel put up Terrence's portable pavilion, plugged in his electric piano, and checked his watch for five o'clock.

The triple-wide mobile homes opened their front doors to hear the music, as Daniel played the only seven hymns he could competently perform from the memory of his lessons long ago. The notes were often struck clumsily, but they reverberated with warmth - with humanity.

People walked their dogs past Daniel's house and occasionally smiled upon hearing the music, and some people even waved before taking their canine companions back to their space-heated garages.

Daniel recognized none of the townsfolk, and no one knew him. But they were charmed by this lonely, handsome, middle-aged man who seemed unable to resist smiling as he played the Lord's songs for the shivering, humble souls of Jackass Flats. He was a veteran of Hawthorn; it showed in the lines of his furrowed brow and his sad eyes. These strangers looked at him with wonder and respect.

Daniel Wright played the piano long after the sun gave up on the day and his neighbors closed their doors. He looked beyond the pavilion and could see every star in the sky, floating and moving ever so slightly like glitter in a Christmas globe.

His fingers were cold, but not numb, and they used their strength to ungracefully strike the black and white keys- sometimes together, which made some good notes sour. It made no difference.

The music that came from Terrence Haight's piano outside that old shack in Jackass Flats reverberated into the universe, delicately and beautifully imperfect.

For as long as there was blood pumping through his veins, Daniel would play the music that his father Terrence patiently taught him. Music served as a reminder to Daniel that the world wasn't always so bad and that you could find pockets of beauty anywhere if you choose to see it. Daniel's hard exhales spat out into the cold and hung around his rosy cheeks for a while - little condensation clouds, as if they were ghosts waiting to greet him - or perhaps, they came out to thank him for finally setting them free.

www.ingramcontent.com/pod-product-compliance
Lightning Source LLC
Chambersburg PA
CBHW030815310726
48980CB00006B/503/J

* 9 7 8 1 6 4 4 4 0 0 6 0 9 *